A Game of Hearts and Heists

A STEAMY LESBIAN FANTASY ROMANCE

GIRL GAMES

RUBY ROE

A Game of Hearts and Heists - A Steamy Lesbian Fantasy Romance

Copyright © 2023 Ruby Roe

The right of Ruby Roe to be identified as the author of this work has been asserted in accordance with the Copyright, Designs and Patents Act 1988.

All rights reserved. No part of this publication may be reproduced, stored in any retrieval system, copied in any form or by any means, electronic, mechanical, photocopying, recording or otherwise transmitted, without permission of the copyright owner. Except for a reviewer who may quote brief passages in a review.

This is a work of fiction. Names, characters, places and incidents within the stories are a product of each author's imagination. Any resemblance to actual people, living or dead, or to businesses, companies, events, institutions or locales is either completely coincidental or is used in an entirely fictional manner.

First Published February 2023, by Ruby Roe, Atlas Black Publishing.

Cover design: Maria Spada

rubyroe.co.uk

All rights Reserved

A dedication in three parts:

*To my stepfather, for tirelessly encouraging me to write
"naughty books". I finally did it.
P.S. thank you for letting me steal your surname.
P.P.S. You're absolutely not allowed to read this book.*

*To Elli Z, for refusing to accept anything less than my best. For
pushing me further than I realised I could go and for never
taking my bullshit. I'm not sure if you're Mother Teresa
reincarnated or a dastardly villainous master mind genius...*

Probably the latter.

*And last, to me.
To the little girl who sat and cried into a book in the school
library at lunch day after day because she had no friends.
I'm sorry I stopped loving you.
I know better now.
I wrote this one for you.*

Note for Readers

This book is intended for adult (18+) audiences. It contains explicit lesbian sex scenes, considerable profanity and some violence. For full content warnings, please see author's website: rubyroe.co.uk.

This book is written in British English.

If you would like to read the free *steamy* prequel sign up here: rubyroe.co.uk/signup

CHAPTER 1

SCARLETT

There are two things I love: winning and angry women. If the two happen to fall together, and I win—or seduce—an angry woman, well, I'll let you work it out.

The problem is, women—and angry ones in particular —never quite play fair. Which is precisely the case for my current angry-woman-play-thing, Quinn Adams. Resident New Imperium medic—she's more commonly known, in my circles, for her vicious skills with poison.

She's also a royal pain in my ass.

Our tête-à-tête started a few years ago. Though if you ask her whether she's trying to screw me over, she'd hang before she confessed.

She is, though.

Trust me.

Stirling, my beloved, but irritating twin sister, kicks her legs up on the outdoor table of our favourite bar as she slurps on a cocktail we can't afford—which also happens to be Quinn's fault, but I'll get to that later. I sip my reluctantly purchased coffee. We could only afford one cocktail between us, and Stirling won the toss. But I guess it's not all bad. The afternoon sun reflects off the table, warmth kissing my skin, the sweet stench of booze and baked goods filling the street. Then I glance at Stirling.

"Must you?" I ask.

"Oh, definitely," Stirling says and oggles the waitress walking inside the bar. The server has an impossibly small waist and tits for days. Exactly Stirling's type.

I lean back in my chair, wondering where Stirling gets the attitude. While I might love the game of chasing women, I'm much subtler than her. I'm more of a power play girl, games of dominance and submission, winner takes all.

Speaking of winning, Quinn—*The Poisoner*—appears at the end of the street. It's those evergreen eyes and crow-coloured curls I spot first. Her hair is as twisted as her heart. Of course I turn away, pretend the sun has blinded me and glance through the bar window. As if I'd let The Poisoner think I was staring at her.

Doesn't seem to matter, though. Normally she won't deign to give me attention in public. But today, I can sense her gaze raking over me—thank you Assassin training. I can play her like this all fucking day. I still my breathing, let my periphery vision work, my hearing stretch, my skin prickle with the vibrations of her movement through the air.

If you weren't paying attention, you'd have missed the flicker of her eyes to mine. It was fast. Not long enough for anyone else to notice.

But I did.

The nanosecond of heat on my arms and neck as her gaze skirts over my body. The hiss and bubble of her anger.

Her lust.

Absolutely glorious.

One nil to me, *Poisoner*.

This is the game between us. She wants to kill me as much as she wants to fuck me. And much to my disdain, the feeling's mutual.

The Poisoner kicks her chin a little higher, walks a little quicker. Her piss poor attempt at snubbing me.

I smirk.

Pitiful.

"Are you quite finished?" Stirling says, glaring at me as she sips her cocktail. The waitress makes another pass as she delivers drinks to another outside table. She tuts at Stirling as she passes, but she also cocks her head, giving Stirling an eyeful of cleavage.

Unbelievable.

I have to physically suppress an eye roll.

This is how it's going to go: Stirling is going to make eyes at the waitress for the duration of our drink. Then, she'll slurp the last mouthfuls of cocktail, kick back the chair, slip to the counter and convince the waitress she needs something from the kitchen. They'll sidle outside and Stirling will finger fuck the poor girl into a leg-quivering orgasm and I will have to hear the sordid details all afternoon.

It's tiresome.

And no, I'm not jealous.

Probably.

"We're approaching thirty for fuck's sake. Shouldn't we have grown out of this by now? Do you ever think about anything other than tits?" I ask.

Stirling shrugs, then pushes a lock of her shoulder length dark hair behind her ear, "Sometimes I think about girls' arses, and the curve of their tiny waists under my fingers, and the taste of their c—"

"—Yes, thank you, sister."

She throws her head back and laughs. "Gods, Scar, you need to find a lady so bad. You gotta lighten up, honey. When was the last time you got laid, anyway?"

I shift in my seat. Hardly appropriate conversation for sisters. Stirling's expression widens. "Oh my. Tell me it wasn't Lara?"

Lara is my ex. She's... it ended in disaster. I say nothing and press my lips shut. She's not the last person I slept with, but Stirling doesn't need to know that. If she wasn't so preoccupied shagging half of New Imperium, she'd remember my last interaction with The Poisoner—Stirling had to help me out of the... predicament.

"Ohhhh..." Stirling drags the word out.

"My sex life isn't actually any of your business," I snap.

Stirling tilts her head to examine me, pausing as she chews her lip. "Tell me it's not the fucking Poisoner."

And she's remembered. I don't respond, just look down the street instead. I don't feel like confessing the fact that I've fucked The Poisoner at least three more times since the particular incident Stirling is remembering.

"Right. That's it," she says, leaning her chin on her hands. "I'm taking you to Velvet Mansion tonight."

"No," I say. It was meant to be a command, but it came out like a whine.

"Yes. I'm going to get you laid. I know a girl."

"I don't fuck on a first date."

"Well, there's a first time for everything."

My jaw flexes. I pull Chance out of my pocket. She's a large double-sided coin that fits snug in the palm of my hand. On one side is an intricately carved YES, laid in ruby.

On the other side is a gilded NO. She's the most expensive and precious item I own, and no matter how little money we have, I won't sell her. Not ever. My father gave her to me. Told me I'd always be a winner if I controlled the game. It's the only thing I have left of him. And I call her Chance because she's a sentient little bastard that likes to play games as much as I do.

"Absolutely not," Stirling says. "You're coming. I'm not betting on that bloody coin."

"One, the coin has a name. And two, if you want me to come, you'll bet on Chance. Feeling lucky, Stir?"

She frowns those dark eyes at me. "I'm always lucky." She glances at the waitress, her lips parting.

"Well, I guess we shall see." I flick Chance up with my thumb and follow her as she spins, soaring up: ruby-gold-ruby-gold.

I use the coin for everything. Nasty habit I've developed. Dangerous too. It's gotten me into more than a bit of trouble. But I love the spontaneity of it. You never know what it's going to land on. I wasn't joking when I said it's sentient. Sometimes the odds are with me, and others, I swear she's a malicious little prick doing the one thing I don't want her to.

Like today.

"Fuck's sake," I growl as the coin lands on YES.

Stirling smirks and folds her arms, and then the smug bitch winks at me. "Guess I'll see you tonight. Better get home, Scar. It will take you a while to scrub up."

She gulps the final dregs of her cocktail and then kicks back and stands up.

So predictable.

"I hope she fakes it," I mumble.

"Darling, please, we both know I'm gifted." She waggles

two fingers at me and swaggers into the bar after the waitress.

Vile.

How I'm her twin, I'll never know. I shake my head and take a glug of coffee. The sun is setting. It coats the mountains at the city's edge in embers; rouge and burnt orange glisten on peaks like flames. The street is bustling, ready for the evening's entertainment. The chatter of expectant party goers, the hum of magic and sweet perfume clings to the air. Every night in New Imperium is a night for hopes and dreams, desires and orgies.

New Imperium is far wilder, far darker than it was before The Tearing. I was only just old enough to go to the clubs when the world tore, but we were a more civilised people then. Now the city seems to thrive on power and sex and all of our darkest desires.

I prefer it this way.

Most don't.

I scan the street, and despite their enormous size, buildings cluster together in the centre of the city. These are full of magic, along with the mansions in the suburbs. It's the smaller houses, the uniform boxes on the outskirts, that don't have any. If you want a power top up, or to gain some new skills and abilities, you come to the centre or the burbs.

The royal palace holds the most magic, of course. It sits in the centre of the city, up a mile long driveway. And then there's the second most powerful castle—The Grey Castle —our old home. I look left down to the square. Our castle takes up two sides of the square. It used to be the centrepiece of the city. A thriving hub of pilgrims travelling, hoping to study our house, our magic, and if the castle deemed them worthy, claiming a piece of our home's magic for themselves. We even had a set of resident Collectors.

Once the house deemed the pilgrim worthy, the Collector would draw magic from the house and tattoo it into the pilgrim, thus allowing the castle to 'collect' them. The ultimate honour. Our castle was so busy, so powerful, that there were times the Collectors had to work twenty-four hours a day.

Not any more. I take a final sip of coffee and drop the last of my change onto the table. I stare at the darkened castle. The crumbling gargoyles. The chipped crenelations, filth covered windows and shattered glass.

My stomach twists. It's not right. Not because our power is desiccating in the heart of the castle, but the injustice of it all burns in my blood. One day I will have my vengeance. One day I will make up for what I've done.

But not today.

I spin on my heel and march up the narrow cobbled street. In a bout of hideous timing, I glance left, my eyes falling upon the alley.

Stirling kisses the girl's neck. Her hand slipped between the waitress's legs. She pants into my sister's ear, gripping her shoulders. Stirling catches sight of me and grins.

She's insufferable.

I pass The Poisoner's apothecary and glare at it. Reason sixty-nine I hate The Poisoner: her store is stealing all my trade. Providing poisons for bored housewives to do the dirty themselves instead of commissioning a first class Assassin like me. I'll have my vengeance on the bloody Poisoner, too. One day.

But not today.

Because today, I lost a fucking bet with my sister.

CHAPTER 2

QUINN

There are two things I hate: playing games and Scarlett fucking Grey. I saw her this afternoon after I dropped a delivery to a client. She checked me out. The arrogance of her to think I didn't notice. She turned her head to the bar window, but I caught her eyes in the reflection; noticed the tensing of her fingers into a fist when I didn't give her any attention.

Her flare of irritation was perfection.

She wants to stab me as much as she wants to strangle me. It's just unfortunate I seem to experience the same dilemma. Fury one day, furiously horny the next.

I sigh and scan my apothecary. It's packed full of conical jars of herbs and ingredients. Shelf after shelf lined with a rainbow of ingredients, poisons, and potions. Everything lined precisely and accurately. Labels out, lids tight.

Everything in here is just so, except the back wall—also Scarlett's fault. But before I can get annoyed, the apothecary shop door opens and a stream of amber light pours in.

The room warms, wrapping afternoon heat around the shelves and poisons. I tut. The shop is cold for a reason. The herbs need a cooler room to stay fresh. This job would be the best if it weren't for the customers.

I glance up from the journal I was reading to see a short man dressed in a butler's uniform. He has an impressively bushy moustache and his eyebrows meet in the middle, not because he has a monobrow, but because they are *that* bushy. It's distracting, and I can't quite look him in the eye for wondering if they'll crawl off his forehead.

"Can I... help you?" I say, forcing my eyes to meet his.

"Madam Lustra sends word of a delivery address," he says in the poshest voice I've ever heard.

"I see, and where does her ladyship wish to meet?"

"The Velvet Mansion."

I put the pen down and stare at him. He can't possibly have said the Velvet Mansion. It's practically a brothel or some such. I can't go there. Not that I'm prudish. I love sex as much as the next person. But I'm a businesswoman and would rather keep business to more professional establishments.

"That's... a joke?" I say.

"Not, in fact, a joke. You're aware Madam Lustra owns the club?"

I wasn't.

He continues. "She has other business in the club this evening and cannot afford the time to meet in a different location. Thus, she's requested your presence at the Velvet Mansion."

"But it's a sex club."

The butler blinks once. A long, slow blink. His eyebrows dip, wriggling like caterpillars. His face twitches. Is the posh bastard laughing at me?

"I'm not sure that's quite the description her ladyship would use, but yes, there's a certain sexual magic imbued in the Velvet Mansion. One for you to try, perhaps? A new Collection tattoo...?"

This time, his moustache twitches. He *is* laughing at me. Bastard. My blood fizzes and heats. I've a mind to shower him in poison and watch as he shits out his insides.

My feet shift on the spot, my lips pressed into a thin line. "I'm not sure what you're insinuating, but I've no need for sex magic. I get ample, thank you. And this is a poisons apothecary."

"I'm sure you do, dear." He pats my hand.

Fucking pats it like I'm six-years-old. The condescending cunt.

Then he glances at his watch. "Well, I must be going. Her ladyship will see you at 9pm sharp this evening. Don't be late."

With that, he disappears out the door, the warmth from the setting sun vanishing with him.

"Bastard," I growl after him. I take a deep breath, letting the air thread through my body and ease the rage. I roll my shoulders and turn back to the journal and the letter I was reading from my brother.

Dearest Sister,

I write with news. I wish I could tell you that things were getting better in the Borderlands, that things between mother and father were fixed, but I think we're both old enough to accept that's never going to happen. They just need to leave each other. It's exhausting.

Father is up to something, I can feel it. There are soldiers everywhere and they're training harder than ever. It feels like something is coming. I wish you could visit. Can you not find

*the time? You know father would love it. He's... none of us have
seen you for months. Plus, there's only so much I'll risk saying
here.*

*Mother is as well as can be expected, though stricken with
worry. I seem to have contracted some kind of flu sickness. I
keep telling her it's a cold and not to worry.*

*Tell me of your shop. How is business? How is that Assassin
you keep battling with?*

*Thank you for the last care package you sent through with
a Border Walker. I'd love to see you, but you know my heart is
here in the Borderlands. So I'm grateful for what you send.*

Yours in blood and bonds
Malachi

I scribble a short note back to him because I don't have
time to write anything longer. I have to make another
delivery before meeting Madam Lustra this evening, and
last time I went, the Velvet Mansion had a required dress
code.

Dearest Malachi

*Perhaps I could send a little more each month, but really,
this is a conversation you need to have with father. He has
more than enough Border Walkers under his finger. Surely he
could smuggle anything you need in? I'll see what coin I have
left after I've paid taxes this month and if I can bundle something more useful together.*

*Have you any news on your voice? Did the books I sent
shed any light on healing options? Or do we still think the
Sanatio is the only viable solution? I'm trying to save to buy a
leaf... it's just... you have to apply, it's not as simple as having
the insane amount of coin you need. I don't know if we'll ever
get a piece. There has to be another option. Keep looking.*

In blood and bonds
Quinn x

Two years after I moved to New Imperium, my brother lost his voice in a random attack. He was sixteen. It's a miracle he wasn't killed. I almost moved home permanently when it happened because the damage to his voice was beyond healing. But Malachi wouldn't hear of it. I was only an apprentice then. I had no chance of helping in any useful way, but I went back temporarily to try. Eventually, he started studying and writing spell work. One of the first things he did was spell this journal. He has an identical one in the Borderlands, and it's the only way we can communicate. The journal is everything to me, especially since I see less of him than I'm happy about. I tuck the journal inside its pouch and into a chest box and lock it under the counter.

The shop door tinkles, and a young man with skittish eyes enters. He's wearing grey magician training robes and has that puppy face expression despite his gangly height. Probably a new apprentice.

"I umm. I have a rash."

Gods.

These young apprentices keep shagging each other senseless. Then they spread these hideous genital rashes and diseases derived from sex magic. Notoriously tricky to get rid of and rather painful, so I hear.

Not that I'd know. I don't sleep around... Or at least, I haven't been since... well, anyway. The Assassin and I have only slept together a few times, and each of those was a mistake. I simply got carried away with trying to kill her and instead we...

I don't want to think about it.

It won't happen again.

The young man's hand slips to his groin and he scratches. My top lip twitches. I have to physically restrain the grimace.

"Middle shelf on the left, blue bottle. Three pills twice a day. You'll want to stay off work the first day you take the medicine. It induces an intense headache and you'll have a raging boner for at least thirty-six hours."

He pales, his sharp Adam's apple bobs as he swallows.

"Th-thanks." He picks up a vial and any remaining blood in his face pools to his feet as he cops an eyeful of the price.

Yes, well. What did he expect? He's come to the best apothecary in town. I'm expensive, darling. Just the way I like it.

He reaches into his pocket, drops the cash on the counter and vanishes. The round coin reminds me of the hole in the back wall display.

The rear wall has a neat arrangement of knives, swords, and blades. It's one part decor, poisons and blades go so well together. And the other part is because I often trade to Assassins. Well, the ones whose business I'm not stealing, anyway.

I purse my lips. There's a gap in the middle of the display. Fucking Scarlett Grey. She stole a blade from me the first time she fucked me. But this particular blade was from my father. It has a stone in the hilt that matches a ring he wears. He gave it to me because he said one day his empire would be mine. It means a lot to me. And she stole it.

I pull a few bottles off various shelves and pull a pestle and mortar close. I pour ingredients in, mixing and grinding harder than necessary, trying to grind out thoughts of Scarlett.

Eventually, I find my rhythm. I could do this blind-folded now. Honestly, I'm tired. I want something exciting instead of this daily monotony.

New Imperium is filled with royals, duchesses, baronesses and the elite high magicians. All of them equally bored with their lives and husbands. Only instead of getting a divorce, they'd rather off their spouses—and not get caught so they can claim their fortunes. And that's where I come in. As gifted as my brother is with spell work, I am gifted with mixing untraceable poisons. Which is exactly what I do out of hours, and I get paid a pretty penny for it too. The apothecary is a front now, although it didn't start that way. Most of my money comes from the poisons.

But, gods, I'm bored.

The same poison, day after day.

The same requests.

The same housewives travelling from different realms to acquire my specialty. I used to be creative. Used to have to use my brain to think and create. Figure out problems, solve medical issues.

Now it's poison after poison.

I finish mixing the solution and decant it into two bottles. I turn off the shop lights, check the journal once more before I leave, and lock the shop up. The sun has set. The evening air is still warm, though. It wraps around me like hot fingers and caresses.

The streets are already busy, the clubs and mansions opening for evening business. Before the realm tore in two, this city was an academic institution. Now it's a debauch pit of desire and lust. Such a shame. I wanted to study here for as long as I can remember, and sure, I got the education I wanted, but... it feels... less.

I walk through the tight streets heading outward

towards the suburbs. I drop the first vial in a public locker and then head home. I shower and shovel leftover chicken and rice. It's dry and tasteless, but it's food. Then I open my wardrobe.

"Fuck."

I have nothing to wear. There is literally only one dress that isn't summery in my wardrobe, and it doesn't even belong to me. It belongs to Tessa, my ex. I swear she left it here to irritate me at this very moment.

"I cannot believe I am going to do this."

I snatch the black dress out of the cupboard and shrug off my shop uniform. I pull the skin-tight cloth on and glance in the mirror.

It's obscene. There's a booster bra inside, so my tits are bulging out of the top. The back plunges so low you can practically see the top of my arse, and although it's a floor length dress, there's a slit to my hip. High enough, I can't wear underwear.

"Fucking Tessa. Why couldn't you have left something more demure?"

My curves are in full force today. I mean... I do quite like the fact I'm curvy, and tonight I'm seriously curvaceous. Especially because although I'm short, the slit makes my legs look long. I decide I'm pretty enough for a pair of heels. My ribs bear the Collection tattoos I've earned from all my studies. They're as bright as the day I got them. I run my fingers over them, remembering the hot sting from the Collector's tattoo gun, the strings of pearlescent magic flowing from the medical mansion walls and floor. Threads of magic poured into the gun, and subsequently, into my body. Each one pulsing and throbbing, filling me with power. When the horticultural castle collected me, its magic had a green tinge to it, never seen anything like it since. I think that was my favourite rite; it was midnight, a full moon. I got collected in the courtyard, so that the building and gardens could pour magic into the tattoo.

The clock in the corner chimes one, signalling a quarter after the hour. I need to hurry. I pull my curls up into a messy top knot and allow a couple of strands to hang free. A smear of mascara and the job is done. I catch sight of myself and tut. What am I thinking? I'm a professional on a job. I'm only going to be in the club for a few minutes. This all feels ridiculous.

I peer at the clock. Too late now, it's 8:30pm already.

I grab the vial of poison and shove it down the side of the push-up bra and slip a small blade into the other cup. You're not really allowed weapons in the Velvet Mansion. You're not allowed them in any of the clubs in New Imperium—they're pretty strict about it. Too much unfiltered magic, The Tearing ruined so many things. But looking the way I do, I want the protection, so I'm taking it, anyway.

This is all completely ridiculous if you ask me. But what madam wants, madam gets. She's paying enough to cover my rent for three months. Who am I to quibble over the when and where's of exchange?

Twenty minutes later, I'm pulling up outside the mansion and stepping out of the carriage.

I give the driver a coin tip and pet behind the horse's ear before hobbling up to the mansion door. Shouldn't have worn the heels. They might make my legs look great, but my feet already hurt.

To my surprise, I'm ushered to the front of the queue, but then the bouncer is an old client. I helped cure his nan of a nasty rash. And yes, it was *that* kind of rash, good for her, still shagging at her age. While poisons are my specialty, most of the medical magicians are useless in New Imperium, so I've ended up with half their trade as well as the Assassins'. I guess I have to do everyone's jobs now.

"Thanks, Jack."

"Welcome. Will you be requesting mansion magic this evening? The Collector is on a break currently and restarting bondings in half an hour."

"No, that's fine, thank you. I'm here to meet a friend."

"Have fun," Jack says, and then his eyes drop to my cleavage and bounce right back up, a hint of pink on his cheeks.

Bless.

Unfortunately for him, cock only ever does it for me if it's strapped to a set of tits.

The woman at the front gives me a violent stare. I give her a 'go fuck yourself, peasant' sneer and enter the mansion.

As I step over the threshold, my body compresses. A fleeting squeeze of the mansion's magic. It's the same in all magical buildings. Only, here, the pressure isolates on my breasts and pussy. I suck in a breath as the pressure stimulates my clit. A heady scent assaults my nose. It tingles with sandalwood and burnt oak and a smidge of spicy clove. Gods, the mansion is on one tonight. As soon as I think it, the club door swings in and slaps me on the arse.

I whip around and glare at it.

"Fucking cheeky house." I rub my ass as the door swings open, a creak in its hinges that sound suspiciously like a chuckle. I shake my head and move down the corridor. The hallway is dim. The walls are deep maroon and black, a filigree wallpaper that's velvety under my fingertips. I step down into the club. There's leather Chesterfield booth furniture around the edge of the main club room. The walls are all black velvet, plush and thick enough I'd like to rub my fingers down them. On the right, is the bar which is rammed three people deep. Great, no drink for me then. To the left is a giant black glass box with a sign saying 'PRISON'. Weird. But the bulk of the club is made up of the dance floor and multiple poles with girls and boys dancing... and... right.

Also fucking, it seems.

One girl has her nipple pierced and is wearing lace panties. She flings her legs open into a split as another woman kneels between her thighs and swipes her tongue over the flesh.

I'm instantly wet. And I'm not wearing knickers thanks to Tessa.

Fucksake.

The woman doing the splits lifts herself up and twists upside down on the pole. I have to swallow down the rush of heat that throbs into my core as she slides her cunt down the pole.

On another podium, one man has his hand wrapped around another man's cock, both of them pumping in rhythmic motions.

The dance floor is more of the same. There are people thrusting and grinding up against each other, some wearing clothes, others with scarcely a nipple covered.

One man? Woman? One person has a gimp mask on and latex suit. They're being led by a collar and chain on their hands and knees by a woman in heels high enough they make my feet ache. There's flesh everywhere: women fucking women, men fucking men, men and women fucking. I walk past a couple, a woman with her hand poised to touch her partner's cock. "What's your safe word?" she says, her fingertips millimetres from his hard flesh.

I don't catch the word. I move past them and leave them to play in peace.

On the opposite side of the bar is a DJ booth, and behind I can just about make out glass rooms with more dancers and poles. Chains hang from the ceilings, along with cuffs, whips, and an assortment of other devices.

I resign myself to queuing and head towards the bar. If nothing else, my feet will thank me for drinking down a few wines before I find Madam Lustra.

My neck prickles like I'm being watched. I squint into the smokey darkness but see no one. As I reach the end of the queue, I spot Madam Lustra. She's wearing a tight corset and skirt, only the skirt doesn't have a front. She's displaying fishnet tights and... that's it.

"Mother of—" I force my eyes up and away from her very bald vagina.

"Quinn Adams, good evening," she says.

I nod because I'm not quite ready to say anything else. Too busy trying to peel the image of her exposed lips out of my memory.

"Do you have my package?" she says.

I nod again, clear my throat and take a step closer. "Care to dance?"

She takes my hand and leads me to the dance floor. There are bodies everywhere, pressing against us. Skin, sweat. Now that I'm on the dance floor, I notice the threads of magic. They flow from the mansion walls, up from the floor. Silver and gold glistening ribbons, woven subtly enough between the smoke that if you're not paying attention, you'll miss them.

The threads wriggle around the bodies, weaving and flowing over limbs and flesh as the mansion chooses magicians to bestow its gifts upon.

Madam Lustra is older than me. In fact, she's probably old enough to be my mother. But despite the fact she's in her late fifties, she looks incredible. She has the skin of wealth. Wrinkle free and slightly too taut, as if it's less flesh and more decades of cream and potion layers. Her eyes have that ocean-deep look that tells you she's holding a thousand secrets. The secrets of her club goers, no doubt. She grabs my hands and pulls me into a spin. My back presses against her chest. My arm and neck prickles again, goosebumps crawling up my skin. Someone is definitely watching me, I know it. But when I scan the room, I can't see anything through the haze of dance floor smoke and laser lighting.

"When I spin you around, slip it to me," Madam Lustra says.

As she twirls me I grip her neck. Her bottom lip drops and she inhales as I slide my other hand out of hers, into my bra and across to her hip. I pull her close. She cups her fingers over mine and the vial passes between us.

We step apart. Her eyes glint under the dance floor lights. She curtseys as a silver shimmer floats up from the ground and flows through her. I move to pull away, but it's too late. She grabs my hand and kisses my knuckles. Her lips are smooth, a ripple of strawberry and wood smoke filter under my nose, a kiss laced with magic.

Fuck.

I sigh, my inhibitions already shedding like snake skins as my veins pulse with the heat of her kiss. A tingly need moves to my groin. Maybe I don't have to leave in such a rush. A couple more drinks won't hurt.

"There's a parcel for you behind the bar. And should you care to dance later, I'll be around." She smiles. It sets those secrets in her gaze on fire. She's stunning. But not my type. I prefer the more commanding girl—a girl with weapons in her hands and murder in her heart.

No surprise that I find myself eyeing the Assassin academy every time I pass it. Who doesn't like watching the girls flinging giant swords around and wrestling each other to the ground? Though I swear ninety percent of the reason I stare is because I'm hunting for Scarlett fucking Grey and hoping I get to watch as one of the apprentices shoves a blade between her ribs.

I head to the bar and nudge my way to the head of the queue. I'll grab my package and—

I'm shoved against the bar as a tall, slender woman wearing an extremely tailored suit inserts herself next to me. Her back is to me, and she leans into the woman next to her.

Fucking rude.

Normally I'd let it go. Normally. But tonight, fuelled by Lustra's kiss and the fucking mansion's magic, I decide this queue-jumping wench needs to go fuck herself.

"ER, EXCUSE ME," I bellow over the music and grab her—

Oh.

"You," I spit. Rage instantly pouring into my chest.

You, I think, and as fast as the rage flows, so too does the hunger. Hot, needy, throbbing.

"Quinn," her eyes glimmer.

"Scarlett. Fucking. Grey."

CHAPTER 3

SCARLETT

The shock on The Poisoner's face is precious. I knew she hadn't seen me watching her from the club's shadows.

Stirling, for all her talk of getting me laid, vanished the moment she saw her friend. And by friend, I mean the casual 'let's fuck every time we meet' kind of friend. I was about to leave when I saw Quinn enter the club in the most spectacular dress. I was taken aback. She doesn't seem the sort of girl to wear a dress like that. Not that I minded. The slit in the black silk cuts over her hip. Easy stabbing access... or easy access for fingers to slide in.

I edged my way around the room, watching. Waiting. She danced with the club owner. It took all my strength not to pull out the blade I'm hiding in my waistband and throw it across the room at Lustra.

I might hate Quinn. But she's mine to fuck with. No one else's. I had to force myself to stay against the wall and watch as she wrapped her fucking fingers around Lustra's neck. I wanted to cut them off, slice Lustra open. That's when I took Chance out. I wasn't going to bother. I would've been happy voyeuring my way through the club, studying Quinn for weaknesses. But she had to go and dance with Lustra, and that pissed me off.

I rubbed the coin between my thumb and index finger.

"Do I go to her? Do I go to The Poisoner?" I asked and flipped the coin.

I knew before I even looked under my hand what it landed on. I've tossed Chance too many times. I know the striations like breathing oxygen.

So here I am, standing in front of Quinn. Her hand is still wrapped around my bicep. I tensed it on purpose. As I strain the muscle, her tongue flicks across her lips and her eyes drop to where she's grasping me.

She releases me, suddenly, as if I'm made of fire.

Her eyes darken. There she is.

Hello, my angry girl.

It makes my thighs heat and my pussy warm, wondering how much I can provoke her. Whether I can coax power from her core, her fury. The angrier she is, the more beautiful she becomes. It's exquisite.

And infuriating.

I decide in that moment I'm going to make her cry my name into the thumping music tonight. Or maybe I could just throttle her and watch as the life slips from her eyes. Both are so appealing, especially after the shit she's caused me.

I make the mistake of lowering my eyes to her cleavage as hers dropped to mine. I wore the push-up bra tonight, Stirling's idea. She made me unbutton one too many buttons on my white shirt, too.

Mistake.

Can't kill Quinn with the way she's dressed. My eyes rove her curves, her leg peeking out from the silk fabric. My breathing hitches faster. It would be too much of a waste.

Can't kill her tonight, anyway.

But I can fuck her.

When Quinn's forest-coloured eyes lock on mine, I swallow. I hate that she has this power over me. Hate that she's crushing my business, destroying my sanity.

She needs to be punished. I'll fuck her until she's orgasmed so hard she can't walk for a week. Good thing I'm packing. I inch forward, the leather straps beneath my trousers pinch against my skin. The cock dangles between my legs and presses against my thigh. Like her, I'm not wearing underwear either.

"You," she spits. And the word curls through my brain like a drug, my vision narrowing until she is the only thing that exists in the club.

I lean down, grab her waist and yank her towards me. "Yes. Me," I breathe into her ear. Her cheek presses against mine, soft, warm. "Good evening, Poisoner."

"I knew you were watching me," she says and shoves me off. "So predictable. Can't get enough of me. It's pathetic, really." She looks up at me.

She's baiting me, prodding and poking to see if I'll bite. This is the game we play. The back and forth, insults, threats, promises. She professes to hate games. It's a total lie. She plays harder than anyone I've ever met.

My nostrils flare. She won't be walking for two weeks for that. I grab her arm and pull her away from the bar and shove her up against the wall. She sucks the corner of her lip.

"Jealous, Scarlett?" The words purr out of her mouth.

Her fingers tiptoe up my abs. I slap them away. And she grins.

Gods. I'm going to ruin her.

"Just because my poisons are better than your blades doesn't mean you can treat me like a rag doll." She gestures at the wall.

I yank out the blade strapped to my waistband and shove it under her chin. But that only makes her smile deepen.

She tuts at me, "And to think I thought you were meant to be the best of the best Assassins."

There's a sharp sting between my ribs. I glance down.

The fuck?

"Wh—" I start.

She leans forward and cuts me off, "—You're not the only one capable of smuggling blades, Grey." Then she sucks my earlobe. My nipples stiffen as she pulls away and leaves the lobe as wet as my pussy.

"You need some new tricks, Old Dog. You're slowing down," she smiles. It's a sneering sort of smile, one I'd gladly wipe off her face.

A looming shadow appears beside me.

Shit.

"Blades," he says. This man is a giant. I'm tall, he's enormous. He holds out his hand, which is less a hand and more a spade, and both of us slap the knives into his hand, our jaws gritting.

"Prison. Now." He glares and points at a giant black glass box on the other side of the room.

"You can sort your differences out in there." He raises an eyebrow, and when neither of us moves, he uses those spade-hands to shove us towards the box.

We're pushed inside. "Jack, please," Quinn says.

She knows his name?

"Twenty minutes. And when you come out, you better play nice, ladies. Blades can be collected from the cloak-room, where you should have fucking stored them in the first place."

Then Jack slams the door shut and clicks the lock.

Brilliant. I flex my neck, irritated. I could have been getting drunk or, even better, hunting for commissions from drunk and desperate guests. There are spotlights on the roof throwing out dim rouge light. We can't see out, no one can see in. Chains and cuffs dangle from the roof, and in the middle of the room is a soft velvet cube. The floor has a velvety carpet too. And there are toys of all varieties in the corner on a shelf.

Quinn rushes up to me and shoves a finger into my chest. "That's the second blade you've stolen from me."

I lower my gaze to her finger.

She hesitates and pulls her finger away.

"That's a good girl. We both know you shouldn't point fingers you don't want to lose."

"I'm serious, Scarlett. I still want that blade back." Her words are as sharp as the blades we just lost.

"What kind of prison is this?" I say more to myself than anything.

"A sex club prison, obviously." She rolls her eyes at me and turns her back on me.

I cock my head at her. "Well, Quinn Adams. You're liable to get spanked with an attitude like that."

"You spank me, and I'll cut your hand off," she's snarling. But she's also leaning back, closer. Her perfume is rich, spicy. The heady scent fills my mind, leaches away rational thought, leaches training and sense. It drives me wild.

"You wouldn't dare. You like them too much." I drag my hand slowly up her bared thigh.

She sucks in a ragged breath. Fury melds with lust as her eyes rake down my body and her tongue slides over her lips. Her fingers flex like she wants to throttle me. But her hips betray her. They tilt towards me.

I smile as I push my fingers higher, sliding them over the rounded flesh at the top of her thigh.

"You have other limbs that can be cut off," she says. But the words are warm now, rumbling in her chest, lust threaded through them.

"The only thing that's going to be cut off," I say, slipping my hand over her pussy, "is your income when I destroy your business."

"Don't be petty. Jeal—"

I part her flesh, silencing her. My finger poised on her clit. She leans her ass into my hand, forcing my finger to move up and down. She lets out a gasp and then a moan as I pick up the pace and rub her core.

She turns round, pushes me to my knees, pulls her dress aside.

She tilts her head, her eyes alive, hungry.

An invitation.

A demand.

When she looks at me like this, I'm never sure if we're going to fuck or fight. Honestly, I don't think I care.

"You know I've punished women for demanding less than that."

Her lip curls, "And yet I'm the only one who can get you to your knees."

This time, I growl. I grab her ass and lift her up. She swings her legs around my neck and I lean into her flesh. I carry her, my face pushed against her pussy, to the velvet cube where I put her on her back. And then I draw my tongue down, parting her.

The moan it elicits from her carves me in two. She sits up, and her hands go to my trousers and crotch.

"Oh," she says as her hand presses against the hard cock. "Oh, that's new."

"Shut up and bend over."

Her mouth twitches like she's suppressing a smile. "Yes, ma'am."

When her ass is in the air, I walk around the cube and take one of the dangling handcuffs. I strap her in one hand and then the other. I yank, testing their strength. There's no way they're coming out of the ceiling.

I pull the key out and slip it into my pocket. Then I lift Quinn's chin up and place a kiss on her mouth. She parts her lips and pushes her tongue over mine. She tastes like forbidden things. Peppery and hot, and the faintest hint of sweet smoke.

I drop her face and move to her backside, hoisting the fabric of her dress up. I slap her ass and she squeals. My clit pulses. I'd kill to ride her face right now, feel her warm mouth lap at my core as I grind into her.

But tonight is not about me.

It's all about revenge for what she did last time. I was on an open commission. This duchess had offered a high reward for slaughtering her rich uncle, open contract, quick turnaround time. Of course, the competition was much stiffer. Quinn and I both turned up to kill off the uncle. We fought. I was an inch from gutting her in the uncle's living room. If it weren't for the fact that I'd slashed her top and she wasn't wearing a bra...

Instead of killing her, I ended up fucking her all over the guy's living room. We broke furniture, smashed vases, ripped cushions. It was... well; it wasn't my most profes-sional moment. After, Stirling had to come and help me make it look like a break in.

Anyway. Quinn must have slipped me some kind of poison because by the time I'd finished fucking her face, my right arm was paralysed and my leg and foot weren't far behind.

She got the kill, of course. And then left me there to deal with the consequences. One nil to her that day.

And to top it all, I was paralysed for two very long days. Stirling had to feed me because I kept spilling everything. Guess she's two nil up.

I owe her.

I owe her big.

I unzip my trousers, pull the cock out and rub it over her pussy. I lean down onto her back, sprinkle kisses over her neck, nipping at the skin.

"Tell me you want it," I say, a growl biting at my throat. This is the best part of the game. Submission. No matter how much she hates me, she wants me to fuck her more.

"I—I want it," she pants, and my jaw flexes.

I shove inside her, shunting her forward into the velvet cube. She gasps out a moan. And then... "Harder, Scarlett."

My teeth grit, my eyes squeezing shut. The demands. It floods adrenaline through my insides, my muscles tighten, daring me to obey, daring me to punish.

The way she says my name, the husky longing. I can't stand it. How dare she command me. And yet... I submit.

I'd do anything to make her scream my name like that over and over.

I thrust into her. Deeper. Faster. Until she's dripping wet and moaning into the velvet fabric beneath her, her knuckles white where she grips the corners.

I trail my hand around her legs and onto her swollen clit. I flick my fingers, rubbing and teasing and thrusting into her until she's wound so tight she's panting out my name like fire and flames. It bores into my mind.

"Scarlett. Scarlett," she breathes, and my soul caves open. She might be the one climaxing, but it's me that's laid bare. She arches up, gripping my arse, pulling me in harder. The chains clank and strain as her fingers squeeze punishingly hard against my skin. It's on purpose. She likes to mark me, I'm sure of it.

I'm hers as much as she is mine to play with. To fuck and discard. To threaten and screw.

I'm glad she's on her front. One look from her would strip me open and tear out my darkest secrets.

She stiffens against me, her world shattering. For a fleeting moment, I wish I hadn't used the cock but my fingers so I could feel her clench me. But there's always next time.

No.

No more next times. I pull out of her, eliciting a sharp intake of breath as she collapses on the cube, the chains holding her arms clinking. This needs to stop. I put the cock back inside my trousers and zip myself up. I check the handcuff key is still in my pocket and then smile.

"Till next time, Quinn. Have a pleasant night."

"What?" she says, still breathless and revelling in the orgasm. The chains clang as she tries to wrench around to see me. She can't turn fully, but she can see enough to realise I have a smug grin on my face.

"Don't you dare leave me in here like this."

I laugh and pull out my spare switch blade—all good Assassins carry more than one—and jangle it against the door lock. It clicks open.

"One nil to me, Quinn."

"I will fucking ruin you. I..." she screams, but I shut the door on her before she can finish the rest of her sentence.

If I strain against the thud of the music, I can still make out her shrieking and the clanking chains.

Glorious.

Utterly, glorious.

CHAPTER 4

SCARLETT

"Did she look for me?" I bark at Stirling over the roar of music. We're on the mezzanine layer above the dance floor. I pass Stirling a fresh drink and we clink glasses. Both satiated for the evening in all the important ways.

"Woman in the black dress? Slit up to her hip?"

I nod. "I couldn't see who it was from up here but, yeah. She came out of the club prison livid. She looked for you alright. Looked like she was gagging for you."

"Yeah, gagging to murder me after what I did."

She huffs a laugh out, "Must you always play games? Why can't you just enjoy the love of a good woman?"

"Says the biggest player I know."

"I resent the accusation," she says, elbowing me.

"I note you didn't deny it, though."

"Go fuck yourself, sister. Who was she anyway?"

I laugh and take another sip of my drink. But ignore

Stirling's questions. Now that Quinn has gone, the evening has lost its sparkle.

Stirling's face falls. "For the love of fuck, tell me it wasn't Quinn?"

I stay silent and sip my drink.

Stirling throws her hands up. "The whole point of coming here was to avoid her. What is wrong with you? I thought you hated her?"

"With all my heart."

Stirling opens her mouth to respond and then closes it and shakes her head. "What about her?"

She points at a tall, thin girl wearing a suit much like mine. "She's a sword maker from the next city." Stirling knows everyone. To be honest, she's probably fucked half of them. She's a Resourcer by trade. It's literally her job to know everyone. Or at least know someone who knows someone who can get the job done, or find the item you need, or source a ship, on and on it goes. There's literally nothing she can't acquire.

It's exhausting. I keep a much smaller circle. I suppose that's the prerogative of an Assassin. Don't want too many people knowing your face. Or that was the case when I still held my rank and legacy.

I shake my head. "Too androgynous. I'm done anyway. Had my fill for the night."

"Ah yes, how could I be so foolish? Fucking the enemy must be deeply fulfilling."

"Gods, Stir, you don't make this enjoyable. I'm going to get some fresh air."

She shouts after me. "I'm just pragmatic."

I head to the rear of the mezzanine toward the stairs. I turn back to check Stirling is okay, but she's already deep in conversation with some guy. Her forehead furrowed between her brows, the way it always does when she's serious. It's probably business. I make my way to the balcony rooftop.

The stars paint a mosaic of diamonds on the velvet black of the sky. The air is frosty enough I need to do up the buttons on my shirt.

Hopefully Stirling can broker a deal with whoever that was. She's far better at bringing cash in. Her reputation wasn't as tarnished by our parent's accusations as mine was. One benefit of being a Resourcer, everyone loves you because you give them exactly what they want.

This is one of my favourite views of the city. Up here, especially on a clear night like tonight, you can see miles across the city. Glistening lights sprawl on the horizon, a lake of glimmering sparks reflecting the sky. Below the club, there are narrow streets and alleys twisting like a maze. Then I spot Alchemists Row. My back stiffens. That's Quinn's territory. Her shop is down there. Not that I frequent it. Mostly, I avoid the area. Fucking plagues of medics and alchemists down there. All of them trying to steal my trade—at least, they are since The Poisoner came on the scene. They never used to bother me. But three years ago, she sprung out of nowhere. Cocky fucking apprentice, newly qualified with big dreams—the usual type.

Except she wasn't. She came in hungry for success. Instead of sticking to her lane, treating and healing, she expanded... into my realm. I don't know how it happened, to be honest. Some bored or desperate housewife without a budget for the likes of a talented Assassin on the dark market must have asked after a poison. I assume Quinn gave it to her, and then when it did precisely what she wanted and offed her husband or uncle or cousin; she talked. And now all of them go to The Poisoner. The richest commissions and they all choose to pay cut prices and off their husbands with untraceable poisons.

It's a disgrace to the industry. To Assassins everywhere.

And sure, I could try to expand into another patch, like politics. But fuck that. I'm good at what I do, and some of the bored housewives like to experiment... they've only ever had a husband, and who am I to say no?

All that's over.

Some weeks, Stirling and I have gone hungry. Once a couple of years ago, we got behind on rent and kicked out of our place. It was only by chance one commission I managed to get had a spare outbuilding and rented out to us because it needed work. Now, we're at a family friend's house who took pity on us.

Quinn, piece by piece, is ruining my life, stealing my clients and fucking with my mind.

And every time I get the opportunity to kill her... I don't. I stall. We end up fucking.

If I can't kill her... maybe I could mess with her instead.

Yes. Maybe that's what I'll do. I take a sip of my drink and glare at Alchemists Row. It's not sporting to off the enemy. When I beat her—and I will—it needs to be fair and square. Yeah. That's the real reason I haven't killed her already. I need to beat her at her own game.

No one ever said you can't have a little fun... a little smack talk. Psych the enemy out.

And I do love a game.

♛

The next morning, I'm jobless. I didn't secure any more commissions last night, and Stirling will sleep for a few more hours. To avoid boredom, I decide chaos is in order.

Especially after Stirling was most disappointed in me for losing interest in finding another woman once The Poisoner left.

But I'm not Stirling, I don't want to fuck around for the sake of an orgasm. I want to hunger for my women.

I let Stirling sleep. I was right. That guy she was speaking to was after her services. She spent half the night brokering a ship deal to transport illegally embezzled coin across the sea. As the middleman, she doesn't get the big money, but she gets to chip a piece off whatever deal is had between the two parties. And thank the gods, because she's keeping us afloat far better than I am at the moment.

I leave porridge half made on the side for her. She'll finish making it when she's up. She hates it if it's left too long. I shower and dress in my training kit. Combat trousers and a tight fitting long-sleeved top and bike leathers on top of them. I braid my hair, save the wind matting and knotting it, and leave. It takes fifteen minutes to ride across the city. I park in the centre, locking my bike to a rack, and tuck the leathers in the box on the back.

Before I get to Alchemists Row, I have to meet a client, Avis. I offed her husband two nights ago, and she needs to pay up. She's inheriting three farms, and enough coin to sink a monarchy. The husband died in an illicit incident, so the papers reported.

He didn't, of course. I hung him and set it up to look like a kinky affair. The perfect murder, you might say. Even the forensic magicians haven't picked up on that method yet. Not that I've used it often, have to keep things fresh.

I smile to myself. It truly was a beautiful killing. I didn't even have to talk to the guy. Got in. Slung the rope over his neck. And down the son of a bitch went.

Easy money. And given the level of notoriety, I charged healthily for it, too.

One moment I'm walking down the cobbled streets of New Imperium and then next I'm yanked sideways.

"Gods," I growl. "You realise most people would lose their life or at the very least a limb yanking me like that," I say.

Avis is short, her greying frizz pulled into a ponytail. She's wearing a traditional magician's robe in dark navy and holding a suspiciously small bag of coin.

"I thought we were meeting at the city park?" I say, my voice rising.

"Yes. Well. Other plans necessitated a closer rendezvous," Avis says.

"I see. Well, I take it you were happy with the end product?"

Her lips press together, her brow furrows. "That is debatable, Scarlett. Questions are being asked."

"Questions?" I scoff. The fuck she mean questions? It was a textbook kill.

She fidgets and forces out a huff. Then presses her lips into a line so thin I swear her mouth has eaten them.

"The forensic morticians are asking questions because of the number of deaths of late."

My chest tightens. That's not good. I also can't afford for her not to pay me.

"We both know those deaths aren't me. Far too crude. And whoever it is needs to be careful. The number of identical deaths is rather telling."

Quinn. Always fucking Quinn. The amateur is ruining everything once again. Greed. That's her problem. If she was pickier, selected her clients more carefully, the entire industry would be better off.

"It appears you're also losing your touch, Ms. Grey. I heard you were the best, despite your parents—"

"—I am the best, Mrs. Randall. And I'll thank you to remember that," I snarl. My hand twitches, itching to reach for my concealed blade.

Avis sniffs. "Yes, well. I am less than happy that I'm being questioned. But I supposed you did as requested and the lawyers have assured me I will inherit the farms."

I lean in, my eyes cold, my face hard. "To payment then."

Avis shifts on the spot, then tips her chin at me. "I'm docking you for the inconvenience of having to deal with the High Magician's questioner and the forensic team."

I have to suck air in, shove it down into my lungs to try and stop the pounding in my ears. I choose my next words carefully. "You'll do no such thing, Mrs. Randall."

She cocks her head at me. "And what, exactly, is a disgraced Assassin going to do about it?"

I smile, letting the sun glint in my eyes. The corner of my lip curling.

She holds out her hand. "Let me stop you there, Ms. Grey. You put a single foot out of line, you're going straight to the dungeons. Who do you think the high questioner is going to believe? A disgraced Assassin and daughter of the map thieves? Or me? A respectable lady of Randall farms, recently bereaved and supplier of Sanatio to the Queen? I think we both know who would come out on top."

"Fuck you."

She laughs, drops the bag of coin in my hand and turns her back on me. Always a dangerous move that. I whip out a blade and in one swing it's under her neck and nicks the skin enough she stills under my grip.

"Quite right, Avis. But you got one thing wrong. All

those things you said don't make me weak or vulnerable. Quite the opposite."

She turns to face me, her eyes wide. Blood pumps harder through my veins. The promise of the kill threading liquid adrenaline through my muscles. We're taught to control this reaction in the guild. When you kill regularly, it becomes a drug. The addiction seeps into your veins, your vision funnels. Nothing else exists except you and the kill. It stops us from being aware of our surroundings, not good when you're infiltrating dangerous realms.

But right now, none of that matters. I've lost the guild, my legacy. Fuck my training, I should do it. I'm tired of this endless boredom. But killing the customer is never great for business. I ease away from her neck, my shoulders loosening.

"Disgusting. Like your parents," she spits on the cobbles.

Oh well. I tried.

I draw the blade across Avis's throat. Stupid bitch. Doesn't know what she's talking about. My parents didn't steal the fucking Queen's map. She's wrong. The Queen is wrong too, and I will find a way to prove that.

Five years ago, the Border Lord set my parents up. All because I didn't follow through on a job he'd given me. The piece of shit screwed my parents up as punishment. Stole the Queen's map and replaced it with a fake one, not that the general populous knows that. He let my parents take the fall. I'm not even sure if the Queen knows.

I drop Avis to the floor. A halo of rouge spreads from under her twitching limbs. I flip her over and fumble in her pockets for a second bag of coin.

There.

In the folds of her thick cloak. So predictable. The entitlement of legacy-borns is unfathomable. And yes, I'm aware I'm a legacy-born, but I've also had the entitlement knocked out of me.

Avis was bluffing the whole time, thought she could get one over on me. I take the second bag and haul her body next to the alley dustbins. Someone will find the festering body in a few days and figure with her dead husband it was a deal gone wrong, or she committed suicide.

I give her a last glance, the bitter aftertaste of my parent's lost legacy clawing at my throat. The injustice of it. The Border Lord needs stopping. He only stole the map to stop the Queen from healing our land. If she heals the land, he loses his ability to tax the Border routes and traders. If it hadn't destroyed my family, I might actually respect the deviousness of it.

So the story goes, ten years ago, the Queen argued with her twin sister and tore their royal map in half. The palace is sovereign land and thus owns Imperium. Any map born of palace magic is powerful in more ways than we can imagine. This map was no different. When they tore the map, it also tore our world in half. Half the city was lost to The Tearing. Swallowed in mist and rumour. It wasn't until a few weeks later, when supplies ran dry and traders needed to cross to the cities on the other side, that the first Border Walkers attempted to cross.

But the Border Lord had already militarised those who were left inside the Border and had survived The Tearing. When no help came for them, he capitalised on the rage of those left and took control. He taxed any trader daring to walk through. Now, both sides of the Border, both Queens, suffer under the hand of the Border Lord and they have for the last decade.

If the two pieces of map could be placed together, I

swear we could heal the land and get our world back. And I, for one, would take great pleasure in executing the son of a bitch lord who ruined my parents' legacy.

I leave the alley and head to Alchemists Row. Avis might be a traitorous cunt, but she wasn't wrong. The poison trade is shrinking my clientele. Quinn's poisons more than any of them. It's time to cause trouble.

Alchemists Row is a thin sapling of a street. It's so tight I could probably stretch my arms and touch the shops on either side. Awnings hang out from the windows like tongues. Magical items, cauldrons, wands, bottles of potions and herbs, wooden bowls, pestles and mortars sit waiting for eager magicians in shelving. The air is thick with the pungent scent of cooking herbs, broths and the bitter hint of poisons.

In the middle of the street is a cluster of shops. I examine them, but the source of my trade issue is obvious. Of the cluster of shops, all bar one look dishevelled. The shop signs are peeling, the windows are dusty and cluttered. But one shop is clean, and sharp. The window organised and dust free.

The Poisoner.

Yes, there's only one shop I need to venture to. The one making all the money. Quinn's Remedies, it's called. I roll my eyes.

How quaint.

How unoriginal.

Couldn't she have come up with something cleverer than that?

I march down the cobbles. They're hard and bumpy

underfoot. The path is so narrow the warm morning sun barely reaches me.

I reach Quinn's Remedies and open the door. A little bell tinkles as I enter. Quinn's mass of dark curls covers her face where she's bent over the serving counter. Her head is buried in a leather journal, ink smeared across her fingers as she drags a quill over the parchment. I can just about make out the page. As fast as she writes, the ink melts into the page. Interesting.

She hasn't looked up, clearly more interested in her note taking than serving a lowly customer like me. How she has any returning customers with manners like that is beyond me.

I enter and close the door behind me, walking around the room, eyeing the shelves of herbs and racks of bottles. Insects and animal detritus all jarred and categorised. Gross. Yes, I use poisons occasionally to help guarantee a death or to hide what I've really done, but it's basic. An amateur Assassin could poison someone. Where's the art? There's nothing better than a blade against skin, the pull and gentle resistance as I slice through layers of flesh. You have to be far more skilled to cover up a murder like that.

I run my finger along the bottles, nudging them this way and that. They were all perfectly aligned. Knocking them out of position is so satisfying.

"Do you mind?" Quinn says, finally looking up. She tuts and moves out from behind the counter. She still hasn't looked at me, but she nudges me out of the way and straightens the bottles.

I step back and fold my arms, watching as she fusses.

Her irritation is enough to get me hot.

I spot the back shelf. A strange array of blades, with one missing. Ah yes, the blade I stole from her the first time we met. My fingers twitch, wanting to move to my waistband, where it's nestled against my hip. But I don't want her getting suspicious. I guess I'll keep it a little longer.

I still remember the first time I picked it up.

The first night I met her. We were at Roman Oleg's annual party. I'm not a huge fan of him. He uses a lot of dark magic, trades in it—all completely illegal, of course. But his party is big business. Most of the year's biggest deals are brokered there. So of course, Stirling was going, and she dragged me too. No weapons, no recording equipment, just you and your charm.

So when I noticed The Poisoner and noticed the curved shape of a blade against her sleeve, she piqued my interest.

I knocked into her, a distraction, slipped it out. It was pathetic, really. Classic pickpocket technique. She didn't have a clue until I'd long gone and was watching her from across the room. The blade had a ruby the same shade as one on a signet ring the Border Lord wore on his pinkie.

I ran my hand over the blade. Its surface was smooth and icy, far colder than the surrounding air.

Odd.

My fingers slipped to the cutting edge. As I examined the shape and lines of the weapon, I drew my finger down the tip. It was so sharp it stung hot and sliced into my skin.

My lips pulled into a dark smile. I didn't push hard enough to cut flesh. The blade was obviously hungry for blood. A drop of red rolled to the metal point, and I swore it vibrated in response: deep, rumbling. Almost as if it was greeting me; one weapon to another.

"Don't you know stealing in a place like this could get you killed?" A sultry voice said.

I glanced up. It was The Poisoner. She'd caught me. And

that piqued my interest in her for the second time that night.

"Good thing I'm excellent at murdering then," I grinned and kicked off the wall I was leaning against.

"I want it back," she said.

"Mmm. No. I'll keep it. But thanks," I said and barged into her as I passed her.

"Be it on your head. That blade belongs to the Border Lord, and he'll want it back."

Strike three for The Poisoner piquing my interest. Because if it really did belong to the Border Lord, how sweet would it feel to push his own blade between his ribs as I watch the light fade from his eyes?

I glanced over my shoulder. "And what's a pretty little thing like you doing with a blade that belongs to him?"

She opened her mouth to answer and closed it again.

I laughed and walked off, pocketing the blade.

That was three years ago, and she's been a fucking nightmare ever since.

"You," she says, wrenching me out of my memories.

I face her, grinning.

"Yes. Me. Good Morning, Poisoner."

She moves back to her counter. Closes her journal. Presses her hand on top of it. It's a protective move.

Interesting.

"What do you want?" she says.

I move closer. She grips the journal; her knuckles white where she holds it.

More interesting.

She slips it off the counter and hides it under the glass serving desk. A plan forms in my mind. A little dose of blackmail, perhaps? Theft in exchange for fucking off out of my territory. What does she need the extra coin for, anyway? She's clearly minted given the quantity of stock in here.

Yes. I like this plan.

She eyes me, her lids narrowing as she looks me up and down.

Hunter.

Prey.

This is my favourite game. If only it would end in the bedroom permanently instead of where it's going to lead her eventually: the mortuary.

Too bad, Poisoner.

Let the games begin.

CHAPTER 5

QUINN

"Well?" I say. My jaw as sharp and pointed as my tone.

I'm pissed. *With her.*

"Out with it, or are you planning on handcuffing me to the counter and leaving me again?"

Yeah, I'm really pissed. I hate games. But that's all we seem to do. Tit for tat. Scar for scar. I wonder if she had to stitch her rib last night. Probably not. I didn't really stab her. More nicked the skin.

Scarlett's lips twitch. My glare falls to her mouth. Bubbles froth in my veins. I glance at the wall and consider whipping down a blade and hacking them off her pretty fucking face.

"I thought you'd enjoy a bit of you time. You're always so tense, Quinn. You need to relax," she says, grinning.

I swear I'm going to poison her in her sleep. I march out from behind the till, a finger pointed at Scarlett's chest.

She juts out her chin and folds her arms. My insides burn. I swear there's a curl of fire fizzing up my throat. This woman is infuriating. How dare sh—

Scarlett's gaze follows the swing of my hips.

Left, right, left.

I bet she's imagining me in that dress from last night, the slit high over my hip.

Unbelievable.

I'll 'slit' her for leaving me chained up. This won't go unpunished. But as I reach her, my finger an accusing millimetre from her chest, the bell tinkles and one of the Queen's guards walks in. I shove past her and approach the guard.

"Can I help?" I say, a little too quick.

"Ms. Quinn Adams?" The guard says.

"Yes?"

"Her Majesty Queen Calandra of New Imperium requests your presence at the palace this evening."

He hands me a white card.

"How unusual."

The guard nods at me, and then his eyes flick over my shoulder.

"Oh," he says. And then walks inside the shop straight up to Scarlett. She's leaning against the counter now.

"This is unexpected," he says.

I gawp as he strides to Scarlett.

"Lady Grey?" he says.

"It's just Scarlett now."

Lady. Pssht. She was never a lady; I don't care if she's a legacy magician. How can you call an Assassin with as much blood on their hands as her a lady?

"But you are Scarlett Grey?" the guard says.

"Yes, that's me," she says, exasperated.

He hands her an identical card to the one he gave me. Her mouth drops open, a furrow appearing in-between her brows as she skirts from him to the card. "You've got to be kidding me?"

"Not, in fact, kidding," the guard says. "Her Majesty has specifically requested the presence of yourself and your sister this evening. And she does expect your attendance."

"Huh?" she says. "But we've been banished from the palace for five years. We weren't even allowed to go back to our own mansion to collect our belongings. What in the royal fuck does the Queen want with me?"

I didn't know that. I mean, I knew she'd been banished. Obviously, I looked her up after the first time I met her, at that Roman guy's party. I needed to find out which soon-to-be-dead-girl had taken my blade from me. But I didn't realise they were forbidden from going home to collect their belongings. That seems... unnecessarily harsh.

"Well, Lady Grey, it seems you are banished no longer... And as for her business, that's above my pay grade, I'm afraid. I'm just here to deliver the message and ensure you come this evening."

Scarlett flips her card over, staring at it. It's identical to mine. On the front is gold foil, and on the underside is the symbol of the Sanatio Plant, the Queen's family emblem. "You're certain this is for me?"

"Unequivocally. Well, I'd best get back to her majesty. Do see that you attend this evening. Both of you."

And with that, he's gone.

I shake my head, turning the card over. This should be good.

"I guess I'll see you tonight," Scarlett says.

I glance up at her. Her face is bright, open. Her eyes,

despite being the ice blue of glacier water, burn with the heat of a thousand flames. I notice a streak of red creeping up her neck, but I can't work out if she's angry or going to cry.

I hesitate, my muscles pushing me forward, urging me to go to her. But my brain forces me to stay put. And then, whatever she was thinking evaporates.

She stands straight, her posture perfect, chin up, neck pale again, exposed.

"Well, this was delightful." Scarlett stares at me, holds my gaze, probing.

The fuck is she up to?

I narrow my eyes at her, which only makes her smile harder.

"For an Assassin wannabe, you're rather attractive when you're angry."

"Well, you're more attractive when I can't see you."

She laughs and pulls open the door. "It was a pleasure, Poisoner."

"Go fuck yourself, Assassin," I spit.

But the door slams and I can hear her laughing as she disappears down the street.

Scarlett Grey.

Absolute dick.

Shamed.

Outcast.

Stripped of her position almost as soon as she was given it, so the whispers say. Father would murder me with his bare hands if I brought a woman like Scarlett home. Not that I would. She's a complete arse. Entitled too, like all those rich legacy brats. Thinks she can take whatever she wants from me.

I return to my counter, my mind still reeling from the

strange invitation. I put the card down, realising I don't actually know why she came here.

She bought nothing. She didn't even really say anything. A cold sleeve of gooseflesh ripples up my arms and down my neck.

"What the fuck?" I freeze. Glance under the glass worktop. I swear I put it there.

I did. I'm sure I did. I'm so careful.

I scramble beneath the till, flinging papers and receipts, poison recipes and detritus on the floor.

"WHERE THE FUCK IS IT?"

My breath comes heavy and hard. Splinters of adrenaline tingle between my ribs. My eyes sting. No. I cannot. I absolutely cannot have lost it.

I shove shit off the glass display, run to the other side of the store and check by the backboard. I check under the racking, on the shelves. I notice the Queen's invite, then peer at the door.

"Mother. Fucker."

I only took my eyes off her for a split second. One second to welcome the guard. She couldn't have.

Why would she?

I glance around the store, the floor, the shelves. Back to the counter. It's not here.

She fucking stole it.

My teeth grind against each other. I'll kill her. It's the most important thing I own. It's the only way I can talk to Malachi.

I wrench the door open, knowing before I even step out onto the street that she'll have gone.

The street is busy. Too busy to see much. It's too narrow.

I let out an exasperated scream. It's loud enough an old

lady in front of me startles. Her eyes widen and then thin as she tuts at me.

"Oh, go fuck yourself. Miserable bitch," I growl as I storm back into the shop.

She will not get away with this. I snatch a vial of poison off the shelf and flick the lights off. How dare she. Too furious to stand and serve in the shop any longer, I grab my keys and lock up.

You don't steal from me, and you definitely don't steal my journal.

This isn't a game anymore.

It's fucking murder.

There are two things I hate: playing games and Scarlett fucking Grey.

CHAPTER 6

SCARLETT

I hide in the alley opposite, waiting for her to realise. Quinn's face is a picture. Fury frothing, features puckered. She barks at some poor old woman. Priceless. I laugh the entire way home.

I unlock the front door and drop the journal in my room. Our house is simple, an old servants' quarters on one of my parent's old friends grounds. The rent is cheap for a reason. The walls are paper thin which means the house is boiling in summer and freezing in winter. But it's ours. And we've made it the best we can. Scrimped for the miss match furniture and wall hangings. Our beds are a little too hard and the sofa a little too scratchy, but it works.

I find Stirling in the kitchen holding her head in one hand, and the other shaking and spilling porridge as she tries to feed herself. Mascara smeared under her lids, her hair a matted mesh of grease.

"You look hideous."

"A pleasant morning to you too, Scar."

"It's the afternoon. Hungover much?"

Her shoulders sag. "When will I actually learn that vodka and tequila, don't in fact, mix?"

"Did you seal the deal?"

At that, she sits up, and a shit-eating grin spreads across her face. She folds her arms and raises a single, slightly smudged eyebrow at me.

"You really are insufferable."

"Say that again tonight when we're eating the most expensive sushi take out in the city."

"Ah. Not tonight, we won't."

A frown passes across her forehead. "Oh?"

I give her the card. Her mouth forms a perfect 'O' as she reads the invitation.

"Yeah, that was my response too," I say.

"But why? We've been banished from any royal property since—"

"I know. Something is up, clearly. I didn't think the Queen would ever forgive our family. So whatever it is, it's big."

I pluck the card from her and put it on the table.

Stirling cocks her head at me. "Where have you been? You're looking unacceptably pleased with yourself for this time of the day."

My mouth falls unnecessarily wide open. I press a palm to my chest. "Why, what on earth could you mean?"

"Don't give me that, you've done something... Or someone, please gods. Anything to lighten your mood. You've been monstrously foul recently."

"I... I may have had some fun this morning."

She rubs her face, smearing the mascara and eyebrows further. She looks like a child puked up a pencil case.

"Kill or fuck?" she asks.

I open my mouth to say neither and then remembered Avis yesterday. "Well. Umm. Actually, I ended up offing my last customer."

"SCARLETT."

"Terribly sorry and all that. But she was a disrespectful bint and I can't have people getting away with that. Tarnishes my reputation."

"And you wonder why your trade has dried up?" She shakes her head at me.

I glare at her. "Piss off. You know it's The Poisoner's doing."

"Her name is Quinn Adams."

"How do you—"

"—I know everyone."

"You could have told me. I would've slit her throat weeks ago and not dealt with a decreasing income."

"And did you?"

"Did I what?"

"Slit her throat?" She looks at me, expectant. "I'm assuming that's where you were this morning? And... if I'm not much mistaken..." she scratches her head, yawning. "Miss Adams was also the furious woman from last night."

I shift on the spot. I should have. Would have solved all my problems if I'd killed her already. I must be silent for longer than I realise because Stirling pipes up again.

"Well, shit. Would you look at that..." She leans back on her chair, her feet against the table so she's tipped and rocking. "You really like her. Not often you pout."

"Do fuck off, Sister."

Stirling grins, the corner of her mouth curling into this deeply vexing smirk.

"You have a problem if you like her and want to kill her."

"Yes, I'm aware of that. Anyway. The invitation," I say, thrusting it at her, desperate to change the conversation.

"Indeed, this is a mystery," Stirling says flipping the invite over, examining the gold foil embossed on the card.

"You've heard nothing through your network?"

"Not a word. And that is most unusual."

"What do you make of it?" I say and snatch the card out of her fingers.

"The Sanatio emblem is the Queen's personal seal as opposed to the sovereign magician seal. So whatever this invite is, it's personal. It's come from the Queen herself."

"Most interesting. We're going then."

Stirling stands. "I wouldn't miss it."

"You better get dressed, then. You'll need a few hours to scrub up," I say and wink, just like she does.

"Hilarious," she says deadpan, and disappears into her bedroom.

Eight o'clock and Stirling and I ride up to the palace grounds. This place used to be a regular haunt for us. While we're not in the royal family, we are legacy magicians. Of high born lineage. We can trace our family's ownership of lands a thousand years. Before the Border Lord destroyed my family, we were part of the Queen's table.

We used to attend parties, and magician rites, ceremonies. My family was a part of the royal High Council. I would have been in line to be head of it one day, too. But all of that's gone now.

"You ready for this?" I ask Stirling through the earpiece.

She clears her throat. Shifts in the pillion seat. "It's weird."

"It really is. I'm not sure I'm that comfortable seeing the woman who ordered our parents' execution."

"Me neither, but it's not like you can refuse a queen's summons."

I can't fathom why we were invited. I pull up to the gatehouse and lift my helmet off.

Stirling follows suit on the seat behind me. Two royal guards extend their arms, and a long spear made of fire shoots out from one of their fists blocking the way.

"Invitation," the other one barks and holds his hand out.

I pull the invitation out of my leather jacket and pass it to him. The guard flips it and waves his fingers over the Queen's seal. It dissolves, and in its place two shimmering heads appear. They're translucent and identical to mine and Stirling's faces.

The guard examines the heads and then glares at each of us. Then he nods to his counterpart, who withdraws his flaming sword and attends to the gate, opening it and indicating that we should pass through.

I flick the bike's kickstand up, ready to drive up, when the first guard grabs my arm. His nails dig into my bicep. I glance down, my lip curling.

"Careful," I snarl. "You wouldn't want to lose those fingers."

"Word of warning, Ms. Grey. Keep your thieving fingers to yourself. You're being watched. Steal anything from the palace and I'll happily sever this arm from its socket. You hear me?"

I lean in close, my helmet pressing against his ear. "You feel that?"

Between the slip of his uniform and the belt of his trousers is my blade. Angled so that if I push hard enough, it would sever his iliac artery. The blade hums in my grip, begging for me to inch it forward. I do, just enough the tip of my blade bites into his skin.

The guard sucks in a breath.

"That's what I thought."

I pull out Chance, flick her up, catch her, and open my hand.

NO.

Too bad.

"Guess it's your lucky day. You touch me again and I'll gut you before your pudgy fingers can flex."

He releases my arm. Sneers at me, as if I were the rude one. I withdraw my blade. There's a small bead of red on the point. The blade is hot where it touches my skin, weightier at the tip, almost as if it's hungry for violence, as if it wants to pull me towards the guard and slice through the rotund flesh and let his guts spill out for being rude. The bead dissolves into the metal like the gold did on the invitation, and the blade settles.

The guard spits at my feet. I twitch, but Stirling touches my arm, urging me through the gate.

"Not tonight," she says.

The guard grumbles curses at our backs, but I rev the bike engine loud enough it drowns him out as we ride up the driveway to the palace. It's lined with trees that bend and curve over the path, twisted branches gnarled and knotted hanging drunk over the road.

We take a few minutes to reach the palace's round courtyard. In the centre, is a patch of green grass and in the middle of that, a fountain. The Queen, her husband and their two daughters moulded in bronze, water flowing from their hands and heads. While the Queen and her husband's faces are finely sculpted, the two daughter's faces are smooth and featureless. The Queen is super protective of her children. She wanted them raised in normal circumstances, away from the public eye. Other than their birth photos, which were released a day after they were born, no one has ever seen or heard from the princesses. They must be in their twenties by now. It won't be long before she has to introduce them to society to take up royal duties.

The palace building is vast. An endlessly large sandstone building, stretching almost further than I can see in both directions. Hundreds of windows dotting the front.

Turrets stretch periodically into the inky sky. Two more guards stand duty beside sandstone pillars lining the doorway porch. A majestic purple carpet extends from the front door. I park the bike in front of the carpet and kick the stand out. We leave our helmets on the seat, and I pocket the keys.

The other guard pushes open the arched, studded door, which groans in response. We step into a long foyer. The moment my body crosses the threshold, it's squeezed. Pressure sliding from head to toe as the palace's magic assesses me. It continues a moment after I step into the long foyer and then must decide I meet its requirements as the weight evaporates. The palace's magic permeates the air. It leaves a clean smell. Mint cloys the air and under it a hint of lilac. It comes from the Sanatio Plant they protect in the centre of the palace, ancient thing it is. The palace was built around it. If you walk the corridors here, the plant has roots and branches that pierce the walls and climb the floors, leaving a trail of thorns and ruby-coloured blossom in its wake.

The foyer is decorated in uniform black-and-white tiles. Ancient oil paintings adorn the walls, the judgmental scowls of long dead magician monarchs staring down at us.

I shiver. I always hated this hallway. On the left and

right are half a dozen state rooms; rooms dripping with jewels, the walls smothered in yet more oil paintings and antiquities worth enough to feed the entire city of New Imperium for a century. The wealth in this palace is obscene and I'm not sure if it makes me jealous, bitter or sad that we're no longer a part of this world. Probably a little of all three.

What it does do, though, is make me wonder what the hell the Queen wants with us. As we near the end of the hallway, a guard nods to us and gestures for us to follow him. He leads us through a series of interconnected rooms and out toward the back of the palace. We pass the inner courtyard; the walls turn to glass and even though it's night; the courtyard is lit up, lights shining bright. There she is, the oldest Sanatio tree in existence. That plant is the reason the monarchy reigns for so long. The Sanatio has healing qualities. It's said it can cure anything, even death, though no one has ever proved that part. I doubt it myself. But it's definitely responsible for keeping the royal family alive longer. Likewise, for the legacy magicians. Those born to money, wealth and power can afford to buy Sanatio and therefore live healthier, live longer.

We pass through an inner door and into the Queen's private residence, a place that even when I was a legacy, I only frequented twice. Once at my acceptance into the circle, and once when I was kicked out of it. The further we walk through the palace, the more constricted my throat gets, a tightness smothering my entire body. How could she? How could the Queen do what she did to my parents? They were nothing but loyal.

Stirling's wearing a bemused expression, her forehead all furrowed and wrinkly. She doesn't speak, though.

Finally, we arrive at the Queen's war room. The guard opens the door and nods for us to enter.

"Well, shit," Stirling says under her breath. "Look at that..."

And I do look. It takes everything I have not to let my mouth fall open. Inside is Stirling's most dangerous colleague, Roman Oleg, and dozens of his gang members. The room is packed. But the odd thing is that we only met him after being ousted out of the magician's circle. The monarchy might have all the legal jurisdiction, but it's Roman who has all the actual power. He controls so much property that he can access an obscene amount of magic. He runs the underworld the monarchy pretends doesn't exist. By all rights, the Queen should not be engaging with him.

Stirling is off before I can confer with her. She sidles up to him, his suit as smart and crisp as his manicured beard. Of all the gangsters in New Imperium, he's the last person I expected to see here. He's responsible for a multitude of high value bank raids in the last few months. Which is bizarre because he owns so much land he's second only to the monarchy in terms of wealth and power.

A huge mahogany table fills the room. It's oval and stretches most of the length of the room. In front of two chairs are brown packets with the Queen's seal on it. They're thick, but both remain unopened.

But I don't see Qui...

I inhale sharply. I sense her behind me before I feel the press of a needle through my trousers. She spins me around, pressing me into the wall.

"If it weren't for the fact I know you're holding some kind of weapon to my thigh, I'd be highly aroused right now."

She inches closer. As close as she can get without it looking suspicious.

"I'd be careful if I were you," Quinn says. "This needle is full of my signature poison. If you don't want to die a very sudden and tragic death, I'd give me exactly what I want."

This makes me smile. She knows about the journal. "Ah, what do you need a dusty old journal for, anyway?"

She steps closer, her body warm against mine. I could simply slide my blade between her ribs and watch as she leaked claret all over the Queen's plush carpet. But then, I'd be arrested and her thieving my patch would be the least of my worries. Alternatively, I could reach down, cup her jaw and pull those soft pink lips to mine. She's a lot shorter than me, especially given she's wearing flat shoes this evening. Several eyes have fallen on us, on her proximity to me.

"I think you're the one that needs to be careful."

Quinn stiffens and eases away, but her hand is still pressed against my thigh and the needle very much poking my leg.

"Journal. Now," she growls.

"I don't have it with me."

She sags. Her hold on my thigh releasing.

I grab her wrist, twist her around and pin her against the wall, the needle in her hand, now caressing her neck. I try to look as relaxed as I can, as if I'm going to kiss her, with one arm holding hers. My grip is tight, my fingers clench her skin. She's grabbed my other arm, her nails digging in so hard it stings. The hiss of heat in my skin pressed against her softness is glorious, like warm silk sheets and sexed beds.

Static hums beneath the surface—but I can't tell if the static is from her or me. I inch closer, heat building between us, between my thighs. Her breath trickles over my skin. I could break her right here. Stab the needle in. Or I could suck those lips, bite a little too hard. Slide my free hand between her legs...

I shake my mind clear.

"Look like you're enjoying yourself or the needle goes in your neck," I say, my voice low.

She's rigid under me, her body hard. Her evergreen eyes round and wide as they pierce my core. A faint quake shivers through her body. At first, I think it's fear, and then her jaw flexes and I realise it's not fear, it's rage. My nipples harden instantly, my underwear wet at her fury. She doesn't even realise how powerful she is when she's angry. Magic billows out of her when she's cross. It's intoxicating, the heady scent of spice and burnt summers. My heart rate increases, the thudding a constant urge to take her, own her, devour her.

Her cheeks pull back, her teeth bared. Oh, she is delightfully pissed over the journal. A smile tugs at my mouth.

"Means that much to you, huh?"

"Why would you take it?"

I cock my head. "It's just a game, baby. Cease trading poisons in my patch and you can have it back."

She guffaws at this. "I'll do no such thing. Those poisons are the cornerstone of my business."

"Yes, and you're destroying the trade of Assassins."

"I do believe I'm destroying the trade of *one* Assassin. I can't help if you're not providing an effective service to your clients and they're choosing me over you."

A growl bubbles up into my throat. I push the needle into her neck. She goes rigid, her eyes flick to my hand. Her nails press into my skin hard enough I hiss. I want to let my eyes roll, the sharp sting, the closeness of her body pushing me towards the line of pain and pleasure.

Focus, Scarlett.

The guards open the doors, and Queen Calandra, along with her personal guards, enter the room. I pull the needle out and drop it into a bin, moving away from Quinn and toward the table. My muscles are still tense. Tense because of Quinn, because of Calandra, and because of the soul-deep rage I have.

I won't lie. The thought of executing the Queen for what she did to my parents passed through my mind multiple times on the way here. It does again, now. The sweet thought of sliding a blade across her throat, the bubble and sticky red flowing like tears down her neck. It would be glorious. It would also be too easy. Where's the retribution? The pay back?

Calandra's wearing a suit. Faint stripes adorn the fabric, and it's tailored to her voluptuous curves. Her hair is light, almost blonde, a sharp contrast to her olive skin. It's quaffed in an elegant up do, the lines of the style as sharp as her power. She holds another envelope similar to the two on the desk and a notebook or journal that reminds me of the one I stole from Quinn.

I glance at The Poisoner, who's flushed and adjusting her clothing. She gives me one last vicious stare before stalking to the other side of the room to lean against the wall, arms folded. Her gaze slides to the journal the Queen is holding. She purses her lips.

Stirling returns to my side, leans in and says, "What, dear sister, did you do to piss off The Poisoner?"

I smirk. "I believe you call it petty theft."

"I see. And will this theft be causing us long-term

issues? Is it about business? Or is this your twisted idea of flirting?"

I place a hand on my hip, my mouth a thin line. Of course, it was about business. Business... and maybe a harmless little game of wind up. Quinn is screwing with my clientele and I need it under control. Is a poxy little journal going to cause us bigger issues? No. Of course not. Who cares that much about a journal? But by the state of the violent glare Quinn is giving me, I underestimated the depths of her rage.

But flirting? Obviously not.

"Why would I flirt with someone I hate?" I say under my breath.

"Well, you seem to fuck her often enough."

I throw Stirling an unimpressed stare. But before I can bark at her, Calandra clears her throat and opens her hand, signalling for silence.

"Roman, I apologise for our meeting being cut short. One of my daughters needed me. Thank you for attending, but as you can see, my next guests have arrived." She glances at Quinn, Stirling and I.

He murmurs 'your majesty' in response, and he slowly leaves. Though he glances back not once, but twice at Calandra, something deep moving through his glance. Once Roman and his men have left, the room feels empty, like he sucked the magic from the room as he went. I shudder, wondering if he has a soul or if he's just made of magic these days.

"Be seated," she says, and Stirling and I take a seat and Quinn sits directly opposite while she confers with her guard.

Stirling glances at Quinn and then at me. She leans into my ear and whispers, "What, exactly, did you steal?"

"A shitty old journal. Worthless. I don't understand the issue."

Stirling looks up at me, her face puckered.

"Alright, I don't exactly know why it's so important. I saw her writing in it before I took it, but it's blank. I checked this morning, the pages were empty. Clearly it's important, though."

"Clearly," Stirling says, flicking her gaze to Quinn. Who fires her a stare so potent, Stirling actually shifts in her seat. Stirling would hate that. She wants everyone to like her. I, on the other hand, couldn't give a fuck if Quinn hated me more than life itself.

Calandra indicates for him to return to his position. He settles against the wall behind her and she then takes a seat at the head of the table.

"I'm sure you're wondering why you were summoned here this evening. You understand that because of your reputations, should you speak of this meeting to any legacy or council members, I'll deny any knowledge." She pauses, glances at each of us. "However, it is these very reputations that I come to seek this evening. I am in need of your help."

Stirling grips my thigh under the table. I slide my hand over hers and squeeze. The Queen needs our help? Ours? It's laughable. After what she did to us?

And yet, it stinks of opportunity. We were told after our parents' execution there was no way back. Banished from our legacy status forever. But if Calandra requires our help... maybe... maybe we can get justice for our parents. Right the wrong done to them.

"I wish..." the Queen starts, interrupting my thought. "To heal our land."

Quinn's mouth drops. "But, how? I thought it was impossible," she says.

"The other map is lost to us. How would we remove the Border?" Stirling asks.

The Queen raises her hands to silence our questions. "I will explain."

We fall silent. The Queen opens the envelope and empties the contents onto the table.

"My husband is sick. He's dying. It's too far gone for the Sanatio to help. I've had medics in from three realms away. There is nothing we can do for him now but pray to the High Magician to take him to his next life."

"I'm sorry," I say, although for what it's worth, I'm not sorry in the least. Not after what she did. But I want to hear out what she's got to say. What this offer might be and how it can help Stirling and I.

Something about how Calandra said her husband was dying makes my mind return to the way Roman looked at her. As if he owned her... or wanted to. Court politics are beyond me, so I shut the thought down and concentrate.

Calandra tries to smile, but it doesn't meet her eyes. "It is most unexpected. He's... he's requested that I try to repair the land before he dies. He would like to pass in our old home. And so," she nods to the envelopes, "in front of you is a set of confidential information."

The three of us turn to the envelopes. I open my packet, as does Quinn. Stirling lets a tiny slip of breath escape her parted lips.

"How do you have these?" Quinn asks. "I thought everything was lost to the Borderlands?"

At that, I glance at the Queen, keen to hear the answer too. Calandra's eyes glimmer at Quinn, the lamplight in the room glistening in her pupils. "An excellent question."

But she doesn't answer. Instead, she steeples her hands.

"I am laying down a challenge. A job, if you like. It is a job not without risk, though."

I pull the sheaves of paper out of my envelope and examine the pages, trying to work out why Quinn was so shocked by the contents. But all I see is a copy of the original Imperium map—the half that the Queen still owns. There are newer maps, structural building designs and schematics.

"These are the sister palaces lost to the Borderlands," Quinn says.

Calandra beams. "That is correct. What I'm giving you is every confidential piece of information the High Magician Council has on the property and city inside the Border. You'll find building plans for both of the palaces, maps, schematics and a selection of documents I think you'll find useful."

"What do you want us to do in the Borderlands?" Quinn asks.

I eye her, but her face is stony blank. Intentionally, no doubt, to hide whatever aspect of her reputation it is that brought her here.

"I think that's obvious, Poisoner," I say.

Quinn's expression deepens from forest to fire, the black of midnight canopies and rotten mulch. "Watch who you're calling Poisoner."

"You're quite right to ask," Calandra says, ignoring our spat. She stands, waves her hand at the wall behind, and a screen drops. One map from the packet appears like a shimmering mirage on the screen. It's a replica of the real map piece she holds in a secure vault.

"The Borderlands contain the missing piece of map. For reasons that remain unknown to me, my sister, when we tore the map a decade ago, did not retain her half of the map. Instead, it was trapped inside the Borderlands."

Calandra turns to us.

"I want you to retrieve it. The High Magician's Council has reason to believe that if we bring both pieces of map together and conduct an ancient rite in the heart of Imperium, we will be able to repair them. Once the map is whole, the world should, in theory, heal itself. That is your mission."

"Sounds great, but there's no way I'm making a deal with the Border Lord, not after what he did to us," I say, frost threading through my tone.

Calandra laughs. "You think the Border Lord would accept negotiations? My dear sweet child. The reason I am laying this challenge down is because the Border Lord will unleash the full force of his power to prevent you from retrieving that piece of map. It is wholly in his interests to keep the maps apart."

"Of course," Quinn says quietly. Her cheeks heat and it makes the green of her irises pop. I flex my jaw, wondering why I'm even noticing things like that.

"If you heal the Border, the Border vanishes and so does his ability to tax the trade routes," Quinn mumbles.

"Precisely," Calandra nods, her smile deepening. "We'll all be better off if the Border is gone. Everyone, that is, except him. This challenge... the mission, if you like, will be incredibly dangerous. Not only will you not be able to walk freely into the Borders, you will be on your own once you are in there. If you're spotted, the Border Lord will send soldiers to attack. If you make it to the palace entrances, you'll face tighter security than even I had when the palaces were ours. You'll have to pass guards, magic rune reinforcements. No doubt the Lord will have booby trapped the map itself, which is harboured in the heart of the palace."

"And then we still have to get out without being caught," Quinn says, kneading her forehead.

"Exactly. A difficult mission, to say the least. And precisely why you'll need a team," Calandra says.

"Will the crown support us and provide resources?" Stirling says, shifting in her seat.

Calandra's lips pinch, her eyes turning down. "I'm afraid not. The reason I've invited you three specifically is because this mission requires a certain..." she waves her hand in the air. "Set of skills and a particular mindset that would be frowned upon coming from the crown. I'd have to use the Assassin's guild who would want planning and to follow the rules and... well, it would take too long, and we all know the Border Lord won't follow those rules."

"So we're completely on our own." Stirling leans back in her chair, blowing a long sigh.

"More to the point, I'm afraid the crown needs plausible deniability. I've hand picked you, precisely because you are the last people the crown would work with."

That hangs in the air, stagnant, thick with the knowledge that we are banished. The Queen washed her hands of our family five years ago. If we're caught and claim to be working for the Queen, no one would believe us.

"Then why should we bother working with you? After what happened to us, the injustice of our—" Stirling kicks me under the table.

And I get it. I'm taking a risk speaking to the Queen like that, but also, fuck her and the crown. Why should we work for her after we were abandoned and banned from the High Council with barely a trial?

Calandra looks down and fiddles with her cuticle. "A

fair question given your history. But should you bring me the map, I will reward you handsomely. We can discuss past misdemeanours and what the future may hold."

Before I can stop myself, the words tumble out. "What exactly does handsomely mean? How handsomely...?"

At this, Calandra glows, "I will grant your team one royal favour."

The three of us draw a collective breath. A royal favour is the highest honour in New Imperium. We could ask for anything. A royal favour can overturn execution sentences, bestow millions in coin, land, titles... it can restore legacies to banished magicians.

"Shiiiiiit," Stirling whistles under her breath. "That is a handsome prize."

"Indeed, Stirling. Your reputations precede you. You are highly skilled. Highly dangerous, and, unless I'm deeply mistaken, the only magicians I know that are capable of pulling off the feat. And the magicians with the most signif-icant grudge against the Border Lord. You have motive, needs and, I suspect, desire."

"What's the catch?" Quinn asks.

"Aside from the fact that if you're caught, the High Magician's Council, the Sovereign crown and the entire legal system will deny any knowledge of such a mission and you will be subject to the laws as a subject of New Imperium you mean...?"

Quinn pales. "Uhh, right, that. Is there a deadline?"

"You have four weeks from tonight. I'll be hosting a royal ball. I'll extend an invitation to my sister and to the kings and queens of the surrounding realms. Four weeks from today will be the greatest ball seen in five decades. It is a Peace Ball, for political negotiations. I am determined that we heal our land for the greater good of all our peoples."

"What are the rules? Restrictions? Is there a line we can't cross?" I say.

Quinn's eyes narrow. She scans my face, probably trying to figure out what line I want to cross.

Calandra claps her hands. "That's the wonderful part. There are no rules. The crown has no knowledge of this mission, remember?"

"And if the Border Lord suffers a fatal accident along the way?" I say, making sure every word is sharp and clear. I want to know exactly how much revenge I can exact.

Quinn has gone still, her face expressionless, except for a tremor that washes through her eyes. Perhaps she hates the Border Lord as much as I do. It would make working with her easier.

Not that I will.

"Let me be clear. Should someone deliver the missing map to me, I can assure you the crown would look over any unsanctioned executions. However, if you or anyone in your party is caught... you're on your own. If you or anyone in your party is injured..."

"We're on our own?" Stirling finishes.

"Which is why you've brought Quinn along as a medic?" I say.

Calandra's fingers skim the journal. She taps it and then nods. "It is. You will need to take a medic, and what better than one who can also provide sleeping draughts, poisons, gases, and other delights that will help you through the palace?"

At that, Quinn and I both glance at each other. There's no fucking way. None at all. Absolutely not in a million years. Stirling, however, nudges my foot under the table. Oh, you have got to be kidding me.

"She's the best there is, Scarlett," Stirling says. "You know it. Her Majesty knows it... Quinn knows it."

"No," I growl.

But as soon as I protest, I know that I have to take this mission on. If we break into his palace, then we can find the evidence we've always needed to prove our family's innocence. And then we can take our legacy back and still be rewarded.

This is... This is the perfect mission. The perfect reward.

"I'm in," Quinn says.

I glower at her.

Calandra beams. "Excellent. Well then, four weeks ladies. No more, no less. I will send each of you an invitation to the Peace Ball. And I hope, very much, to see you holding the map in a month's time."

She walks to the door, places her hand on the frame, and then turns to the room.

"Be safe. And good luck. You're going to need it."

And with that, she vanishes, and the three of us gawk at each other.

CHAPTER 7

QUINN

A royal favour? A fucking royal favour. Gods, I could ask for anything. Join the High Council, ask for immunity for my father, or even a piece of Sanatio. Then I can use some to make a medicine strong enough to repair Malachi's voice.

And then my thoughts turn to Scarlett, what she said. Whether she said it outright or not, she implied she was going after the Border Lord, after father...

I can't have that. I have to be on their team. Be close enough to stop her. She's a trained Assassin, she'd slaughter him in an instant... even with all father's security.

I'm out of the war room, running down the hallway towards Scarlett and the woman with her, Stirling, I think it was. Pretty sure I've met her before. I scratch my mind, trying to remember when I've done business with her.

"Scarlett," I say.

The pair of them halt. Stirling turns, and as soon as I see the unlit cigarette hanging from her mouth, I remember.

"I remember now, fire-suffused tobacco. You located me a batch for an outbreak of ice boils that swept New Imperium a while ago."

Stirling winks at me. "I certainly did."

I glance between the two women. Realisation dawning on me. They have the same crystal eyes. The same defined jawline and red tinge to their hair. Scarlett's hair is long and braided, whereas Stirling's is shoulder length and angled. Stirling is shorter too, slightly curvier than Scarlett's pencil appearance. But what confirms it is the way they hold themselves. The weight of their legacy status pinning their shoulders back and chins up—no banishment can get rid of that, it's in their blood: entitled. The arrogance runs through both their expressions. Stirling, though, she has a distinct air about her, warmer, cockier, as if she knows how attractive she is and uses it freely.

Scarlett is far subtler. Her quiet command melting my insides, making me desperate to submit to... I focus. "You're twins?"

Stirling grins. "She's lucky, aren't you Scar... having a sister like me?"

Scarlett rolls her eyes. "I see you two are already acquainted."

I nod.

"And it seems you are the best Poisoner and medic in the city."

I stand a little straighter, try to brush the compliment off. "I think I probably cause more deaths than I save at the moment. But I trained as a medic initially."

"Excellent," Stirling says. "So we have our medic then."

"Absolutely not," Scarlett barks so loud it startles me.

"Oh, this is going to be fun," Stirling says, smirking. "Whatever your little domestic is, and we all know I know exactly what this is about... Spoiler, it's not your trade war... you need to shape up and get on board because we're teaming up. Deal with it."

"I mean, I'm game," I say. There's no way I can go in alone. Father would realise exactly what was up, and I'd be sent straight to his palace. All the guards have known me for years. But if I come in under the cover of a team and change my appearance a bit, I might get to him before Scarlett does.

"You sound like you want to assassinate the Border Lord," I say. "You'll need help if you want to get past his soldiers."

"Yeah," Scarlett says, narrowing her eyes at me, "and what's a Poisoner like you going to do that a High Assassin can't? I'll just cut my way through."

I snort and rock on my heels. "Ex-High Assassin. And I would like to see you try to get through his soldiers."

Scarlett's face shakes. A shimmer of red flashing up her neck. I love annoying her. Her muscles tense and those... well; they are glorious. One nil to me, Grey.

"And what do you know of the Border?" Scarlett says and takes two steps closer. She towers above me. My eyes slip to her arms, the bulging muscle under her skin-tight top, down further, around her tight waist. She doesn't curve like me. She's straight up and down. I swallow hard, wondering what it would feel like if she picked me up, slammed my back into the wall and ravaged me.

Gods.

This is not what I should be thinking about. Not when she's intimating going after father. And yet, I can't help it. She smells like worn leather and metal, cool and fresh and a little like wind.

"I've spent time there. I was born in one of the towns

lost to the Border. The Queen probably chose me because I'm familiar with the area."

And there's no fucking way I'm letting you murder my father. Even if he's not exactly innocent.

Stirling jabs her sister. "See. Told you. Insider information. And a medic. Do I really need to convince you? This is a win-win, Scar."

Scarlett snaps to her sister, "Oh, really? And what exactly are we going to do with the prize? Because she—" she thrusts a finger in my direction. "—doesn't need her legacy reinstating. We get one royal favour."

I fidget on the spot. I'm losing her. She's right. One royal favour. I hadn't even considered that they'd want to spend it, but how the hell else can she get her legacy back?

"Maybe she will give us a favour each," I say, but my words are weak.

"It's a nice thought," Stirling says and gives me a limp smile.

We're silent for a while until a guard enters the hallway and encourages us to keep moving.

We pass through hall after hall of low lighting, giant oil paintings of monarchs past. Then we enter the heart of the palace and we pass the central courtyard. A regal Sanatio tree stands tall. It's centuries old. So old, it almost outdates magic itself. The wealth and power that one tree bestows upon its owner, the palace, is almost eye watering. But it gives me an idea.

"You had land and titles and enough coin to fund an army when you were legacy magicians, right?" I ask.

Scarlett glares at me, her face dark, fury burning in her expression. "What's your point?"

"Take the prize, but use your money to pay the rest of the team. I only need enough to buy a piece of Sanatio."

"That's pricey," Stirling says.

"And the mission is dangerous. Which is why it would have been my royal favour. But the hows of how I get a branch don't really matter. What matters is I have access to it, so I can... well, anyway. I need a piece."

Stirling pulls on Scarlett's arm. "Scar. This works. We could negotiate with a technician, a transporter, magician..."

"And if we don't? If we're caught? Killed? Then what? What if we get there and can't secure the map? How do we pay everyone for the time? No. This is ridiculous. If we do this, we're doing it alone. It has always been me and you, Stirling. And that's the way it's going to stay." Her eyes flash at me. "Poisoner. It was intensely displeasureable meeting you. Stop stealing my fucking clients. Good night."

She marches off.

Stirling touches my arm. "Don't do anything rash, okay? I'll convince her. Nice seeing you again, Quinn."

She squeezes me, then she's jogging off after her sister.

Fuck. This isn't good.

The longer I stand in the corridor, the further away they get. And then they're out the front door and vanish into the night. I'm left knowing my father is going to be assassinated, and there's nothing I can do about it.

CHAPTER 8

SCARLETT

"Are you out of your fucking mind, Stirling? How could you ask, nay, demand that woman be on our team? She's crucifying my business and, by default, our living standard. What is wrong with you?"

I march down the street, pounding the cobbles, needing to burn off the frustration cording its way through my veins.

"Would you slow down and let me explain?"

I halt in the middle of the street, and Stirling walks smack into my side.

"You are most irritating this evening," Stirling says, brushing her skewed hair off her cheek and giving me a shove.

"Get on with it," I growl, and put my helmet back on. I pass Stirling hers, and we both get on.

"Well?" I say through the earpiece. I flick the engine on, kick the bike into gear, and unleash the throttle. We race up the drive, the exhaust screaming as I bend left and right down the long, winding driveway.

"Slow the actual fuck down. I'm getting nauseous. It's not a fucking racetrack, Scar." Stirling squeezes me where her arms are around my waist and I relent, easing off the throttle.

"You're not going to like this, but hear me out before you make a judgment. Okay?"

"I'm listening," I say and pull out onto the main road.

"I watched you tonight and the other night in the club, when you were around her."

I sit straighter, my arms locking out on the handles. Stirling's right, I already hate where this conversation is going.

"You basically spend all your time either eye-fucking her or eye-murdering her. Your expressions are so similar I can't quite work out when one flips to the other."

At this, I turn my head. I can't quite see her without twisting dangerously. But Stirling taps my belly to silence me.

"Regardless. Fifty per cent of your time, you want to bang her brains out."

"Where are you going with this?"

"We bring her onto the team, get to know her. I dunno... maybe let yourself be happy? I mean, she spent as much time eye-fucking you as you did her."

"And?"

"And you fall madly in love, finally accept it and give the rest of us a break from having to deal with your pining."

I tut. "You are a giant cock. You know that?"

Stirling laughs. "Be serious though. Maybe you should give her a chance. You might not want to admit it, but you like her. Besides, in the meantime, we can be a team. She will bring her knowledge of the Borderlands."

"I suppose," I sigh.

"What's the alternative? Seduce her, get close to her, earn her trust so you can find out the secrets of her poisons? And then sabotage and drive her business into the ground..."

I sit higher on the bike.

"My Gods, Scarlett, it was a fucking joke."

"Was it?"

"YES, you fool. Don't even think about screwing her over." Stirling smacks me on the shoulder hard enough it makes a thump, and the bike wobbles.

I decide not to respond, but her words sink in, a plan forming. Revenge is always a good idea, right?

We streak past mansions and castles, the night air cutting through my leathers. Finally, we leave the legacy region of New Imperium and drive through the narrower, darker, dirtier streets. Houses without magic crammed together like candy in a packet. Because they're magicless, the houses are smaller, their brickwork crumbling instead of polished. The windows netted instead of lined with plush fabrics. The air is thicker here, full of smog and the leftover essence of borrowed magic, brought here from the mansions in the heart of New Imperium. Five years ago, I'd never even been here, never deigned to visit the poorer areas of the city. Would never have dreamt that coming here would eventually feel like coming home. Where magic hums in the air and tingles your nose with cinnamon, static, and a little bit of grease instead of it living in the walls of your castle.

We reach our place and I park the bike.

"What if I can't do it?" I say as I pull my helmet off and take the ear piece out. Stirling already has hers off.

"Then you'll have fallen in love and... gods, I dunno, Scar... be happy?" Stirling winks at me.

My eyes widen. She throws her head and laughs, trotting off to the front door.

"You're insufferable," I bellow after her and lock the bike up.

She sticks her head around the side of the house. "And you might get laid along the way which will also be a bonus for me, because I won't have to put up with your whiney uptight ass anymore."

I scramble up and chase after her. But she's too quick and has the door open and slammed in my face.

I finger our dented and chipped letter box. The flap is hanging off at an angle. I open the door and pull the letters out. There's two thin envelopes with the Queen's personal seal.

"The invitations," Stirling says.

"I guess we're doing this then, four weeks and counting."

I hand her the invite addressed to her and then open the next letter. I skim the text, blood draining from my face.

"What's wrong?" Stirling says.

"Shit. Shit. Shit."

I slide down the door and hold my head in my hands. Stirling takes the letter and mumble reads it aloud.

"Dear Ms. Grey, it is with deep regret and sadness that I have to write and notify you of your eviction notice. While I have been deeply grateful to you both for how you've looked after the property, I am experiencing financial difficulties and need to sell the house. I do hope you'll understand. I require you to leave four weeks from receipt of this letter. Yours, Wilbert."

Stirling crunches the letter up and dumps it into the bin. "Two nights. That's what we have once we return from the mission. Two nights after the Peace Ball to get out. We have to get that fucking map, and you need to find a way to get on with Quinn because otherwise, we're both royally fucked." She storms into her room and slams the door.

The following morning, I decide to investigate. With the eviction notice hanging over our heads, there's no question now. We have to take the Queen's mission. I send Stirling off to reach out to her network for any intel they have on the Borderlands, and specifically, any contacts we could use inside the Border. And on her way home, to source some cardboard boxes so we can start packing our belongings. That leaves me with visiting the physical Border itself. I can combine it with a training session, anyway. I slip on a crop top and lycra compression leggings and strap a pair of Katana swords to my back. The bike scowls at me from its parked position. But I decide the run will be a good warm up, and I make my way to the Border. Five minutes in, I'm already grateful for it. My body is full of frustration. Some people prefer massages and relaxation when they feel like this. I prefer to hurt; the intense burn of lactic acid and endorphins is a meditative experience for me. The searing in my thighs spreading to my mind, clearing it of everything.

I pound the streets, breathing in the smog. My lungs humming with static and cinnamon. But it's not long before the roads widen, the houses grow bigger and the air clears. I take half an hour to run to the Border. It's at the edge of what is now New Imperium. Though the city was three times the size before The Tearing a decade ago.

Suddenly, the houses run out, and that's how I know I've arrived. There's a wide strip of grass as the houses stop and then a wider plain of concrete up to the Border.

Behind me, New Imperium sprawls. And in front of the gap carved through the city like a scar, is the Border. If you didn't know what you were looking at, you might not even realise. In the distance, sat upon a hill, is the old palace, and beneath on the undulating hills, a mosaic of city mansions.

It's all a lie, of course.

It's why the Queen demolished all the houses sat on the boundary. In the early days after the Border was formed, dozens of people were lost to it. My guess is they weren't concentrating and because the Border is a mirage, they'd bumble down the road and find themselves crossing into the Borderlands without realising. Poof, they'd vanish and never be seen again. So the Queen demolished every house that sat within 100m of the Border and, instead, situated a permanent base of royal guards the entire way up and down the strip.

Now, combined with the Border Lord, there are passports, access papers, specific trading routes. It's a lot, and security is... tight, shall we say.

I spend another twenty minutes running along the Border, checking out all the security points, wondering how the fuck we're going to get in without passports or papers and without the Queen's permission. Each gatehouse is precisely far enough away from the next that they can reach anyone trying to. The wall of guards is relentless. No gaps. No space for errors.

This is going to be much harder than I thought.

I find a large patch of grass in front of a woody area. While it's still near the Border, it's secluded and the streets are empty. I pull to a stop. I take out the Katanas and practice a series of attack and defence moves and a variety of parries until a sheen of sweat lines my brow.

I drop to the grass and do pushups, situps, mountain climbers. I jump up, high knees, tuck jumps. I pump out jump squats until my thighs are screaming so bad I collapse in muscle failure. Now that my body is warm, I pause a minute to recover and then pick up the Katanas again, close my eyes and train blind. Pushing and stretching the remnants of my magic. I breathe deep, let the thread of my senses pulse. The air fills with iron and coal, but the harder I try to reach for the magic, the more it pulls away. I swear and throw the sword to the ground. I pant, hands on my knees.

"Fuck's sake." I refuse to give up. The more I sweat, the deeper the burn weaves through my muscles. I like it. Crave it. The endorphins kick in, I push harder and harder, more reps. Fuck the magic. I can rely on my senses without the heightened abilities. I grab the blades, swipe, swipe, duck, spin my leg out. Drop my arms, turning kick, sidekick, reverse kick. Jab, jab, hook, duck, kick to the knee.

Over and over.

Harder and faster until I bend over, buckling on the grass, and hurl my guts up. I collapse, my chest pumping so hard I can't work out if I need to be sick again or pass out.

My whole body courses with adrenaline. Everything is louder, brighter, with endorphins flowing through my veins.

When my heart rate comes down, I get up, sleeve the katanas and take a slow walk towards the main Border gatehouses. By the time I get there, there's a queue four dozen people deep.

I pause on the peak of a small incline in the road and stare out over the view. It looks like the city always did, as if nothing ever changed. But if you scan the horizon carefully, it glimmers. The mirage shudders. If you catch it at the right moment, you can see the city inside. But it isn't so much a city anymore, as a nightmare. Dark billowing clouds, the sun mostly blocked, light lost to the in-between. A broken city, trapped between the here and there.

Not quite either.

I shiver, and the mirage snaps into place.

One of the Queen's guards catches my eye. I'm pretty sure he watched me run past earlier.

His royal ruby uniform is pressed and starched to within an inch of its life. The fabric is the same colour as the Sanatio blossom. I flash to the ceremonial swords on his back and suppress a sigh. Fucking guard wouldn't know how to use a sword if it gutted him over coffee. They've all spent so long at the military barrack mansions that they've had the mansion's Collection tattoo inked on them: giant swords down both forearms. They could swipe their blades through the air, and the mansion's magic would make the swords act for them. Where's the skill? The skin on my arms, where my tattoos were stripped from me, itch. The scars are no longer angry and livid but pale and watery, echoes of the power I used to draw on.

Bastards. The Queen isn't innocent either. She might offer us an olive branch now, but she sanctioned my parents' execution. She's as culpable as the Border Lord.

I'll have my retribution, or I'll die trying.

The guard approaches me. His face is full of scars, striations tearing up his skin. Long faded, like my own scars, but on his face they're savage.

But it's not the guards I'm afraid of, it's what lies beyond the Border I'm curious about. How the hell am I going to get inside to find out enough information?

The queue up ahead moves forward in a slow constant shuffle. That's when I spot The Poisoner. She waltzes straight to the front of the queue and past all the Border Walkers and traders, and the guards wave her through like she's a fucking celebrity royal. And then, just like that, the canny bitch vanishes through the other side.

My jaw drops.

What. The. Ever. Living. Fuck.

She said she had grown up there, had access, but that's... Stirling is going to have a field day with this. How the... If she can just...

"Oh, for fuck's sake. I hate it when Stirling is right."

The guard approaches me. "Don't be fooled, missy. I seen you looking at the Border."

I frown at him. His name label reads Gale. "What do you mean?"

"I see you. I been watching you watch the Border. It don't look like that inside. It's a devious bit of trickery. A mirage if you like. One of them magician illusions. I thinks it's the mansions inside. They're all pissed at us for fucking up the maps."

"Is that so?" I smile, brighten my expression, feign interest. He's not told me much, but perhaps he knows something useful. I can work with this, embody my inner Stirling and pump him for info. She's all charming, bright smiles or some shit like that. Gods, killing people is much easier than having to talk to them.

"It is. The Border shows you what it thinks you want to

see. That's how it does it. How it lures in the unsuspecting. Makes them think it's candy and cuddles inside."

"And I take it it's not."

He guffaws. "I only went in once. That was enough for me."

"Why?" I say, trying to scrunch my face into some semblance of an afraid little girl. It works because he shakes his head, wipes his hand over his mouth.

"You ain't thinking of going in there, are you?"

I shrug. "There's something I want in there. I was considering it."

"You gotta get the right passes and what not, you know?"

I grit my teeth and nod. I want information from him. Not him extracting it from me.

He reaches out to touch my arm. I resist glancing down at his pudgy fingers gripping my forearm. Resist snapping them off.

"Do yourself a favour. Don't bother. Don't even consider it."

Unlucky for me, we're way past not considering it. I need to get that map, restore my legacy and be done with The Poisoner, too. There's no way I'm not going in. I place my hand over his and gasp. "Why? What's so deeply terrible about a city that used to be part of ours?" A haunted look passes across his eyes.

The soldier pulls himself back, disentangling from me. He eyes me with a narrowed gaze.

"Because, missy, there are a thousand nightmares in there. A rotten, decaying world with rotten people, rotten creatures, and all of them want to eat you. Or at least it was in them early days. Traders and Border Walkers say it ain't too bad these days. But I ain't risking it. Some of them... the ones who veer off the routes, they don't come home looking so good."

I shiver under his gaze. It was full of shadows and the icy prickles you're left with after a fright. Whatever he'd seen in there had him spooked.

"You walk in there alone, you won't last three seconds," he says. "That's if you can get in without a pass. Which I'm assuming you don't have. And if you don't, you won't get one."

Well, The Poisoner just walked in. But I wasn't going to bring that up. Whatever she had on the guards that enabled her to get through like that, is something I need to know.

I'll torture it out of her. I might enjoy that. Fuck her until she screams her secrets at me. But I'm instantly annoyed because what I want to think about is torturing her and flailing the skin off her bones. But instead, my mind drifts to thoughts of my bare hands spanking her arse cheeks and tweaking her nipples, leaving marks of me on her flesh. Gods, Scarlett, get a grip.

"Are you listening, miss?" the guard says.

"What? Yes. Of course. I'll get a pass."

He sniffs. "Look. I watched you train. You got some skills, I'll give you that. But I was in one of the early teams to investigate the Borderlands. There were ten of us."

Were? My blood cools. Stories that start in the past tense never end well.

"I might not look it now," he pats his paunch, "but I was in the Queen's Guard squadron. We went in all young and cocky, like you. Thought it would be a breeze. It was our city, after all. We'd all lived in it our whole lives. Yeah, the city was torn in half, but it was still our city."

He lowers his eyes. Rubs a hand across his face. "Two of

us made it out. But Freddie didn't last the night. I tried to keep him alive, but he... he didn't make it."

"I'm sorry for your loss," I say.

He nods, swallows hard. "If you go in there, make sure you're not alone or you might as well kiss whatever it is you're hunting goodbye."

"GALE?" another soldier calls from up ahead. His beret as ruby coloured as his uniform. A Sanatio symbol on his epaulette. He must be the captain of the squad.

"Thanks for your help," I say. He nods and walks to his post.

Even after Gale took his place back at his post, as he settled and his shoulders relaxed, the harrowed expression never left his eyes. Whatever he'd seen, whatever happened, it haunted him deep. Ghosts of monsters and nightmares furrowed in between the lines of his scars. All of them wrinkled and etched into the grooves of his face so he'd wear them close and never forget.

My stomach tightened. He was right. I might be an Assassin, but what do I actually know of the Border? I've never been inside, not since we escaped The Tearing. Neither Stirling nor I have. She may have some contacts that have intel, but clearly, The Poisoner wasn't lying when she said she knew the Borderlands.

I hated it. I hated that Stirling was right, that I'd have to grovel my way into The Poisoner's good graces and ask her to work with us.

I'm spiralling, turning everything over and over. There's only one way to settle this. I pull Chance out of my bag and rub her edges.

"What should I do? Yes for team up. No for go solo." I kiss Chance, flick her up, and she spins through the air. When she lands, I drop her onto the back of my hand.

YES.

"Fuck's sake."

But the more I think about it, the more I realise Chance is right. If going in alone is really as much of a risk as the soldier made out, then there's no way I'm putting Stirling in jeopardy for the sake of my pride. I don't give a shit about me. I won't put my sister in harm's way for the sake of our legacies. No. We're going to need a team. I'll go to The Poisoner's apothecary tomorrow and ask her to join. I suppose the best bit is that I can do exactly as Stirling said. She was joking, but perhaps there was something to it. If I can needle into The Poisoner's heart, I could uncover something. The secret to her infamous poison... I could sabotage it, crush her business the same way she's been throttling mine.

Yes.

Now this is the kind of plan I like.

CHAPTER 9

QUINN

It worked. Scarlett saw me stroll past the queues and straight through the Border. I don't often take to stalking women. But I had to make sure she saw. How else could I convince her I'd be useful? I entered the Border and then raced down to a gatehouse further down. She doesn't need to know I didn't spend long inside or what I was doing. As far as she knows, I've proven what I said to be true.

And it is true, of course. I do know the Borderlands and the palaces. I just can't tell her why. Not if she's really going to hurt my father. I wish I understood what he'd done. Why she's hell bent on hurting him.

If I can convince her to work with me, I can find out what her problem is and rectify it. Then everybody wins.

I know my father. He's done some nasty shit. Killed a few men even. And yes, he might tax the trade routes. What else was he going to do? Weeks went by after The Tearing, and no one came for us. No one helped. We were trapped with supplies running out, and someone needed to take charge and get control. Without him, we all would've died. He keeps everyone in line. Stops the looters and Border gangs from attacking the traders. He does a good job. I can't imagine what the issue is. But if we work together on this mission, I'll be able to sort it out. And Stirling can help me negotiate.

It's early afternoon by the time I get to the apothecary, and I'm dishevelled and in need of a shower. The Borderlands are hotter than New Imperium in the day and far, far colder at night. The weather is a monster all of its own in there. Storms like I've never experienced. Heat that makes water pour from your face, cold that should only be found in the most northern regions of the realm.

Scarlett and Stirling won't know what hits them when we get through the Border. How the hell I'm going to drag a team through undetected, let alone into the old palace and through my father's security, I have no idea. But I suppose I have no other choice than to try. I have to protect him.

I pull my hair into a messy bun, hair and fly aways springing around my face. Fucking hair. I should cut it all off. The only reason I haven't is because father loves the way the curls frame my face. And that's when I realise cutting it off is exactly what I should do. Father and the palace soldiers will all recognise me. I've always had long hair. If I want to get through the Borderlands undetected, I'm going to have to go in disguised.

I close the shop early for the day and go to the barbers. I only have to wait a few minutes because it's drop in.

"Are you sure?" the barber says, his eyebrow set to firmly raised.

"Billion per cent. Get rid of it. Leave styled curls on top and shave the sides. I'm over it."

"Right you are, Ma'am."

I hesitate and shut my eyes the moment he takes the scissors to my hair. There's a grinding slice, slice, slice, and then my head is lighter.

I grin. Totally the right decision.

As he cuts and trims and uses the clippers against my scalp, my smile gets wider and wider. It makes my neck and jaw look more defined. I'm never going to be thin. I like my tits too much to even try. But this new style definitely makes my face brighter, and I love the smile that will not leave my mouth.

I thank the barber and leave him a generous tip. Then head home for a quick shower and change. I'm hoping Scarlett will bite today. She saw me, I'm sure. If she has any sense, then she'll come and find me. There's no way she can go with just her and Stirling.

I shower, threading my hands through my hair. It's so short that my hands pull away faster than I expect. The sides bristle against my palms. And then I'm imagining not my fingers, but Scarlett's, caressing the sides, stroking my head.

The space between my legs heats. Even though I'm in the shower, I'm slick. I bite my lip. This is a dangerous game to play. She wants to murder my father. The last thing I should do is have any untoward thoughts. But... But I'm alone...

My hand slips between my thighs, my fingers finding my apex, rubbing rhythmically as images of Scarlett flood my mind. I close my eyes. Scarlett appears beneath me. On her knees, her braid soaking from the shower raining down. Mentally, I strip her clothes away, imagine her watching me as I pleasure myself. Her hands grip my thighs hard. Her grip presses into my skin hard enough to bruise. A moan escapes my lips at the thought. She pushes her face into my flesh, her tongue lapping at my core. Heat courses through my body. My legs tighten as I imagine her standing, pulling me towards her, kissing me so I can taste myself. My fingers sliding to her pussy. The higher I push my body, the more I picture, the faster my core reaches its peak. Images of Scarlett shoving me against the wall, worshipping my stomach, biting my nipples, gripping me like she owns me. Her hands roaming everywhere.

I can't take it anymore. My thighs shudder as waves of pleasure ripple through my core.

It takes me a moment, but I pull myself together and realise what a stupid mistake that was. The last person I should masturbate over is fucking Scarlett. And yet... and yet it was almost as good as the orgasm she gave me in the club prison.

"Fuck's sake," I scream and slam the shower handle off.

Okay, that is absolutely the one and only time I ever do that. There's a thousand women in the realm. I do not need to come over her.

I dress in a tight top that clutches my skin like a hug and a short skirt. My breasts bulge out of the top, but I don't care. I look good today. I rub curl cream through what's left of my curls, swipe mascara over my lashes, put some sandals on and glance at myself in the mirror.

"Damn. The haircut is on point."

This is the most me I've ever felt. I practically dance out of the apartment and all the way to the apothecary. I wasn't going to go, but there's a delivery due tomorrow, and I need to move the stock around the warehouse.

I unlock the warehouse door at the back of the shop and slip in. It's dark now the sun has set. But the warehouse has no windows, it's dim at the best of times. As I make my way through the aisle, my skin prickles and cools. I freeze. Glance left and right.

I strain to listen for anything unusual, but the warehouse and the shop are silent. I shrug it off and continue to the apothecary front to grab my stock journal.

I reach the counter and ice threads under my skin like worms. I reach for a hairpin beneath the counter and pull the cap off, careful not to touch the poisoned tip. Slowly, I step toward the door for the light switch.

Someone is inside. I can throw a mean hook, but I'm short, and having a weapon would be far more advantageous. I hazard a glance to the rear wall where the blades are on display. Too far.

My breath kicks up a notch, clawing like granite in my throat. My heart matches my breathing, thudding against my ribs.

I notice an umbrella in a tall vase bucket by the door. As I flick the light switch, I spin round and grab the umbrella.

And then I scream.

It rips through my lungs, a shrill piercing sound that echoes around the shop as I launch the umbrella at the counter.

I stop screaming, and a roaring laugh comes from under the counter.

"You absolute mother fucker. What is wrong with you?" I shout.

She stands, gripping the counter with one hand, bent double, holding her stomach with the other, tears of laughter streaming down her cheeks.

Dick head.

"One... One..." Scarlett pants through the laughter. "Nil to me."

"Oh my Gods, you're... I hate you so much." But that only makes her laugh harder.

And to my irritation, a hysterical bubble of giggle wobbles up and out of my mouth. When we've both finished laughing, I'm still shaking. The shock not quite out of my system. Scarlett pushes a lock of loose hair behind her ear and then rubs her lobe.

"I didn't mean... Sorry," she says, realising I'm shaking.

"It's fi—"

Suddenly, she's round the counter, her arms wrapped around me, warm, safe. I stiffen against her, but it makes my teeth chatter.

"Relax, and let me make you feel better," she says and tugs me in a little tighter, a little safer. "I didn't mean to scare you that bad. I was only playing."

"You're still a cock of the highest order," I mumble into her chest and then relax, letting my arms drift around her waist. The soothing heat of her torso encloses me like a caress. I push the thought away and detach myself from her.

I brush my curls behind my ear. Now awkward and unsure of what to say.

"That was n..." Scarlett starts. I glance up. There's a strange expression on her face.

Heat rushes to my cheeks. We might fuck, but we don't hug. The realisation makes my insides knot. "Thanks. For erm. Helping me calm down or whatever. We probably shouldn't do that again. Anyway. What do you want?"

I'm rambling. I shake my head, brush the curl away. Fucking thing won't stay in place. That's the only downside of new hairstyles, takes a minute to work out how they sit best.

Scarlett takes my chin and lifts until my eyes meet hers. "You cut your hair."

She lets go of my chin and runs her fingers across the shaved patches. The brush sends a shiver of pleasure down my spine. My eyes shut, my mind drifting to the shower and how much I wanted her to do this. My lips part. This is...

We don't do this.

"Yes," I say, stepping out of her reach and returning to the counter to put the cap on the hairpin. "Fancied a change."

"It's really... it suits you."

I look at her for the first time. She's wearing sports kit. Gods. I need to stop ogling her. She has legs for days and her abs are big enough I can actually see them through her skin-tight top. She has those little cuts that run from the hips into her trousers. I swallow hard, hoping it'll suppress the urge to run my tongue down the lines of her muscles.

Nope.

Didn't work.

It is entirely unfair that Scarlett fucking Grey is the most attractive woman I've ever seen, and she wants to slaughter my father.

There. That's better. I needed to remind myself of why I hate her. And there are so many reasons. Entitlement. Yes. That's one. Plus, she stole my father's blade and let alone the journal. The first simmering bubbles of rage feed into my lungs, breathing the anger like air. This is better. This is where I should be. Because this... between Scarlett and I... it's a game and nothing more, and it never will be.

It's a game I have to win. There's no way I'm letting her anywhere near my father. Steel settles in my gut, a coldness in my throat. I want my fucking journal.

"So," I say, my voice thick and chilly. "Can I help?"

Her eyes rake up and down my body, and I swear to gods it's like the silk of her touch. Focus, Quinn.

"I like it. That was all I meant," she says, her gaze hungry.

My fingers mindlessly run through my locks.

"Anyway," she says, arrogance oozing through her tone. "I owe you an apology."

My mouth drops open. I slap my palm to my mouth, a devious grin in my eyes.

"From Scarlett Grey? How controversial. Tell me, what did you do that means I'm bestowed with such an honour?"

Her jaw flexes once. It makes the ice-blue of her eyes darken for a flash. Oh good. I'm getting to her, scratching the edges off that one nil.

"It appears that you were right," she says, her mouth a tight pinch. I bet she hates having to admit that.

"I waaaas?"

She glares at me, knowing I'm drawing this out for the simple pleasure of having her tell me I'm right.

"About the Borderlands. It seems it's going to be more difficult than I assumed to get in. And other than the packet of schematics for the palace, and the information the queen gave us, we have very little other intel."

"I see," I say and lean on the counter, my breasts plump and billowing out of my top. Scarlett, though, doesn't bite. Shame. Every cell in my brain knows I shouldn't want her. But my shower orgasm is well and truly gone. And she looks... I sigh mentally.

"And so you're here, why?" I ask.

Like I don't already know.

"My sister seems to think we'd make a great team. Gods

knows why. But having investigated the Border this morning, it does seem like we're in over our heads."

I nod, stoic, my face expressionless. Internally, though, I'm wearing a shit-eating grin and feeling delightfully smug. One all, Grey. One all.

I lean forward. "For once, I agree. The Borderlands are far more dangerous than you realise, and I have experience that would be invaluable."

Scarlett steps closer. Her eyes flicker to my cleavage so fast I almost miss it.

Two-one to me.

"Right. Yes," she gestures in the air, "that's why I'm here. The only time I'll grovel. But I've reconsidered my earlier position and think it would be best if we maybe..."

"Yesssss," I say, inching my arms together, bulging my tits out higher, fluttering my lashes at her. Shameless Quinn, fucking shameless.

"If we work together," she says.

This is where I see my opportunity. I move out from behind the counter and step right up to her. So close that the air between us heats and tingles, our breath mingling. She smells like hot rose, leather and warm skin... I need to control myself. I am in control here. She's here because I designed it. This is my court, my game. I've got this.

"On one condition." I tiptoe my fingers up over her abs. She stands straighter, that viciously sharp jawline flexing. It does bad things to my pussy. I have to take a breath, push the urge to grab her and fuck her on my counter away.

"And what is the condition?" Scarlett says. She leans forward. Pins me against the counter with her body. Her arms lock me in place where she grips the glass on either side of me.

I could lean back, hitch my ass onto the top, spread my

legs and present myself to her. I could reach out, take her hand, slide it up my bare thigh. She's worked out today, I can tell. The veins in her arms and hands stand out. I doubt it would take much for her to pick me up and throw me onto the counter, pin me down. I glance at her crotch. She's not packing, I'd get to feel her hard fingers as they pumped in and out of m—

"Quinn?"

"Huh?" I say, snapping out of my thoughts. The heat in my groin shoots to my cheeks, like she caught me out, like she knew exactly what I was thinking.

"The condition?" She's so close, her lips part as if she wants to kiss me. I can't concentrate. I can't think. She's a fucking parasite wheedling her way through my focus. All I can think about is how much I want her to push me down, part my legs and...

FOCUS QUINN.

"Right. Yes. The condition. Give me back my journal and I'll do whatever you want."

Shite. I did not mean...

Scarlett cocks her head, her tongue slipping over her lips and her ice-cold eyes now ablaze. "You'll... do whatever I want?" Her gaze slides down my body like she's peeling my clothes off. Gods, I should not want this. I'm furious with myself, and yet... I move a millimetre closer, a temptation, an offer, a tease.

I drop my voice, let a little husk into it. We can both play games, Ms. Grey. "What I meant to say was, I'll help with your team."

She laughs. It's light, fluttery, like my traitorous fucking stomach. She leans in. I close my eyes as her breath trickles over my cheek. The space between our skin is volcanic hot. I have to force my lids open. She holds me captive, time slows, and I'm certain she's going to take me right there and then on the counter. But then...

"No."

The word slices through me like diamonds and ice. I push her away, the air alive. My body fizzes a raging internal war; the cold arctic fury she inspires against the feverish need of my clit.

"What do you mean, no?" I grind out.

"I'm keeping it as leverage. Don't think I've forgotten our little business tryst. You help me win the chall—"

"Us," my eyes narrow. "You mean, I help *us* win. If we team up, we're in this together, and I want a blood pact that you'll give me the money for the Sanatio."

She shrugs, examines her fingers. "You'll get your money for the Sanatio. I'll get my legacy status back. And we'll all win."

"And if we don't secure the map? What about my journal, then?"

"Then I guess we can come up with another kind of deal." She drops her eyes and smiles. What does... Is she suggesting...

"You know, something like agreeing trade areas, given you're screwing my business into the ground," she says.

"Right. Yes, of course. That's what I thought you meant."

Lies. It was entirely not what I thought she meant. I need to take a cold shower. Clearly pleasuring myself earlier was insufficient.

"We're agreed?" I say.

"We complete the mission. You get the journal back. I pay you coin for the plant, and we use the royal favour to get back our legacy status, titles and land."

"And if we don't succeed?"

"Then we figure out a new business agreement. You get off my trading land, I'll keep off yours. And I'll consider giving you back your journal. Agreed?" She reaches out her hand to shake.

I reach out. "Deal."

She grips my hand and gives it a firm shake, then she bends my fist until she holds it to her mouth and places a kiss on my knuckles. I suck in a sharp breath. Her lips are warm and soft, and what if she kissed...

"The best deals are always sealed with a kiss," Scarlett says, a devious glint in her eye.

She releases my hand and stands straight. "Tomorrow eve, then?"

"Where?"

"City Centre New Imperium Park. 9pm. There's a stone arbour in the park on a hill. We have a full 360 degree view, and we'll know if anyone approaches. We'll be able to discuss plans in private."

"Till then," I say. Then she's gone, and I'm left standing in my apothecary wondering if I really have hold of this or if she was winning all along.

CHAPTER 10

SCARLETT

Stirling and I spent the evening packing the living room, boxing our meagre belongings and binning anything we weren't going to keep. When I finally crawl to bed exhausted, it's Quinn I'm thinking of.

That fucking skirt she wore, the way her breasts bulged out the top. The sharp lines of her undercut. It was torture trying not to stare at her curves, her arse, the way she leant on that fucking counter. I swear she did it on purpose. My neck and traps ache from physically restraining myself. All I could think of was pinning her to the counter and fucking her until she sobbed with pleasure. As I roll over and drift off to sleep, it's with fury in my heart; I still don't have new clients. I'm livid I've had to accept Quinn on the team. And so horny I swear my clit is swollen. As sleep drags me under, it's Quinn I dream of, and instead of walking out of her shop, I stay, do exactly what I wanted...

"You want me," Quinn says. Her deep green eyes boring

into me, a glint curving her gaze. It sends fire through me. She sets me alight. My nerve endings burn and throb. How dare she presume such a thing.

"I want to kill you. Destroy your business," I say, heat laced through the words.

"Liar," she says, and her tongue wets her plump lips. I want them. I need them tracing smouldering kisses over my skin.

"You want to take me on this counter and fuck me until the only name I ever scream is yours," Quinn says, her gaze so intense it makes my body vibrate. She hops onto the counter.

I march forward. One pace, two. Three. The space between my thighs hot and slick. Desperate for me to do as she says. To submit myself to her. Take her on the counter and taste her. Make her mine. Make her beg for everything I will give her.

"Tell me you need me," I say.

Her gaze darkens, a twisted smile curving the corner of her mouth.

"Beg." It's a demand.

This makes her smile harder. She shakes her head and jumps up on the counter, her floaty skirt lifting and flashing a hint of flesh and lace. I'm instantly wet. My legs and neck are tight, straining to hold me back.

Quinn brushes her freshly cut hair, nudging the curls aside. The lines of her neck are smooth, her skin bare, empty, begging to be ravaged.

Her hand slips down her front to her thick thighs. I suck in a breath. Slowly, torturously slowly, she pushes the hem of her skirt up.

With each millimetre her skirt rises, her eyes never

leave mine. Her expression darkens until her fingers nudge the lace aside and she parts her molten core.

I can't take it.

I'm on her.

My hands grip her thighs, pulling her toward me, toward the edge of the counter. I shove my way closer, and she responds by wrapping her legs around my waist, locking her feet so I can't escape. My lips meet her neck, fast and hungry, smothering her skin in kisses and bites. She smells like summer gardens and herbs, like deep, heady lust. I want her. I need to take her.

I nip the skin at her throat. She moans under me, wrapping her arms around me and digging her nails deep into my flesh. The sting sends pulses of pleasure down my spine. I pull her chin around. Push my lips over hers. They're so soft, warm. She tastes like honey and cinnamon, like fire and magic. She pushes her tongue inside my mouth and it drives me wild.

She pulls my skin-tight top and sports bra off. Exposing my nipples to the air. Her mouth drops to the hardening nibs. Her teeth scrape the buds, and I can't help but let out a guttural moan. My hands grasp her arms tighter.

I slip one hand to her leg, inch it up slowly, slowly. Teasing her the same way she did me. The heat increases the closer I get to her lace. She releases me and slips her top off. Her bra is lacey, her brown nipples peaking out.

"Say it." It's a command. I'm not messing around anymore. I need her. Need to taste her.

She grins at me. Places her hands on my shoulders and pushes me until I'm kneeling in front of her. All I have to do is lean forward, pull her knickers, and I'll lay her bare. My tongue will make her come undone.

I just need her to say it.

"Do you want me?" she says.

"Don't play games with me, Quinn."

She closes her legs, hitches her bottom up, and takes her lace panties off. She dangles them in front of me.

"I want you," she says, "to tell me exactly how much you want me. Tell me how much you want my cunt." And she drops her panties to the floor.

I'm soaked between my legs, my whole body quivering with need.

"Well?" she says. She leans down, her breasts threatening to escape the lace fabric. I need all of her. To own her. Dominate her. Desire consumes me, fuelling my body like oxygen and fire.

She cocks her head, leans back, and spreads her thighs.

I inhale a sharp breath. The flowing fabric of her skirt covering her flesh. I want to see her, to touch every millimetre of her skin and savour every kiss. I want to feel her clench around my fingers, knowing I've made her body melt.

"SCARLETT?" A voice cuts through the reverie.

"Show me," Quinn says and pulls me between her spread legs.

I'm shaking. My body is rocking. But it's not Quinn. She's not touching me.

"Scarlett? Get the fuck up."

I peel my eyes open. My whole body still aching from sleep, from the dream. From the need.

"What's your problem?" Stirling says. "You look like... actually, I'm not sure what you look like. But it's time to get up."

She takes a bite of an apple.

"Where the hell did you get that?" I ask. Fruit is expensive, we don't normally keep it in the house.

"I know a girl," she winks at me.

I rub my face, the fragments of Quinn's sultry voice and her demands slipping from my consciousness.

"I need a minute," I say, trying to work out whether I'm furious about the dream or disappointed it's over.

"Hurry up, we've got shit to do today." Stirling leaves and slams the door shut, and I lie down. Every time I blink, there are flashes of Quinn. Her thighs, the way her hand slipped up her dress. The way her mouth curved around my breasts. Her hands gripping my shoulders, demanding I fuck her.

"Fuck's sake." I slip my fingers beneath my pyjama waist band and over my pussy. Like the dream, I'm soaked. What is wrong with me, that my enemy can arouse me like this? I close my eyes, but all I see is Quinn. Her beautiful evergreen eyes. Stupid curves I want to drown in. My body stiffens as I move my hands over and over myself. I'm not gentle. I ravage my core harder, faster, rubbing the rage away, the fury that she could do this to me. How dare she. But no matter how many times I close my eyes, try to blink Quinn away, it's her I think of as my clit swells and throbs and tips me over the edge until I'm riding a wave of ecstasy, of her. It's Quinn my body aches for as I lie back in bed and grunt out a frustrated moan.

"I have to end her. Forget trying to screw her business. I'll kill her instead. No one gets this much power over me," I'm mumbling to myself, but Stirling has reappeared at the door, her arms folded as she leans against the frame with a pinched expression on her face.

"Oh dear, The Poisoner's really got her claws into you, hasn't she?" she says and takes another bite of her apple.

Cocky twat.

"Don't you have some deal to go negotiate, supplies to source?" I say as I stand up.

"It's not me you're pissed at. Are you sure you can keep the feelings at bay?"

"I don't have any feelings," I bark at her.

But she tuts at me. "Scarlett. You know I was joking, right? I don't actually think you should go down the path of luring her in only to fuck her over…"

"Too bad it was a good idea, and now I can't let go."

Stirling rubs her forehead. "Er, no. It's a terrible one. All that's going to happen is you'll bring her in and fall for her and then not be able to go through with it."

At this I march up to her. "I am a trained Assassin. A fucking High Assassin, no less. I don't have feelings. They took them all away. I'm dead on the inside, like she will be when I'm done with her."

Stirling sniffs and shakes her head. "Don't say I didn't warn you. You can still walk away from this. Don't mess with her. Why don't you… oh, I dunno. Be happy and date her?"

"How can you say that? You're supposed to be my sister. She's screwing with our lives. Our businesses. She needs to pay."

Stirling kicks off the frame. "Does she though? Have you ever considered that maybe, just maybe, you could let yourself be happy? That legacy and status isn't everything. That being in love is enough?"

I snort. "Coming from the biggest player I know?"

She looks at me with a pained expression, her eyes dropping to the floor.

"You don't want to hurt her, Scar. For once, let it be."

"I'll be happy when I'm standing on the carcass of her

business as High Assassin, holding the keys to our mansion."

"It's your funeral." Stirling walks off and out the front door, slamming it as she goes. She doesn't look back.

She's wrong.

Obviously.

CHAPTER 11

SCARLETT

Stirling and I arrive at New Imperium Park early. The park is an odd shape, most of it is a giant hill that overlooks a lake and a wooded area. The stone arbour we're meeting at is at the top of the hill with an amazing view of the city, and if you strain hard enough, you can make out the shimmering haze of the Border in the distance. Stirling and I stand under the arbour for protection from the rain, which is spitting.

I notice The Poisoner before she sees me. Her head is bowed, her breathing elevated as she trudges up the giant hill. A flicker of irritation passes through me, that I'm not the one making her pant. I suppress it. Stupid thought. She's wearing jeans that hug her curvy hips and a tiny crop top. A slip of flesh showing between her belly button and waist.

I swallow.

"And you don't like her?" Stirling says, shaking her judgmental head. "Put your cock away and stop drooling."

I glare at her, refusing to bite. "Go do a final scout around. Make sure we've not been followed. Make sure there's no one in the park."

"Just think about it... about letting it go and being happy," she pouts at me, but I point at the park and she leaves, stepping into the growing rain and jogging to the edge of the woods at the bottom of the hill.

She runs the periphery of the woods, a giant circle around the base of the hill. But the park is empty. It's late, for one. Second, it's starting to rain. And third, my senses aren't prickling. That's one of the first things they train you to heighten in the Assassin's guild. I trace my fingers down the tattoo that's now a scar. Even though I'm not connected to the Assassin's guild building anymore, I still have my natural born magic. Sure, it's not as powerful as it was when the guild building had collected me. But I can still tap into my training, my skills. We're safe here tonight.

The Poisoner finally looks up, her eyes dart to Stirling running around the hill. Her cheeks are rosy, where she powered up the hill. We'll have to train her hard the next couple of weeks before we go into the Borderlands. If we're trekking through the city on foot, there's no room for stragglers.

Much as I try not to let it inside, I smile at the prospect of making her sweat. But I'm not sure if it's because I want to make her sweat in the gym or the bedroom.

I knead my temples. This is going to be hard. But I'll be damned if I'm telling Stirling that. I'll prove her wrong. I'll seduce The Poisoner, find some incriminating evidence to cripple her business and then leave her heartbroken.

I've changed my mind. It can't be that hard, can it?

But then she crests the hill and smiles at me, and the rest of the park disappears.

"Hi," she says and looks up at the sky, her eyelids fluttering as droplets of rain patter against her cheeks.

"Hi." I need to relax my jaw and stop grinding my teeth. It's deeply unattractive. I gesture at the arbour behind me. "Shall we?"

"Sure," she says and hustles the final few feet. She's got to be almost a foot shorter than me. Gods, she's going to slow us down in the Borderlands. This was a terrible idea. As if she can read my mind, she strides out in front of me, marching to the other side of the arbour.

My eyes slide down her back to her arse.

It swings from side to side. Boom, boom, boom, as her hips kick out.

No. It's just an arse. Nothing special.

Whatever.

Stirling, thankfully, is jogging up the hill, a welcome distraction. The rain grows heavy, droplets pounding a rhythmic beat on the arbour roof.

"So," The Poisoner says.

"So," I say.

Stirling appears at the entryway drenched, water peeling off her in long threads of dripping splashes. Her hair sticks to her face in strings.

Stirling glances from me to Quinn, her features pinching. "Well, this is delightfully awkward. Shall we make a start?"

We move into the middle of the arbour and stand there, as awkward as Stirling said. Oh, this is ridiculous. I open my mouth to start, but The Poisoner butts in.

"We should address the fact none of us trust each other," she says.

I press my lips shut, narrow my eyes at her. Nice point. Alright, I'll give her that.

"I agree. Let's lay everything out on the proverbial table. Why we're doing this. What we want out of it," Stirling says.

A thick silence follows. When no one offers anything, The Poisoner thrusts a hand on her hip. "Fine. I'll start. I have a sick relative, and none of the training I've had as a medic is working. The only thing I can do now is try a piece of Sanatio. But I can't do that because it's prohibitively expensive and most of the time, you don't even get your application authorised to buy a piece, never mind the money."

Stirling folds her arms. "An honourable motive, for sure."

"And you two?" The Poisoner asks.

Stirling looks at me. I take a breath. "We need to right a wrong against our family."

"Your legacy?" she asks.

I nod.

"But your parents tried to steal the map. They were caught, were they not?"

Stirling stands straighter, the muscles in her neck stiff, her veins popping as she flexes her jaw.

"We don't believe it's true. They were framed," I say.

"Then why not prove it?"

"There's no evidence."

"I see," The Poisoner says.

"But that's the reason we want to go after the map," Stirling says. "If we can retrieve the map, we can ask for our legacy status to be reinstated, and then we'll have access to the resources we need to prove our parents' innocence."

"Another honourable motive," The Poisoner says, repeating Stirling's comment. "We're all in this for the right reasons. That, at least, will make it easier for us to trust each other."

I start to pace. "How the hell are we going to pull this off? Not only will we need to infiltrate the old palace, we'll need to get across the Borderlands city, and that's all besides the fact we need to enter the Border undetected."

"Well, that's why the prize is so high," The Poisoner says. "I can sort the way in if you guys are able to source team members. The city is about fifty miles across, it will take us two days to get to the palaces if we're on foot. The actual city crossing itself won't pose much of a problem. It's the entry and the palace that will be tricky. We're going to need ample supplies, and carrying them might slow us down."

Stirling glances at The Poisoner. "How is it that you know so much about the Borderlands, anyway?"

Quinn takes a deep sigh. "For one, I was born and grew up in that part of the city, and two, I have relatives inside that survived The Tearing, so I try to visit when I can. Which means I've spent more time there than most, given I have a resident's permit."

Stirling and I both frown. But I open my mouth first. "A what? How did you get one of them? You had to be inside The Tearing when it happened to have one."

The Poisoner shrugs. "I was."

My eyebrows shoot up. I look at her anew, a wave of respect washing through me. I didn't know that about her, but it makes sense. The toughness, the ruthlessness by which she's encroached on my territory. I wonder if she's sending money home. The Tearing was horrific, so the stories go. The earthquakes, the skies ruptured, winds tore through the city, buildings collapsed. Ice fell, crops died, the magic went on the fritz. And they were all trapped inside. It wasn't until the land settled that the Border allowed people through, started swallowing passersby.

Stirling pipes up this time, "Then how are you out here living in the new city? I heard there were only a handful of people allowed out."

Quinn looks at the ground. "There are. The Border Lord keeps most residents inside the Border. You might hate me for taking your commissions, but it's the same talent with herbs that got me out. Plus, I pay Border taxes. I guess that helps. Or it could have been luck." She shrugs.

I glance at Stirling, my brow furrowed. Do I believe her? Seems... I'm not sure. Suspicious. Though, if I think about it, she really is that talented. Not that I'd admit it to her. But I've never seen poisons like it. Once I'd gone on a job in the southern quarter of the city. A woman wanted to kill off her husband, who was a nasty piece of work. Not my normal work, but thanks to Quinn, I couldn't afford to be picky. Anyway, I'd waited until the end of the husband's shift. It was twilight at the steelworks and he was the last one there, locking up. I was ready to pounce, make it look like a random mugging. When fucking Quinn stabbed me in the neck with a needle. I have no idea what she injected me with, but she managed to paralyse half my body. I had to drag myself one armed, one legged out of the industrial estate. And then there was the time she blinded me for a day with some powder after we both turned up to a locker location for a job commission. I'd got there first, we fought, we fucked, and then she blinded me. Thankfully, it was only temporary. Still, I can't deny she's skilled.

"I don't believe in luck," Stirling says.

The Poisoner stands straighter. "Then I guess I'm that

talented. And given the way I've crippled Scarlett's business, stolen her clients and completed commissions she couldn't, I don't think any of us need to question that."

Heat instantly bubbles in my chest. I need the reminder that the only thing she's interested in is destroying me. And as for completing commissions, I couldn't. The only reason I couldn't complete the drowning kill was because she blew puke poison in my face and I was too busy retching my guts out to hold the guy's head under the water.

She's here to ruin me, remembering that will make it easier to gut her life when this is all over. Instead of knocking her out, which is what my Assassin instinct wants to do, I smile sweetly and say, "Well, perhaps you can teach me the tricks of your trade, then. Make it a fairer competition."

She smiles, a thin, malicious thing.

"The only competition here is securing that piece of map before the Border Lord catches us and hangs us all. We both know I've already won the murder game."

Prickles of hot, spiked rage course through my veins.

"Watch your tongue before I make you kneel and punish you."

Stirling wipes a hand over her face. I ignore it because The Poisoner steps up to me, her mouth twitching as if she's suppressing a laugh. She pulls my chin down to meet hers, "Calm down baby, it's just a joke. We'll all be winners at the end of this, remember?"

Her stare drives right through me. Into my heart, my skin, my bones, as if a piece of her buries itself in my soul.

She's infuriating.

I hate her.

But the soft warmth of her fingers on my chin against

the chill breeze whipping under the arbour is enough to calm me down.

I place my hand over hers and gently remove her fingers.

Stirling coughs. "Right, well. When you two have finished verbally fucking each other, shall we begin?"

I pull away, glaring at Stirling, who will absolutely get an elbow in her sleep for that comment tonight.

"Do you have a suggestion, sister?" I say through gritted teeth.

Stirling's pout is all pinched and tight, like she's also trying not to laugh. They can both go fuck themselves.

"I do. We're going to need resources, right?" Stirling says, looking at The Poisoner, who nods.

"Yeah, even if we were super fit—"

"—I am," I say a little too sharply. "That fit."

"I'm sure," The Poisoner says. "Ex-Assassin and all."

"High Assassin."

"Ladies. Can we stay focused?" Stirling says. "It's a fifty mile walk. Unless we can find a transport guy with connections inside the Border, we're on foot, anyway."

"We need to be on foot. Smuggling us into the Border will be hard enough, let alone with vehicles," The Poisoner says.

"Right. On foot, then. And we'll need supplies to last two days," I say.

Stirling paces around the edge of the arbour. "We can't take two days' worth of supplies. It's too risky. We'll need to carry four days' worth to be on the safe side. That will impede progress. Especially the bigger the team gets."

"How many do you think we need?" I ask.

"Five? Maybe six?" Stirling says.

The Poisoner frowns. "Why so many?"

Stirling halts her pacing and counts on her fingers. "Scarlett, as Assassin and primary protection, makes one. You," she points at The Poisoner, "as medic with insider knowledge, is two. Me, as team Resourcer, coordinator and map reader, is three. We'll need a transport and supplies guy to get us out. That makes four. Then we'll need a security and rune hacker to actually help us break into the palace, which makes five..." she trails off.

"Oh, shit," I say.

"Oh shit, what?" Quinn says. She has this little confused wrinkle between her brows and it makes her whole face crumple.

"Oh, shit, the sixth is a Collector," I say, tearing my gaze away from her.

Stirling nods. "And the best Collector we know is my ex."

"Ah," The Poisoner says.

"And things didn't exactly end well. Did they?" I throw Stirling a pointed stare.

She presses her lips shut and shakes her head. "Might be somewhat of an understatement. We umm... look, that's old history and doesn't matter right now. The point is, she's the best."

The Poisoner groans. "Right. And I'm guessing there's no one else?"

"I mean. There is. I know some magicians, but no one like Morrigan. Last I heard, over sixty mansions have collected her," Stirling says.

The Poisoner whistles. "That's a lot of magic to have access to."

"Exactly, and she has palace magic," I add.

"As in...?" The Poisoner asks.

"As in old palace magic from the Borderlands," Stirling answers.

"Shit." Quinn sits down in one swift huff. "How the hell does she have palace magic?"

Stirling tilts her head. "I never actually asked. I guess why doesn't really matter. What's important is that she's the best, and if we want a powerful magician as a backup, power supply or basically anything we're not qualified for, then she's it."

"I guess you better put your most charming smile on and buy some flowers or whatever you do to win a girl's heart back," The Poisoner says.

"Flowers?" I snort. "You can tell you don't date very often." I cross my legs to sit with her, and Stirling follows suit.

"Says the woman who steals pretty girls' journals?" The Poisoner bites back.

Stirling rubs her forehead, glancing at me and Quinn. "Are we going to be able to get through this without all-out war between you two?"

The pair of us glare at Stirling.

"I'm serious. We need some agreements. No fucking, no fighting. Fucking leads to fighting, fighting leads to fucking, and we don't have time for either." Stirling stares at us both, but neither of us responds.

"So we have a Collector. Who's next?" The Poisoner says.

Stirling lets out a grunt of irritation.

"That leaves a transport and supplies guy," I say and turn to Stirling. "You thinking who I'm thinking?"

She nods. "I know this guy, Jacob Jones."

"And then you said a security and runes specialist?" Quinn asks.

"I'm guessing from the schematics the Queen gave us that the palaces are heavily guarded and, unless the Border Lord has a rune specialist in there, the security systems will be a decade old. Then again, we have no idea what upgrades he may have put in place now."

"I might," Quinn says. "Or at least I'll be able to find out."

I scowl at her. "How?"

Quinn hesitates. Something flashes through her expression, but it's gone before I can work out what it was. "My relative works for the Border Lord."

Stirling can't have noticed as she rubs her hands together. "Excellent. This is all coming together nicely. And as for the security and runes specialist, I know a girl."

"Of course you do," I say.

She throws me a vicious side eye. "I mean... It *is* my literal job."

I'm not even dignifying that with a response. "Who's the girl?"

Quinn is shifting from foot to foot. Rubbing her hands together. What's her problem?

"You don't know her. But she's good. Really, really fucking good. But she's also constantly in demand, so it's whether we can get her or not," Stirling says.

"Okay then, we have a plan and the bones of a team. We'll start recruiting tomorrow," I say.

"The Rune specialist..." Quinn starts, and then shakes her head. "Never mind. It can't be. I heard they weren't in business anymore. Let's meet mid-morning outside my shop? I have to open up for my assistant anyway," Quinn says.

I scan her face, trying to work out what the issue is. I hold my hand out, and Quinn slides hers in to shake on it.

Where her skin meets mine, I swear heat pulses into electricity. Stirling places her hand on top of our clasped ones, and we shake. And as we do, I catch that familiar unreadable expression flicker through The Poisoner's face, and I wonder exactly what it is she's hiding.

CHAPTER 12

QUINN

The next day, I meet the twins mid-morning as planned. I worried yesterday that they'd seen through me, that they didn't believe what I was saying.

I tried to keep as close to the truth as I could. I do have a relative in the Borderlands who works for the Border Lord. What I didn't add was that it was the Border Lord himself. They'd never trust me if I said that, and then I'd never get my journal off her. The fact I have a resident's permit because he's my father is beside the point. In all honesty, the only reason he let me out is because I'm talented. That was the truth. He sent me out to learn the world, build my skills independently without his support, to understand how hard it is to survive, and realise the enormity of what he'd done and had to fight for. So that one day, I could take over the reins from him as Border Lord. And the taxes bit is more or less true. I send money home. Okay, it's not taxes, but it goes to my mother and brother. Father is tight, despite the accrued wealth. I suspect because he's terrified of losing it all and having to live like we did after The Tearing.

I figure the closer I keep to the truth the better. The more lies I tell them, the more I have to keep track of, and I'm bound to fuck up at some point.

No. This is the easiest way. Tell as many truths as I can while avoiding answering the shit I need to keep quiet.

Scarlett and Stirling set a gruelling pace, marching across the city. I was sweating after the first ten minutes. I had a stitch after fifteen, and I wanted to be sick after twenty. They're both tall and long legged, and I am most definitely neither of those things. The cobbled streets are killer on my ankles and it's chilly, as if rain is singing somewhere in the distance. We're at least three miles out from the centre of the city now, and I've no idea how much longer we have to go.

"Guys, for the sake of my dignity, could we slow the ever loving fuck down?" I moan.

Stirling cocks her head over her shoulder at me. I'm trailing at least ten feet behind them. "You're aware we're going to have to set this kind of pace through the Borderlands. Better to practice now, don't you think?" But she's grinning, a little twinkle in her eye.

"You're a dick. And I'm hailing a carriage." I'm puffing as I try to keep up with them.

"We can't aff—" Stirling starts, but Scarlett digs her elbow in her ribs.

They can't afford it? How badly were they ex-communicated from their legacy?

"Were you not allowed to keep your inheritances?" I say and immediately regret it. The words spilled out before I could stop them. I don't mean to pry. "I'm sorry, you don't need to answer that."

Scarlett puts her hand up. "No. It's fine. And if you must know, no. We were banished from all our properties, all our banks. The only coin we were allowed to keep was whatever was in our pockets. Which, given we are... *were* legacy magicians, meant we were still living at home. We hadn't inherited anything, as our parents were still alive. We had barely enough coin for a room for a night."

This makes me stop mid-stride. "I didn't know. I'm sorry." It makes me see her in a new light. They'd spent their whole lives with everything handed to them on a plate. I can't imagine the culture shock of having it stripped away. I get why she fights hard for her territory. No wonder she hates me when her clients are all she has. How strange that she went from everything to nothing as I went from nothing to everything.

"We don't need your pity. It is what it is. Five years we've lived like this, and we've done fine. But when we get the map and have our titles restored, our banks unfrozen, and our legacies returned, we won't forget those who shunned us."

"The carriage is on me," I say.

Scarlett stiffens. "We don't need your money, either. We can pay our way."

Stirling places a hand on Scarlett's arm.

"We're a team, are we not?" I say.

Scarlett nods.

"Then we can all chip in and do our part. A carriage and perhaps even a pizza this evening is my shout."

This, at least, makes Scarlett smile. "I haven't had a pizza in years. It was my favourite."

"We have a deal, then?" I ask.

"You and your deals, Poisoner. I'll tell you what. We can go in a carriage today. We can eat pizza tonight. But from tomorrow, you start training with me. The whole team will."

My face pales. Scarlett is super fit. I watched her working out near the Border the day I snuck in. She'll probably work me to death or something horrific. As if she can read my mind, she says, "Don't worry, we'll go slow..." She leans close to my ear, so close her breath trickles down my neck. It's warm against the chill of brewing rain in the air. "I only like to break you in the bedroom."

I swallow down the images of Scarlett between my thighs, sat on my face. Her naked flesh.

"Enough. I told you. No fucking on mission," Stirling says, rolling her eyes.

"Fine. Carriage and Pizza. Tomorrow we train." I stick out my hand, but as she stretches out to meet me, I pull away.

"And I want my journal. Today. I want to look inside it."

Scarlett's jaw flexes. "Hail a carriage, Poisoner."

I do, and half an hour later, we pull up to an enormous glass-fronted building. The car park is full of predominantly motorbikes, the odd car scattered between. The windows are equally filled with motorbikes, both stationary on the ground and hanging from the ceiling. To the right is a garage. Flaming wheels hang on racking, exhaust pipes with green smoke, chains and bits of cogs lay discarded on the ground.

"What is this place?" I ask.

"This is where we find Jacob Jones," Scarlett says. "Notorious underground racer. Can drive, fly, operate any machine. And a dab hand at fixing them, too."

"Right, and this is... what, a racetrack?" I ask.

"Bingo. Jacob is also deadly fast. Which is precisely why we need him on the team," Stirling says, and hops out of the carriage.

I pay the driver, ask him to wait and get out. Outside, a group of unnaturally large magicians appears. Each one looks more buckled, broken and deranged than the last. One has what I can only describe as a spade for a face, the next has a black eye and a scar that cuts through his lip and gives it a ridge. The following two have shoulders as wide as the cars they're standing in front of.

A considerably shorter man with salt and pepper hair, dressed in leather magician robes walks between the rows of bikes, a deep set of lines scouring through his forehead. "Can I help you?" he says to me, and then Stirling appears from behind the carriage.

"Stir, darling," he says, his expression opening up and brightening. "What are you doing here?"

"Business Reece, I don't suppose your main man is here?"

"But of course, he's on the track now. You can watch his last race if you like. I'll take you to the box."

Stirling waves Scarlett and me over. "Super. Although I don't know whether you'll be as happy to see me when I tell you the favour I need."

Reece frowns. "I think a favour is the least I can do for you after everything you've done for me."

I glance at Scarlett, wanting to know what exactly Stirling had done. She leans down, her lips brushing my ear. It sends sparks of heat down my neck, and I have to close my eyes to keep control of myself. That's the second time today. Remember, this is a game. I need to get my journal and to prevent her hurting my father, and then I can put all this behind me. We can go back to hating each other over territory.

"She helped negotiate the deal that got Reece this race-track along with a string of others. If it weren't for Stirling, he wouldn't be where he is today."

"That's a good thing, no?" I mouth.

"It is, but, Stirling is about to ask for his best racer, and that means less income from sponsors and racers for the best part of a month. He won't like it."

"I see, a tricky negotiation for sure."

"It is, but she's the best deal maker I've ever met." Scarlett glances at Stirling, whose arm is wrapped around Reece's shoulder like they're old pals, and I suppose they are. But what takes me by surprise is Scarlett's demeanour. Her shoulders back, chest thrust out, a gleam in her eye as she stares at her sister. I remember watching Malachi do his first spell, I had the same expression in my eye then. I'm so used to seeing fury crease lines into Scarlett's face, or the deep gaze that tells me she's about to fuck me senseless, that I'd almost forgot she could have other emotions.

We enter the building and a rush of flutters curls inside my tummy, I've never been to a racetrack. My legs urge me on, the adrenaline pushing me towards the track. A fleeting thought runs through my mind, wondering what it would be like to drive around the track fuelled by engine and fire magic.

We entered the foyer, it's spacious despite the quantity of bikes in here. It's bright, too, the walls clean white. Photos of magicians in leathers holding helmets in front of bikes and racetracks. I don't recognise most of them, save for a blonde woman who's infamous for her antics on and off the track. I can't remember her name now, but she dated one of my ex-girlfriend's mates. I noticed her in passing at a few club nights and parties but never spoke to her. There are several tall glass cabinets filled with trophies that shimmer and have phosphorescent whorls flowing up from the goblets, a nod to the fire magic used in the bike engines no doubt. In the middle of the room is a receptionist. But she looks at Reece and waves us through.

Reece guides us up a set of stairs and into a suite that's long and thin and stretches the entire length of the pit lane below. I rush to the stretch of window and peer down in the pit lane. It's alive with mechanics and bikes and racers. There are technicians holding balls of fire, their hands lit with sparks, others wield burning cogs. The garage section is littered with spare parts, racking of tyres, exhaust pipes, handle bars, wires, tubes and fire boxes to hold fuel. The teams make the lane look like a rainbow where they all wear bright coloured uniforms.

"Woah," I breathe. I peer at the racetrack and my stomach rolls, only this time the adrenaline has vanished, and a queasy nausea fills my gut. The track has a slight tilt and the way the motorbikes whizz around the corners, their riders knees grinding against the tarmac, it's like ants jacked on speed and makes me want to hurl. I change my mind, racing is considerably less appealing.

Round and round they go, faster with each progressive lap. I try to keep up. The glass window must be thick because I can't hear the engines. I stare in astonishment at the speed they ping, ping, ping down the track. Two bikes near each other as they curl around the bend. I gasp, wondering how the hell they didn't collide. Then the bike numbered six veers around the other and accelerates. They're so close I swear their thighs must be touching.

I stagger away from the window.

I can't watch. My heart pounds in my chest, no wonder

people get addicted to watching. I stumble over my ankle as I step, but Scarlett's there. She grips my arm and waist. Her touch is firm, secure, safe as she hauls me standing.

"I. Umm. Thanks," I say, brushing her off me.

"Have you never been to a race before?" she says.

"No, never. I've spent my life studying or working. This is... this is awesome but completely terrifying." I'm grinning like an idiot.

Scarlett's staring at me with a strange expression.

"What?" I glance behind me, wondering if someone walked in and rub my face in case I have something on it.

"Would you..." Scarlett starts and then hesitates. She pulls out a coin. It's red on one side and gold on the other. I think there are words printed on it, but she's twirling it between her fingers so fast I can't make them out. She rolls it onto her thumb and then flings it up in the air. When it slams down on her fist, she covers it and then lifts her hand, and a deep grin spreads across her mouth.

"You know what. Fuck it. Come with me." She grabs my hand and pulls me towards the stairs.

"Wait. What about Jacob and Reece?" I say.

"Jacob's on the track, I saw him. Reece will be there when we get back. Stirling will need some time to negotiate, anyway."

She hustles me down the stairs and towards the rear of the building. She pulls open a wide door and the roar of engines and cheering booms around us. I flatten my hands to my ears to dampen the noise.

"Holy shit," I bellow.

And Scarlett is beaming. "Amazing right?"

"It really is."

The air smells like hot tyres, smoke and leather. There's a bowl next to the pit lane gate full of ear buds. Scarlett grabs two sets and hands one to me before putting her own set in.

"Come on," she says and gestures for me to follow.

We walk down the tarmac lane. There are people everywhere. I love the race suits dotted with logos and badges over their chests and down their arms. People hold their hands out as they levitate tires and engine pieces. Another technician has a piece of silver piping hovering between his hands and tiny fire threads flowing from the middle of his palms as he solders it to another piece of metal someone else is holding.

This. Is. Incredible.

The motorbikes racing peel off the track and into the pit lane. Each one going to their respective teams. The clamour and rumble of exhausts and engines reverberates through my entire chest like thunder and drums. A bike pulls to a stop in front of us and the rider pulls off his helmet.

"Ms. Grey. What do I owe the pleasure?" The biker is tall. Much taller even than Scarlett, and she has to be approaching six foot. This guy dwarfs her. His hair is long, and the creamy coloured waves flop around his ears. His eyes are brown, but so light they almost match his hair. He has perfectly trimmed stubble around his chin and cheeks, as perfect as I suspect his ego thinks he is. I've dabbled with men, though I much prefer a woman's body, a woman's sex. But even I can admit, Jacob is extraordinary to look at.

"Stirling's upstairs."

His shoulders sink. "Well, that is less good news! That woman always gets what she wants. And what she wants, is rarely what I want."

This makes Scarlett laugh, and to my surprise, it's light and infectious and despite trying very hard not to, I smile in response.

"Isn't that the truth. Do you mind?" She gestures at the bike.

He raises an eyebrow. "When was the last time you rode?"

"Get fucked Jones. You know I kicked your arse last time I was on the track."

He grins, "In your dreams, Grey," and hands the bike over. "Be careful, she's pulling a little on the straights when you let the throttle out. Smith dropped some potent fire-catalysing combustion agent that he tweaked with magic into the engine pistons, but it's made her a henny beast in the runs. We're still working through the niggles."

"Alright, I'll be careful. Grab me two helmets?"

He nods and vanishes into the garage.

"Wait," I say, having processed what she said. "What do you mean two helmets?"

Scarlett glimmers, a slow, delicious smile that expands across her lips like sunrise on the horizon. "I'm taking you for a ride."

"Er. No." My stomach instantly shrivels up, and I'm pretty sure the sour taste in my throat is vomit that is very ready to escape. "Definitely not."

Jacob reappears, hands Scarlett a leather overall, then one to me and places two helmets on the ground.

"I am one hundred percent not getting on that bike."

"You one hundred percent are," Scarlett says.

"But we didn't plan it. I haven't researched the safety or thought it through. I can't possibly get on that bike," I say even as my body betrays me and I push one foot followed by the other into the leather suit.

"Sure looks that way too," Jacob says chuckling.

I fire a glare at him. "I'm... I can't get on. I'll die."

He helps velcro me into the suit and taps my shoulders. "You won't die... probably."

My eyes widen.

"Stop winding her up, Jones," Scarlett says, nudging Jacob out the way. She finishes zipping up her leathers and checks mine. Tugging straps and zips. I try to ignore the pressure of her fingers tugging me closer to her.

"Live a little. Not everything needs to be precision perfect. We can do this. Just hold on to me. Okay?" She says and cups my cheeks. "As long as you hold on, you'll be fine."

I'm shaking. I'm not sure if it's nerves or excitement or a bit of both. Definitely both. The fact she used the word "we" didn't go unnoticed. The only we I'd ever thought of in relation to Scarlett was how much *we* hate each other. I let the word settle in my mind. Settle next to her name and this spontaneous death trap we're about to ride.

"Do you trust me?" Scarlett says.

"Absolutely not."

She erupts in laughter. "Good. Get on the fucking bike."

She lifts me. Literally picks me up by the fucking waist like I weigh the same as a toddler and dumps me on the bike. Then she points to the pillion pedals and shoves my feet into place.

My eyes widen. "We... this... how the fuck is this happening. Are you even qualified to drive this... this machine? I don't understand how this contraption works, I need to kno—"

"—One. It's a motorbike. Two, I am a race champion. Three, you don't need to know everything, sometimes you can flip a coin and take a chance. And four, put this in your ear. It's an intercom. You'll be able to speak to me."

"Curse you more like it."

"You're a magician, not a witch. Don't pretend you know how to hex me."

"If I die, if you murder me on this track, be assured I will come back and haunt your sorry ass for the rest of time." I take my current ear bud out and push the intercom in instead.

"You're going to love it."

I say nothing because I'm fairly sure if I open my mouth I'll be sick. I pull the helmet on and the cacophony of noise in the pit lane drops to a low rumbling. Instead, it's replaced with the thundering storm that is my heartbeat.

Scarlett flips my visor up to talk. She fiddles with the straps under my chin, her fingers warm where they brush against my neck. Then she's slipping her own on. There's a crackling in my ear and Scarlett's voice appears.

"You know you'll love it, and you can thank me after when you do."

I glower at her, entirely unconvinced.

She checks my helmet one last time and then looks me dead in the eye. "You're safe with me."

I can only see her eyes through the gap in her visor. They're pale, but this afternoon they sparkle. I haven't seen her this excited before. I like it. It changes her whole face. Makes her warm instead of full of ice.

"I promise," she says. I can't see her mouth moving, but her expression tells me everything.

"Okay," I say.

She gets on in front of me. Her arse shifts until it's pressed right up against my thighs which suddenly feel very warm. She wriggles until she's as close as she can be.

"Hold on," she says and pulls my hands around her waist. Despite the tremors running through my body, her torso is thick, strong, like mountains and granite. She is utterly still beneath my fingertips and her assuredness, at least, gives me a little confidence and slowly my trembling ceases. That's the second time she's made me feel safe. I push that knowledge aside. It's not something I want to acknowledge. This is a fun—

My whole body tightens and a scream rips from my lungs as Scarlett opens the throttle and the bike explodes down the pit lane.

"FUCCCCCCCCCCKKKKK MEEEEEEEEEEEEE," I squeal.

But I'm drowned out by Scarlett's cackle. Between huffs of laughs, she spits out, "I told you this would be amazing. Now. Are you ready?"

We slow down as we reach a set of lights suspended above us.

"What? I thought that was it?" I stammer, my whole body shaking.

"Oh, Poisoner, no. We haven't even started. When I curve around the bend, lean with me, okay?"

I nod. "If I'm going to die, you can at least call me by my name."

"When we survive, I will. I promise." She slips her hand over mine, her fingers looping in. "I promise you. I won't let anything happen to you."

She squeezes and then lets go, and where the imprint of her hand was is a cool patch.

"When the lights go green, I'll go. We're only going to do one lap as the racers will be on in a few minutes. I'll take you off the track to a spectator patch at the end of the track."

I lean against her and try to swallow the desert mouth that's currently clawing the insides of my throat.

"THREE. TWO. ONE," Scarlett says, and then the entire world vanishes in the shrill ringing of my scream, the rushing pressure of air around us, and the high pitch whine of the engine.

And Oh. My. God.

This is the best fucking three minutes of my life. I cling to Scarlett's back as she shouts messages of encouragement down the intercom.

We curve around the bends, my knees pressing into her thighs as I hold on for dear life. My breasts push into her back and my arms tighten around her as we drop low to the floor. The hum and vibration of the tarmac skimming the plastic plates rattles through my knees.

The world streaks in the rush of wind against my overalls. The pressure from the gusts is surprising. Even though she's taking the brunt of the force, I still have to use my muscles to stay in place.

And then we hit the straight and Scarlett gives the bike everything. She opens the gas and I swear I almost pee. I'm laughing and screaming. The track is zooming past and my heart is in my throat thumping to the rev of the engine. Then we're slowing down and pulling into a slip road off the track and up towards tiered seating. She slows to a stop around the back. And holy shit I want to do it again.

Scarlett puts the bike on the kickstand and pulls the helmet off, her plait all static. But her face is beaming and bright, and fuck, I want to kiss her. I yank my helmet off and jump up and down, and then I don't know what I'm thinking, but I leap into her arms. And Scarlett, bless her Assassin soul, catches me.

My legs lock around her back. My arms around her neck. Her eyes are totally focused on me, as if nothing else exists. It's intoxicating. The adrenaline coursing through my veins is replaced with something deeper, hungrier. How dare she just take me on the bike like that, take my life in her hands at two hundred miles per hour.

"That was... I didn't want to go on the bike," I say, trying to add acid in my voice.

She holds my gaze, the intensity between us infinite, consuming. "Yes, you did."

Yeah, I did.

"I didn't want to be driven at speeds like that."

"Yes, you did."

"You don't know me, Scarlett."

She brushes a stray lock of curl away from my cheek. Such an intimate, soft movement. All the while, her eyes never leave mine.

"Yeah, Quinn, I do."

"It was... it was incredible. Like you promised."

Her mouth twitches, a whisper of a smile. And I realise she used my name. She's never used my name. And, using my name is the second promise she's kept. It breaks me. I can't hold out any longer. I plunge my lips onto hers.

It's not gentle, it's not clean. It's hard and messy and wanting. Heat billows between us, my hands sliding up the back of her head into her hair. I squeeze my fingers through her braid, just hard enough she hisses and then drives her mouth over mine. She walks me to the stand and pins me against the wall. The thud as my back meets wall echoes through my torso. My core slick and hot already, the throb of her energy consuming me. Her fingers dig into my thighs, the pressure reminding me how much she wants me. Wants to own me. Wants to make me moan.

And... despite everything, I want to let her. My body craves her like oxygen. Even though I shouldn't, even though she knows she shouldn't. We hate each other. Don't we?

I pull away from her mouth, gasping for air; trace her neck, her jawline. My hands glide around her waist. I need her. Need her to take me until there is only us.

I'm ripping at her zips, the velcro, there are too many layers of fucking clothes. She lets me slide to the floor as she slips her hands to my jaw, her thumb stroking my cheek. A gentle caress for a moment that is anything but. The air between us is electric. Neither of us can rip the clothes quick enough.

Everywhere her lips meet my skin it tingles, as if she is the power and I am her spark. How is it she can drive me mad, terrify me with speed and still make me feel safe? And still, I hate her.

I hate her. I hate her. I hate her.

Hate what she stands for. Her fucking legacy. Hate that she's going after my father, her fucking ego. Hate that she can make me do things, try things, make me livid with rage.

But in this moment, the only thing I can think about is her mouth on my body. Her tongue sliding between my flesh, lapping at my core. I'm gasping, desperate to be naked, to let her have me. Who cares that we're outside, that there are people on the track. I'll fuck her while they watch, let them see me come undone.

I moan as she tugs off the upper overalls, pulls my bra straps down and plunges her mouth over my hard nipple. She kneels before me. Exactly where she should be, beneath me, submitting to me. Her crystal eyes meet mine, and the hunger in them makes my pussy slick. Her hands tug at my overalls and clothes.

"I...I... I want..." I'm panting.

"Ahem," a restrained cough startles me out of the moment.

"Fuck." I pull up my bra.

Scarlett drops her head, leaning against my waist. She lets go of my body and sighs a deep, breathy noise. "Stirling."

"Sister," Stirling says and takes a bite of an apple, her leg cocked back against the stand where she leans. Stirling, at least, doesn't look at us. Which enables me to keep my dignity.

"Inconvenient time?" Stirling asks with the hint of laughter beneath her words.

"What. Do. You. Want?" Scarlett says, standing up. Her posture is rigid, her jaw stiff.

"Negotiations done. It's time to get the rune specialist."

Stirling pushes off the seating, Scarlett flicks the kick-stand up and wheels the bike after her sister, and they leave me to pull myself together.

"Where did you get that apple?" Scarlett asks.

"Told you, I know a girl."

Scarlett grumbles. Then, I swear, as they step out of earshot, I hear Stirling say, "Don't do this. You'll regret..."

But by the time I catch up to them, they've changed the subject, and I'm left wondering what exactly it is she's going to regret and why I have a sinking feeling it's me.

CHAPTER 13

SCARLETT

"Don't do this. You'll regret fucking her over, Scar."

"Don't preach at me. You don't know what you're talking about."

"Oh, really?" She swings me around. "So that intensity between you? That's acting, is it?"

I shrug.

"For the love of my sanity, stop. It's obvious you like her. I don't have to be your twin to see that."

"I hate her. She's fucking ruined everything. She's paralysed me, blinded me, made me shit my insides out. Stolen three quarters of my regular clients. I received a note that Mrs. Winters was no longer in need of my services the other day. Yet another client lost. She is a constant pain in my arse."

"And yet you kiss her like she's oxygen. Like she's your everything."

I grit my teeth, staying silent.

Stirling shakes her head. "I'm asking you to be reasonable. To listen to this." She places her hand above my heart. "I love you, Scar, and I want the best for you. Yes, you two have a messy history, but maybe that's how the best love starts. Think about it?"

My lips purse as I take in her words. Love? Is she right? Of course I don't love Quinn. Do I? The more I think about it, the more I wonder how different love and hate really are. We reach the pit lane, and Stirling leaves to find Reece. I take my leathers off and hand them to a race technician, and then return the bike and helmet. Quinn hands her suit and helmet over too as Jacob, Reece and Stirling reappear inside the reception. Quinn and I enter the reception area as Stirling is shaking Reece's hand.

Reece is sweating and pale. Which is exactly how Stirling usually leaves everyone in a negotiation. I still don't understand how she does it. But then I suppose that is how she was trained. Charm, woo, and win. I glance at the scars peeking out from her sleeve and neckline. Her Collection tattoos used to be on her shoulders. Hers burnt off like mine when we were banished from the legacy community.

One day, Stir. One day, I swear to you, we will get them back, only bigger and better.

"Do I get to find out what the hell you've negotiated me into?" Jacob says to Stirling.

"In the carriage. You ready to rock?"

Quinn and I nod.

"Jacob, you're with me. I'll explain on the way to the carriage." She turns to Reece and slaps him on the shoulder. "Pleasure doing business with you as usual, Reece."

Reece sniffs. "Go fuck yourself, Stirling." But he's smiling, so whatever Stirling bartered for, he must have come out reasonably satisfied.

I get in the carriage, my mind still trying to reconcile everything Stirling said. The carriage rattles down the cobbled streets, rocking my body. Quinn sits opposite me, Stirling next to her, and Jacob to my right. Jacob and Stirling are deep in conversation about racing, but Quinn stares out the window, her expression distant and unfocused. Her dark curls flop in her face, a face that plagues me whether I'm awake or asleep. Too often I've thought of her, raged about her, fucked the hate away. But for the first time, I wonder what it would be like to stop.

Stop hating. Stop raging. Just be. To exist in a world with her where we work together. Quinn pulls her knees up under her chin. She glances at me, our eyes meeting, and it pushes a rush of heat up my neck.

No. I turn away, forcing the heat down. I don't need anyone wheedling their way in or making me weak, distracted. I have to focus on finding this piece of map for the Queen, digging up evidence on the Border Lord to prove our parents' innocence, and getting our legacy reinstated.

The carriage driver is one of those drivers that seems to think he exists outside of time. He takes a leisurely pace, waving at magicians on the street. I'm about ready to knock him out when he pulls onto a dusty track.

"Where in fuck's name are we now, Stirling?" I say, frowning.

"We're close," she says and continues her conversation with Jacob.

I don't recognise this place at all. The road is barely passable in the carriage. We'd be better off on dirt bikes, not that Quinn could drive one, but I'd take her pillion. It's muddy and bumpy and dark as sin. The sun is setting, the dense trees on either side of us swallow the remaining orange hues. The rustle of branches and leaves rolls through the cabin in waves, rhythmic enough it lulls me into a daze.

The driver pulls to a sudden stop.

Quinn lurches forward in her seat. Head. Shoulders. Her entire body lifting out the seat. My instincts kick in. Body moving before my brain registers what's happening. My arms swing out, my body braced for impact as she slams into me. I wrap my arms around her, catching her. We drop to the floor. She's shaking. I stroke her hair away.

"You okay?"

She nods. She could have been flung into the wall. Broken her neck, cracked her head open. My throat dries, my vision tunnels. "What the fuck is wrong with you?" I snarl as I punch the driver, a little harder than necessary, on the shoulder. Blood pounds in my ears, my breathing elevated. My face contorted with lines and wrinkles. I want to scuff this twat by the neck and yank him out of the carriage. Beat the snot out of him.

No one hurts Quinn.

The thought hauls me to my senses. I was literally about to slaughter the carriage driver for *almost* injuring her.

No one hurts Quinn. I won't let them. And that is the most surprising thought I've had... ever.

"Watch it, missy, or I'll fling you out and leave you here." He points out the front of the carriage at a giant deer standing in the middle of the road.

I slump in my seat and wipe my face, trying to clear the fog. I glance at Quinn. Annoyed that my body seems to perceive things my brain doesn't. I can't do this with her. I won't. A rising hiss floods my veins. I glare at her. "Put your fucking carriage belt on." It's a vicious snap, and I don't mean it. Her brow folds, a tight knot pinching at her forehead. I squeeze my eyes shut and rub my chest.

Her belt clicks, and she mumbles, "Thanks," but she doesn't look at me. The only person looking at me is Stirling.

Her eyebrows raised, her lips pressed thin.

"What?" I mouth at her.

She shakes her head and stares out the window.

A few minutes later, the driver slows to a stop and pulls up his sleeve, displaying a set of Collection tattoos. There's a series of lines inked onto his skin. They're kind of pearlescent, like a lined drawing of the city. In the middle is the blacked out shape of a mansion. He waves a hand over his arm, and up shoots a glistening map. It's translucent and shimmers. But it's a map nonetheless.

"What did you say the address was?" he asks.

"It's the old steel mansion. They used to forge all the katana swords for the guild there, imbue them with magic before the building died."

He prods the translucent map hovering out of his arm, spins it with his other hand, and pinches and opens his hand, which zooms the map in an out.

Then he drops his hand, and the map vanishes into his arm.

"We're here. I have business to run while you're here. I'll return in an hour."

"Umm..." Stirling says.

But the carriage driver pushes a button and the doors pop open. "Out, I'll be back later."

Stirling glares at the driver but dutifully gets out. The rest of us follow suit and we're left alone.

Night has settled over the sky, stars gleam and wink at us. Acres of trees stand sentinel behind, and in front, an empty field. One road in and out and absolutely no sign of runes specialists or a building.

"You're certain it's here?" I say to Stirling.

"Hundred percent. She was on a job. We were meant to meet her as she was finishing up." Stirling scratches her head and then turns to me. "Stay here for a second. I'm going to search the field. Maybe the mansion is on the other side or something. You know what drivers are like, one field or another, all the same to them. They get paid no matter where they dump us. Assholes."

She sprints ahead, and Jacob turns to me. "This supposed get rich scheme... We going to spend a lot of our time in fields? Or do you guys actually have a plan?"

"One. Go fuck yourself. Two. Yes. Three. She's handling it. Give us a second and we'll have your princely arse in the warm, okay, baby cakes?"

Jacob snorts and ruffles my hair. "There she is. Gods, I've missed you on the track. You really need to stop working so much and come back to racing. I always thought you'd make a better racer than Assassin."

"I'd be delighted to if someone stopped pilfering clients, taking my commissions after I've already accepted them, and appearing on jobs they're not meant to be at. You need coin to race." I fire a glare at Quinn, who is quietly shivering on the side of the road.

Oh, Gods.

I shuck off my jacket and hand it to her. "Stop shivering, it's pathetic."

A single wrinkle forms between her brows. She scans my face as if she's trying to figure something out. "You taking it or not?"

She nods and slips it over her arms and instantly stops shivering.

I double take. She's wearing my jacket. I mean, of course she is, I just gave it to her. But as I stare at her, something shifts inside me. I enjoy seeing it on her. And not because it's tight and pushes her tits together. But because of how it makes me feel.

Seeing her wear a piece of me, as if she is mine. As if we belong, and I really don't know how I feel about that.

Stirling is up the track now. She steps off the road and on to the field and...

Gone.

"What the..." I say and my feet move, automatically pounding the track. The crunch and slap of boots on a gravelly road ringing out.

I reach the edge of the field where she disappeared and shout her name. But nothing. Jacob and Quinn appear behind me.

Then, in a single flash, Stirling reappears, stepping on my feet and collapsing both of us on the ground.

"Where the hell did you go?" I mumble into a mouthful of her shoulder.

I shove her off me, and her face is stormy as she takes me in.

"Why were you standing there?"

I haul myself up. "Because you literally vanished."

"No. I took a few steps onto the field and then started calling you over because Remy is right—" she glances at the empty field and then at me, then laughs and shakes her head.

"Clever bitch. It's an illusion field. No wonder she isn't getting caught," Stirling says and stands herself up.

She gestures for Quinn, Jacob and I to follow her, and she steps onto the field again and vanishes.

I glance at the other two, shrug, and follow suit. The minute I step onto the field, there's a brief rushing sound in my ear and then the field blares to life.

"Caught doing what, exactly?" Quinn asks.

"Only illegal stuff," Jacob smirks.

Quinn is grey. The pallor drained from her cheeks. "Remy... Remy Reid?"

I narrow my gaze at her. "Yeah. How did you know?"

"She's... I... I mean we." She looks up at me, her throat bobs where she swallows. "It was a long time ago."

Oh. My stomach hardens, my rib cage burns. I can't bear the thought of her with someone else.

"I see. Well acquainted already then." My words are bitter. I don't care. Obviously. I have ex's too. The lesbian world is close knit. There's very few of us who don't know each other—or have dated each other.

Doesn't matter.

I don't even care.

I turn to the decrepit mansion in front of us. The windows are all smashed, the turrets that clearly used to thrust into the sky are crumbling and broken. There's ivy crawling up most of the brickwork and burrowing its way into the cracked windows. Gargoyles litter the floor, broken in two like cracked teeth, and one side of the house roof has fallen in.

But surrounding the house is a circle of magicians, all with their hands raised and facing the house. And from the mansion flow strings of pearlescent light. Streams of it pouring into the hands of magicians.

It's a drug. The magic of a dying house. They're not supposed to take it. The magic is supposed to be lost when the High Council demolishes a building. But when you have a runes specialist as good as Remy, it would be rude not to siphon the last of a house's magic.

It's potent. Like really potent. Some magicians liken it to a death rattle. The house's last whisper, an expulsion of all its magic. And if you time it right, if you have the right magicians, then you can siphon that shit and sell it for serious coin.

That is why Remy is rolling in dough. It's not her upstanding job in the day. It's the drugs she peddles at night. I don't blame her. If I could do it, I would.

The last strings of magic stream from the house in flowing silk like ribbons, and then the mansion visibly sags as if relieved it's over. A few tiles peel off the roof and smash on the floor and the grey bricks darken.

It's dead.

The magicians circling the house take a step forward. They crouch to their knees, with orbs of the mansion's magic still hovering above their palms. They kiss the orbs and then pinch a tiny piece of magic off and bury it in the ground. A last rite. A final goodbye.

Several of the magicians pull chest-like boxes in front of them and pour the magic they took from the property into the box. When it's done, they hold their hands above the lock and seal the boxes.

They stand, move their hands and fingers in a series of interconnecting loops and flicks, and then each of them inclines their head at the building.

Finally, Remy breaks the circle and turns to greet us.

"The Grey twins. To what could I possibly owe the pleasure?" she says and then stops as she notices Quinn.

"Quinn," she says, her face brightening. And the wider she smiles, the tighter I grip my fists. Jacob slides an arm around my shoulder, as if he can sense what's brewing inside me.

"Long time." Remy leans in and kisses Quinn on her cheek, the other one, then on her lips.

My whole body lurches forward, but Jacob grabs my hand and holds me in place.

"It's good to see you, Quinn," Remy says, still smiling.

"You too, Rem."

Rem? Fucking Rem.

Stirling glances at Remy and Quinn and then at me. She flusters and promptly shoves her way between them, separating them.

Remy is tall enough she dwarfs me. Her shock of ice white hair is shaved on the sides and spiked up into a quiff. Her eyes, though, are such a dark brown, they're almost black. Thin limbs float at Remy's side, making her more skeletal than human. She wears black boots, combat trousers that have seen better days and a vest top that shows her oddly large breasts. She holds herself upright, in that knowing fashion. It's commanding, confident. Alluring. I get why Quinn dated her.

I hate her already.

Stirling pulls Remy into an embrace. "Hello, old friend." They fist bump, and then Remy drags her in for another hug.

"Been a while," Remy says into Stirling's shoulder as she slaps and rubs her back with equal measure.

Remy holds Stirling by the shoulders. "Let me see you. Older, cockier, not sure about wiser though."

Stirling laughs and shoves Remy off her. "I missed you."

Remy and Stirling go way back. They shared a class or two at the guild, were constantly in trouble. Remy would crack the security runes of a ton of illegal meets, of clubs and places neither of them should have been. But of course, how else was Stirling going to build her network than attending these places? What I didn't realise was that Remy and Quinn were connected. But like I said, what lesbians don't know each other in this city?

"You missed my genius, more likely," Remy says and grins.

At this, Stirling rolls her eyes. "We have a business deal to offer you."

"Ahh, and the perfect timing, too. I just finished this job. They're demolishing it this weekend. I'll let this lot take the goods to the club and we can discuss. Do you have transport?"

Remy squints at Jacob. "Aren't you that bike racer? Gods, you're not driving us, are you?"

"I'm a world class driver, I'll have you know," Jacob says, his eyebrows pinching into a frown.

"I've no doubt. But I'd prefer to keep the contents of my gourmet dinner this evening inside my body rather than spewing it on the road or footwell."

"Well, I guess you're safe then. There's a carriage on the way back," Stirling says.

Finally, Remy turns to me. I force myself to smile, but it's stiff. The way her eyes search my face tell me she realises too.

"Scarlett."

"Remy." I nod and stick my hand out to shake hers. I grip it. A little tighter than necessary. And she tilts her head, assessing.

I let go, stand straighter. My shoulders tense. Stirling glances at me and then steps in. She wraps her arm around Remy and tugs her toward the now derelict mansion. "Let me explain the deal. We've got another twenty minutes before the carriage returns, anyway."

They saunter off into the distance. Jacob glances at me, his eyes dance to Quinn and back again and he says, "You know... I think I could do with hearing the details again. I'll leave you guys here." And then he's gone too.

"So..." Quinn says, toeing the grass with her boot. "Are you cold? You can have your jacket back if you need it."

Her lips are blue, her legs covered in gooseflesh, and she's shivering harder than ever.

"You look ridiculous standing there like that. Come here."

She hesitates but eventually strides over.

"I thought you hated me," she says.

"I do," I say and open my arms. She tucks herself around me. She's like a little block of ice, and I can't help but notice that she fits perfectly inside my grip. Her head tucks under my chin as she presses her cheek to my chest.

"You're not bothered that Remy and I..." she says and inches her hands around my waist and under my jumper.

I stand a little straighter.

"Obviously not."

I feel her smile against my chest.

"That's what I thought. So, it doesn't help to know that it was ages ago, and I don't find her attractive or care one dot about her."

I relax a little. "No."

She nods against my chest. "But in case it did matter... we really are just friends now."

I lock my hands around the back of her waist, pulling her closer to me. Her breasts push into my ribs. Her shivering slows the longer she's pressed against me.

"You keep talking, and I'll have to punish that mouth of yours."

Her eyes glitter and darken. "I shouldn't tell you how long we dated."

My fingers slip to her ass, grip it and haul her up. She locks her legs around my waist. "Not unless you want to get spanked."

She fake pouts at me. I know because lust glimmers in her eyes. "Then I definitely shouldn't tell you about the time we fu—"

My chest flares hot. My fingers jerk, aching to pull a blade, hold it under her chin. But we're a long way past that. I want something else, something better.

"Another word, Quinn Adams, and I will handcuff you to that tree, strip you naked and fuck you till you come all over my hand."

She bites her bottom lip, her stare deepening. She wants it; she wants me to fuck her.

Remy, Jacob and Stirling reappear. Stirling is staring at me. She doesn't need to speak for me to recognise that her head is bent at a '*the fuck you doing?*' angle.

I drop Quinn to the ground and shrug at Stirling. "She was cold."

Remy's eyebrow is cocked, a knowing smile at the edge of her lips. Oh, whatever. She can go fuck herself, too.

Stirling points up the track. "Carriage awaits, ladies."

I follow the group. Remy and Stirling deep in conversation with Jacob about some illegal race Remy did the security for. Quinn trails them. I bring up the rear, my mind distracted, unable to think about anything other than the way Quinn looked in my jacket, how it made my stomach knot and my chest ache. The way she locked her fingers behind my neck.

How she smells of summer and fresh herbs, like her shop. The way her scent lingers in my nose, long after she's gone. The fact she fits perfectly pressed against me like a puzzle piece.

My mind is distracted because Quinn is supposed to be my enemy.

She is ruining me.

And yet, I can't quite remember what it felt like to hate her anymore.

And that is utterly terrifying.

CHAPTER 14

QUINN

Scarlett waltzes around, pretending to be heartless. I mean, truly; the girl is a vicious killer when it comes to assassination. And yet, she lends me her jacket, lets me steal her body heat... and my gods, she was so warm she felt like fleece blankets and curling up in front of an open wooded fire. She felt like warmth on the coldest days and that... that is very confusing. She acts like she wants to hurt me, but I'm not sure she does anymore. And if she doesn't. Where does that leave us? I don't know how to be around Scarlett if we're not fighting and fucking.

The way she looked at me when I wore her jacket. It was... I don't even know. And what about the carriage? The speed in which she reacted. If she hated me that much, she should have let me fly out of the car and hit the windshield. I'd have been dead in seconds and she could have been rid of me. But she stopped me. She protected me, and that is...

Confusing.

The more I think about our past, the more confused I

get. My fingers skim up to my shoulder, to the inch long scar she gave me when she stabbed me last year. It was payback for poisoning her at one of Roman's parties. I dropped the most pungent dust into her drink. She would have been puking and shitting for days.

But the night she stabbed me, she'd gone on a job. It was dangerous too, from what I made out. She knew the legacy family she was there to slaughter. I followed her into the castle. Work had quieted that week. I needed to check whether she was doing something to win back the clients I'd charmed or if it was a slow week.

I watched her loop a rope around a ceiling rafter and haul fourteen stone of man up to hang. Watched as she revelled in the pleasure of her victim's death. Gods, she loves her job. There's a moment when her victim's life evaporates and Scarlett's eyes are wide, her mouth opens, and all the tension loosens from her body. It's sheer pleasure. When he was good and dead, I clapped from the doorway. Her face flushed. Rage pooled in those cold eyes. She could have killed me then, too. But she didn't. She had to finish the job, for one, but I wonder if she enjoys the game too much. She pinned me against the wall, finger fucked me until my legs quivered, and then pinned me to the wall with a one inch wide blade straight through my trapezius. Fuck, it hurt, but it was only a surface wound and it healed in a couple of weeks.

And that's the thing with us, I realise now. A lot of threats, a lot of foreplay. But any time I've been in danger, she's protected me.

And I'm not really sure what that means.

I pull myself out of my thoughts and ask, "Where are we going now?"

There's only one seat left in the carriage. Surely we can't have many more stops.

I'm sat next to Scarlett, seat belt on this time.

"To the hardest sell of the evening," Scarlett says, staring out the window. I notice she's not looked at me since we got in the carriage. As if she's actively avoiding looking at me.

"Oh? Why is it going to be a hard sell?" I ask.

Stirling folds her arms. "Because I fucked up."

"You... I don't understand."

Jacob laughs in the corner.

"You're kidding me? We're recruiting Morrigan?" Remy asks.

"Unfortunately," Stirling says.

At this, Remy snuffles out a stifled laugh. "Morrigan is her ex-girlfriend. And things... Well... Let's just say their breakup is legendary in our circles."

"Legendary? What happened?" I ask.

"And that is where I'm out. That's not a story I'm going to tell. That's all Stirling."

But Stirling stays quiet in the front and no one else offers anything. I wait, watching the scenery change from the leafy trees and forests of the suburbs to the narrow streets and finally the cobbled stones of New Imperium. Another twenty minutes later and we're through the city centre and heading towards an area I'm unfamiliar with. Instead of tight clusters of flats and newer buildings mixed with mansions, there's row after row of castles and mansions, each one bigger than the last. Finally, they grow further apart until the driver slows to a halt.

He turns over his shoulder and says, "Get out. One hour. I'll be back. Got another drop."

We stumble out of the carriage, and the driver leaves.

"You alright?" Scarlett asks Stirling and squeezes her shoulder.

Stirling takes a large breath and sighs it out. "No. But I don't know another Collector who would do this, do you?"

Scarlett shakes her head. "Not one with connections to the Borderlands. I'm pretty sure she's the only Collector I know that actually has Old Palace magic."

"Exactly. What choice do I have?" Stirling asks.

Scarlett sighs. "Do you know what you're going to say?"

Stirling rubs her forehead. "Erm. I was thinking I'd start with sorry."

Remy coughs. I glance up at her and her lips are twitching like she's holding in a smile. "I, erm... I think I saw a food stop half a kilometre up the road, Jacob. You with me?"

"One hundred percent. I don't think I want to witness this bike crash."

Stirling glares at him. "Get fucked. For that, you can bring me a burger and fries and a drink. I'll take whatever they have, and if it's got alcohol in it, even better." She pops a gum in and chews furiously.

Jacob, grinning, looks at me and Scarlett. We both nod in agreement.

"Same, hold the booze though," I say.

Remy and Jacob leave, and Stirling marches forward towards the mansion. This one is huge. Its brickwork is more ochre than sandstone, and there are acres and acres of fields surrounding the house. It has two giant circular turrets on either end of the building, and in the middle of the central building, a large arched door. It feels familiar, but I can't place why I know it.

When I glance into the fields, I notice dozens of horses. We're at a stables? I confirm my thought as we approach the house and I realise that behind the main building is an enormous set of wooden units.

"Does everyone like horses?" Stirling asks.

"Yeah, beautiful animals, very regal. I'd love to ride more. I learnt a bit as a kid, but most of the horses in the Borderlands didn't survive The Tearing."

"As long as you like them, the house will let us in. This mansion is renowned for horse magic. Breeding, breaking, training, blacksmithing, incredible leather work too, I recall."

"Oh my gods, is this where they hold the realm-jumping trials every year?" I gasp.

"Yes, have you ever watched them?" Stirling asks.

"Not in person, but I've always wanted to." I realise now why the mansion is familiar. I used to watch the trials as a kid when I was still having riding lessons.

Scarlett reaches the door first and holds her hand up to knock.

"Are you ready?" she says to Stirling.

"To see the love of my life that I abandoned because I'm a complete idiot? Absolutely not."

Love of her life? Oh, this is going to be messy.

"Close enough." Scarlett shrugs and pounds her fist on the door.

It takes a painfully long amount of time for it to open. At first, I wonder whether the mansion is going to let us in. Perhaps it doesn't like strangers. But finally, as the frosty night temperatures eat at my bones and the shivers set into my legs, a rather short man wearing a butler's uniform opens the door.

"Yes?" he says.

Stirling fidgets, "I'm here to see... umm. I'm led to believe Morrigan Lee is in residence tonight?"

The butler nods. "Do you have an appointment?"

"Alas not. But if you tell her I am here, she'll allow us to be seen."

Really? From everything I've heard, Stirling is probably the last person Morrigan wants to see.

"And you are...?"

Stirling scratches her neck, glances at her sister and then says, "Scarlett. I'm Scarlett Grey."

Scarlett stifles a laugh and rubs her arm over her mouth as she tries not to let it out. The butler scowls at Scarlett, who raises her hands at him.

"I ate pecans before getting here. Sorry, caught in my throat."

The butler presses his lips into a flat line but pulls the door open. As we enter, the familiar press of magic slides over my skin. The pressure bringing with it a hint of manure and hay and the rich earthy smell of horses and leather. And then I'm through the door and the smell evaporates.

The foyer is huge. The floor checked in those typical black and white diamonds all legacy mansions have. To the left of us is what I can only assume is the kitchen, the smells of roasting chicken and boiling vegetables and garlic drifting into the foyer. The butler leads us through the entrance and down a long corridor. We pass a wide, red-carpeted staircase that twists up and disappears into the upper floor. The house bustles with staff, people carrying leather saddles, helmets and other paraphernalia. There seem to be two different uniforms. One, similar to what the butler is wearing, a navy-coloured suit and white shirt, which I assume are all the house staff. And then another set of staff wearing beige jodhpurs, knee-high boots and a navy jacket to match the house staff. These must be the staff working directly with the horses.

Finally, the butler stops outside a lounge-like room. Its windows face the stables outside. In the room are plush Chesterfield sofas, and oil paintings dot the walls filled with regal horses and even more regal owners sitting proudly atop.

Ornate chandeliers hang from the tall ceilings and in the heart of the seating area is a woman leaning over an arm chair tattooing a Collection onto a girl. Next to her are three enormous piles of books. In fact, there are books on the floor and arms of the woman's chair too.

The woman grips the Collection gun, her jet black hair and blunted fringe hang in front of her focused gaze. The needles in the gun vibrate against the skin of a girl, punching in and out of her skin. All around the pair are threads of pearlescent magic stretching from the walls and floor and into the gun and, subsequently, into the girl in the chair being collected by the mansion.

"Oh, cute. We're at a Collection rite. Congratulations," I say, bouncing on my feet. I love moments like this, the moment a new power surges through your body for the first time, the connection you have to a place. The feelings of home, knowing that in this place, the people here are part of your family.

"Indeed," the butler says. "Loren is one of ten being inducted this evening, but she's going first as she came top of the apprenticeship class."

"That's wonderful," I say. "Congratulations again."

Loren, while looking relaxed leaning back in the armchair, has a line of sweat beading on her forehead. She tries to smile, but it looks more like a grimace. And trust me, I get it. Every one of these Collection tattoos is fucking painful. I mean, you're literally being bonded to the mansion and having a dozen needles stab into your skin with power simultaneously surging through your body. It's glorious and horrendous all at once.

The girl, who I assume is Morrigan, is yet to look up. She pushes her fringe out of her way and that's when I notice how many tattoos she has.

Holy mother of gods and magicians. No wonder Stirling and Scarlett want her on the team. I think she's the most collected magician I've ever seen. The tattoos start on her hands and crawl up her sleeves. They're on her neck, even one on her ear. She must be insanely powerful.

The longer Morrigan doesn't look up, the more Stirling shifts on the spot beside me. The butler reappears with a trolley of tea and sandwiches, fruit, and the tiniest cakes I've ever seen.

I practically bubble at the sight of the cupcakes and reach out for one. I pop it in whole and let a little groan out at how moist and sweet the sponge is. Scarlett's expression twitches into a smile as she looks at me.

"That good?" she whispers.

"You have no idea," I say around the cake.

I scan the plate and pick up the darkest one with black icing. "This one matches your soul..." I say to Scarlett.

She tuts at me but takes the cake. "You'll ruin my physique feeding me like this."

"That's my plan... I'll beat you by inducing a heart attack."

She smiles, and then leans into my ear, her voice low, "And then who would make you come all night long?"

I grip her arm, my fingers sinking into her hard bicep. "You keep talking like that and that's exactly what I'll make you do tonight."

The room shudders, the paintings juddering against the walls. And then, the streams of magic cease, and the last threads float towards Morrigan, the Collection gun, and Loren.

Loren shivers and sweats. Her teeth clamped together, eyes squeezed shut. She lets out a grizzled cry as the last threads flow through the gun and bury themselves into her skin. And then, just as fast, it's over and her face relaxes.

"Congratulations," Morrigan says. Her voice is deeper than I expected, husky as if it aged years before she did. "You're officially a magician."

Loren squeals. "One house down, many more to follow, I hope."

Morrigan smiles at her and says, "I'm sure they will. Keep studying and you'll have as many as me before you know it."

Loren flings her arms around Morrigan. "It was an honour to have you do my first. Truly, I can't believe it."

She bounces off the chair and runs into the corridor. It is at that exact moment that Morrigan clocks our presence. Her eyes falling on Scarlett, then me, then Stirling.

Scarlett swallows down the last bite of her cake, she skirts from Morrigan to Stirling. The lights in the room flicker in time with the twitch in Morrigan's eye. Shit, she is powerful. Never have I ever seen fury burn beneath the surface of an expression like I have right now.

Thunder burrows in the wells of her pupils. Murder and blades and all things vicious. I blink and she's vanished and reappears in front of Stirling. She can translocate? My jaw drops. I don't know anyone who can do that. I can't even fathom the power she must hold. She has to have legacy blood.

Scarlett scrabbles to wipe her mouth and shoves me

behind her as Morrigan approaches. Once again, her instinct is to protect me. Stirling slowly moves into the room, hesitant step after hesitant step.

But Morrigan holds her palm out and Stirling, I shit you not, halts mid-stride. Frozen solid, arms mid-swing.

Okay, remind me never to fuck Morrigan off. I glance at Scarlett, giving her a *what in fuck's name have we let ourselves in for* expression. But she waves me off.

Stirling starts, "I'm sor—"

Morrigan swings out and slaps Stirling across the cheek. It's loud enough the sound rattles in my head.

Ouch.

Next to me, Scarlett's face is turning a delightful shade of red, her neck threaded with pulsing veins. Scarlett and I don't do caring gestures. We don't do softness, but in this moment, knowing her, knowing that she's one slap from punching Morrigan and probably getting killed, I decide to slide my hand into hers.

It startles Scarlett. Her glance drops to our clasped hands, her mouth forming a tiny 'O'.

"I deserved tha—" Stirling starts. But Morrigan throws another brutal slap at Stirling's cheek.

Scarlett's jaw tightens as her body lurches, but I hold her tight, my grip keeping her in place. The air between Stirling and Morrigan fizzes with tension and heat. I guess it's not just Scarlett and I that have bullshit.

Morrigan leans in towards Stirling. She raises her hand, but this time, Stirling catches it as Morrigan whips out another slap.

Stirling yanks Morrigan's fist away and then grabs her by the neck, swings her around, and shoves her against the wall. Morrigan plunges her lips against Stirling's and... and... What the fuck is even happening?

They moan into each other. Stirling's mouth drops to Morrigan's neck as she peppers it with kisses.

Morrigan slips her fingers to the back of Stirling's hair and yanks her head, spinning her and pinning her against the wall. They glare at each other, panting. A confused frenzy of thirst and tempers twisting through their expressions.

Morrigan yanks Stirling's hair tighter. She winces, but the rest of Stirling's face is relaxed. Morrigan loosens up, pulls Stirling in for another, slower kiss. And then she breaks away, shoves Stirling and retreats to her chair.

"What the fuck do you want, Grey?" She waves her hand at Stirling, who is a dishevelled mess. She stands straight, brushes her hair down and adjusts her clothes.

I raise an eyebrow, glancing between the pair. I can't decide if I'm horrified or turned on. Morrigan leans in her chair, kicking her legs up onto the arm.

"Well?" she says and pulls out a cigarette. She puts it in her mouth, her index finger twitches and the fucking thing lights, just like that.

Oh my gods, she's incredible.

Stirling brushes her hair flat and wipes her mouth. Her fingers skim what is now a delightfully red, raw handprint on her cheek.

"And don't bother starting with an apology. Spit it out and then get the fuck out of my presence before I make you puke your intestines through your nose."

I swallow and step a little closer to the door. Morrigan must notice because her eyes flick to me.

"Who are you?" she says.

"Quinn. Quinn Adams." I give her an awkward wave and then her face brightens.

"You're the infamous medic with the poisons."

"Nice to meet you." I give her a little bow of my head and that seems to satisfy her.

Stirling moves forward. But Morrigan's eyes snap to hers. "That's quite close enough. You're lucky I don't tear your throat out. After what you did."

"We need your help," Stirling says.

This makes Morrigan roar. A deep throaty laugh that echoes around the room. She throws her head back, and when she rights herself, there are tears in her eyes. But Stirling's face is expressionless. When Morrigan catches sight of her, she stops laughing abruptly.

"Oh fuck me, you're not joking," Morrigan says.

"No. Not, in fact, joking," Stirling replies, her voice mousy. I've never heard her so sheepish. Usually she's cocky and full of it.

"This is where we exit," Scarlett whispers and tugs my hand, pulling me out of the room.

"Oh man, we were getting to the good bit," I say.

Scarlett laughs. It's that soft, bright trill. It still surprises me she laughs like that.

"Trust me, the grovelling Stirling is going to need to do to convince Morrigan to join us... none of us need to witness that level of dignity loss. She's taking one for the team."

Scarlett leads me further away from the room. She has to stop and ask for directions, but eventually we find ourselves outside near the stables.

She's still holding my hand. And I don't know if she realises, but her thumb is rubbing rhythmic circles over my hand.

A lone horse trots and jumps and flicks its feet out as it prances around the field. Its owner or trainer running after it, a whisper of pearlescent magic trailing from her hands through the air as she runs. The night air pierces right through Scarlett's jacket. I pull the zip higher. I don't understand how she's not cold. She's not even wearing sleeves. But there are no goosebumps on her toned biceps, no hint of a shiver. I, on the other hand, am instantly icy. My nipples harden beneath the layers of clothes. I hesitate. She was warm earlier, I wish I could snuggle in. But before I pluck up the courage, she must have noticed how cold I am. She looks down, tuts, and unzips her jumper. It's an invitation...

"What did Stirling do?" I ask as I slide my arms around Scarlett and inside her jumper. This place, my arms locking into her like they were always meant to fit; it's too familiar, too warm, too much.

"You can't just use me for warmth, you know," she says, but then she pulls me in tight, sharing her warmth.

"I'm not enjoying it, if that's any consolation," I mumble into her chest. She's like a furnace, and I instantly warm. It's delicious.

"Liar."

"Narcissist."

She laughs. A billow of bubbling sound reverberates through her chest and into my body.

"Seriously though. That was quite the welcome Morrigan gave us. What the hell happened?"

Scarlett sighs. "They fell in love. That's what happened."

I lift off her chest and gaze up at her. "But that's a good thing."

"Is it? Love doesn't make someone slap you that hard."

"Maybe. Maybe not. It definitely makes someone kiss you like that, though."

Scarlett nods. "Stirling promised herself to Morrigan. Promised she'd be there for her, and then she left. Broke her vow. She abandoned Morrigan when she needed her most."

"But why?"

Scarlett shook her head. "That's not my story to tell."

"Do they still love each other?"

Scarlett shrugs. "A love like that never goes away. But I also don't know if they'll ever get back together. They have a ton of history and mess."

"Lesbians are good at mess, though."

Scarlett smiles. "Then perhaps there's hope for them yet."

"And for us, too." I don't mean to say it. It just comes out. Heat rushes up my collar and into my cheeks.

Scarlett releases me, a bitter rush of air sucked between us. She tilts her head, and her fingers meet my chin, lifting it up.

There's a softness in her expression I've never seen before. Her features smooth, lips part. It's the first time she's looked at me as though she wants to kiss me instead of kill me.

My heart thuds a hesitant thrum against my ribs as our eyes meet. She holds me in her gaze like old souls and precious memories. As if nothing else exists but me. The way she stares at me steals my breath and slows time.

She inches down, her lips moving closer to mine. She smells like strength, like leather and steel and the safety of home. Our breath mingles in the freezing night air. I inch up closer on tiptoes.

Scarlett's thumb traces my cheek, leaving trails of tingles in its wake. Her lips brush against my cheek. Soft, warm, gentle.

"Perhaps there is..." she says and slides her hand to my

neck and pulls me to her. Scarlett's lips brush against mine. I close my eyes.

"Ready?" Stirling says, ripping me out of the moment. I swear Scarlett will murder her sister in her sleep.

Scarlett and I spring apart as if electrocuted.

"Yeah. Yeah, we're ready," she says, shoving her hands in her pockets and stepping away. The distance between us is cold, a cavernous, aching ocean of space. As if whatever almost happened didn't.

Maybe it didn't.

Maybe there isn't hope after all.

CHAPTER 15

SCARLETT

"You dreamt of her last night, didn't you?" Stirling's face peeks into my bedroom doorway, wearing a devilish grin. "Uhh, Quinn. Ohh, baby... Come for me, Quinn... Come for m—"

I launch a pillow at her head, which gives a delightful thud as it smacks her head and the door.

"My Gods," I groan and roll over, flinging an arm over my face. "What time is it?"

"Late, eleven. Was it a good dream?"

I peer out from under my arm, squinting in the mid-morning light. She bounds into the room and slams herself down on my bed, bouncing my body up from the mattress.

"If you're going to attack me that viciously, you could at least bring me coffee."

"We're out."

"Well, seeing as you're disgustingly perky this morning, didn't you think to... Oh, I don't know... maybe go and fucking get some?"

"One, I am not perky. Two, you're only miserable because it's been that long since you got laid that your own dreams are having to masturbate for you."

"Well, if you stopped cock blocking me, I could get laid."

Stirling curls into me so I can spoon her.

"You smell like sweat and feet. You need a shower," she says, but hitches into my stomach anyway, and I slide my arm over her waist. "You realise why I keep interrupting?"

"I assume this morning's torture is going to involve a lecture. Please enlighten me if it will lead me to coffee faster," I groan into her shoulder.

"Because you're not ready. I really want you to be happy," she rolls over to face me, "to let yourself be happy. Let yourself do what your heart already knows it wants."

I purse my lips together. It's far too early for this. She picks at my pyjama sleeve, threading her finger through a hole. "You don't have to look after me anymore. We're not kids. I know you felt responsible for me for a long time after they died, but... we're okay. Yes, it's been tough, but whose life isn't? You're allowed to do stuff for you. To choose happiness."

"Am I? And what about you, hmm? Miss secretly happy because the love of her life is suddenly back on the scene."

She stops fiddling with my top. "It's not about me this morning. Don't fuck this up, okay? You have the potential for a good thing with Quinn."

I lean down and kiss her on the forehead. "Go away and find me coffee. I need a shower."

"That deal I was brokering in the Velvet Mansion is sinking. I need to manage it ASAP. I'll be home before we need to go to Quinn's this evening. What time was it again?"

After we finished recruiting we went for pizza, like Quinn promised, and then agreed to meet at the back of her shop tonight ready to plan and train.

"Six."

"Alright, see you tonight."

She closes the door.

"I still want that coffee," I shout after her.

"You've got legs," she bellows, and then the front door slams shut.

I get up, shower, and get dressed. When I'm ready, I open my rucksack looking for my purse. My fingers fumble across a hard leather book.

No. Not a book.

I pull Quinn's journal out and flip it over and over. I'd almost forgotten I lifted this from her shop. Our whole house is a mess of boxes and white walls. We've spent so long packing everything up, I've not taken anything out of a box or bag in days.

I smile, imagining the absolute furor she must have made when she realised. She looks all sweetness and light on the outside, but I see her dark side. It's the vicious gleam buried in those green eyes that I love the most.

My fingers caress the spine and run down the pages. Should I open it? See what's inside? I hesitate. I didn't take it to invade her privacy. It was a joke, another way to wind her up. I pull Chance out of my pocket and run my thumb over the gilded letters.

"Tell me what to do," I say and flick her up. She spins in the air, red-gold-red. She lands, and I flip her onto the back of my hand.

Gold and ruby red shine at me.

"Guess I should open it then."

I peel the front cover open, genuinely expecting it to be blank or filled with scant notes about herbs and poisons.

But that's not at all what I find.

There's a note in there.

Dearest Sister,

Where are you? We're worried. We've not heard from you in days. Is everything okay? Is the shop busy? We're hopeful it's just a busy trade period and not anything troublesome.

Father is antsy. He misses you but doesn't want to beg you to come home—too proud, as usual. He also fears trouble is brewing. The atmosphere here is unusual. Heightened security. Guards tread on eggshells, and there are dozens of them everywhere.

Mother, of course, is dealing with it by drinking herself into a stupor. And of course, that makes father fly into his usual rages.

We tried the recent herb mix you suggested for me. No luck. It didn't work. But then neither of us really expected it to, did we?

Why don't you spend your time on other things? Dating perhaps? Rather than working all the time.

Isn't there a lovely woman locally? What of that meddlesome Assassin you speak of? Mother talks of finding you a nice legacy magician. I scoffed, of course. We're not of that calibre, no matter what father does.

Please reply. I need to know you're okay.

Yours in blood and bonds

M.

Well, well, well, Ms. Adams. It's not a blank journal after all. This has to have been touched by a spell worker. And Quinn has spoken of me to her brother? Interesting.

And of course, once I start thinking about her, I can't get her out of my head. Over and over, my thoughts drift to Quinn. Always fucking Quinn. She's a parasite invading my mind. One minute I'm plotting how to crush her business, the next it's those plump lips, the way her hips are wider than her tiny waist. The way we almost fucked against the race stand, the way I had to stare out the carriage window to stop myself from ravaging her body inside the carriage. She's a kind of madness I don't know how to deal with. This is futile. Stirling is right. I can't pretend to woo her because I actually want to win her as much as I want vengeance. How can I have both?

Because when I imagine bringing her body close to mine and slipping the blade between her ribs to nick her arteries... When I picture the light fading from her eyes forever, I can't breathe. My chest tightens and my lungs cinch. I have to physically bend forward and clasp my knees.

I wipe the thoughts away, a haze of confusion filling my mind.

And I'm left with one horrifying prospect.

If I'm not going to kill Quinn, what the hell am I going to do about my business?

CHAPTER 16

QUINN

Tonight is the night. The team is coming to the shop, and we're going to discuss the plans. I hope I'll be able to gather enough information to work out what exactly Scarlett has planned. Then I can create a secondary plan to protect my father.

Before we said goodnight, Scarlett was clear. We all needed sports kit ready for our first training session this evening.

Which is how I've ended up standing in front of a shop assistant with my hand on my hip, wildly unimpressed.

"Is this a joke? Are you fucking joking?" I say, my eyebrow high enough it practically crawls off my face.

I dangle the offending items out at her. She simply shrugs at me, flicking her long brown hair behind her shoulder. She chews a piece of gum noisily, blowing and popping bubbles.

"What? You said you wanted an outfit, and you have killer abs, so, like... show them off."

"IN A CROP TOP? This is a training session. Gods. Don't you have anything... anything more?"

"Sure," she shrugs and disappears into the shop. When she returns, she dangles a top that has so little fabric it looks more like a ball gag.

"I said more?"

She blows a bubble and pops it. "This is more. More, *extra*. Duh."

"We have different definitions of more."

She shrugs. She's one of the lucky ones who looks about twelve despite being in their twenties and will still appear thirty when she's fifty. Her jaw grinds the gum as she stares into the void, and I wonder when she lost all her fucks.

"Gods. Fine. I'll take what I'm wearing. I haven't got time to change again. Can you price it up for me?"

She leaves without a word.

I catch sight of my abs in the changing room mirror; she has a point. They're not defined or anything, but I have a small two pack under my ribs that slides nicely into a chunky belly and enough hips for at least three women. I turn this way and that. The crop top cuts me at the perfect position to show my ample breasts and... fuck's sake. Maybe she was right. I would never have chosen this for myself, but I don't look too bad. I suppose I don't have a lot of choice now, anyway.

I pay and leave, returning to the apothecary warehouse at the rear of the shop. It takes two hours, but I create a vast space by pushing all the herbs and ingredient racking to the edges.

I order in chicken, salad, breads and a range of drinks. I don't have time to cook, and I can't imagine anyone else will have thought of organising dinner.

There's a knock at the door. I open it to find Stirling, who whistles, giving me a very obvious glance up and down. "My sister is screwed," she says and slides into the warehouse.

"Ooh, dinner. Thanks Quinn," Stirling shouts as Morrigan, Remy and Jacob pile into the warehouse.

Then Scarlett appears in the doorway and halts. Her bottom lip drops as her eyes rake me up and down.

"Oh," she says, her lips parted.

And immediately my skin heats, the way her gaze swallows me, the shortness of her breath, the way her throat bobs. She's either peeling my clothes off inch by inch or plotting ways to kill me. Either way, it makes my knickers wet, my apex throb. I could shut the door, step outside, let her fuck me up against the alley wall. My nipples harden at the thought. Scarlett's eyes find my breasts under the skintight fabric. As if she knows what I'm thinking. Knows why my nipples are erect.

I cough. I have to scrub the thoughts from my mind. Focus on the task at hand. Getting my journal back and finding out what she's planning to do to my father and why.

"You can't wear that," she says, her tone steely.

"How dare y—"

She pulls me outside, shuts the door and pins me against it, exactly as I hoped. Her hands are on either side of my arms, locking me in place. Her breath is heavy, her cheeks rosy. She pulls a blade out from a thigh strap and hooks it under the band of the crop top, pulling it taut, taut enough a breeze rushes against the bottoms of my breasts.

"Watch it. That's new," I snarl, my core heating as my teeth clench.

"Well, you can't wear it."

"And why the hell not? Who are you to t—"

"—You can't wear that unless you want me to cut you out of it and make you come all over your shop."

She tugs the blade against the waistband, making the fabric ping against my flesh, a warm glimmer in her expression. She closes her eyes and leans her forehead against mine. Her fist slams against the door.

Oh. I see.

"What are you doing to me?" she says and lifts off my forehead. I slide my fingers to her waist, tug her close. Slide my hand to her waistband. It's evening, the sun has set, and no one comes around the back of the warehouse. Perhaps a little fun wouldn't hurt.

I pull at the top button, unhooking it. There's a frisson of heat between us. She caresses my cheek; I lean into the warmth against her hand.

The warehouse door creaks, wind whistling through. "We should go inside."

Scarlett sighs and looks down at me. "You're going to have to pay for what you're wearing, you know." There's a glint in her eye, a smile curving her plump lips.

"Am I?" I purr, sliding my hand between her thighs. She catches my wrist lightning quick, gripping it tight. It makes me gasp and my pussy clench.

"Don't make it worse, or I'll tie you up and spank you before I fuck you."

I step into the warehouse, grinning hard. I glance over my shoulder. "We both know I'd like that."

Her jaw clenches and her knuckles whiten over the hilt of her blade. Gods, I love that I can make her react like that. I smirk. "One nil to me."

Perhaps games aren't all bad after all.

We make our way to the table I set up at the corner. Everyone grabs a plate of food and takes a seat. Stirling has already rolled the maps and information the Queen gave us out onto the table. She's shovelling food in when Morrigan twists and folds her fingers over a stick, the familiar pearlescent hue of magic brimming under her hands. She shoves the stick at Stirling.

Stirling picks up the stick, and a beam of light shines out the end, forming a dot on the map. Stirling's face brightens. She mouths *thank you* at Morrigan, who folds her arms and turns her head away.

They've not made up then?

"Right, let us begin," Scarlett says.

She stands after swallowing a bite of food and moves to the head of the table. Then she paces in front of us.

"Tonight, we plan, and then we train. We've got three weeks to get as organised as possible. The Queen has asked for us to deliver the map on the night of the Peace Ball, which is under four weeks away."

"Three weeks to train, one week to execute?" Jacob asks, gnawing chicken off a thigh bone. When he's done, he pulls his hand through his creamy locks. He really is rather handsome.

"Correct," Scarlett replies.

Remy leans forward and pushes her clean plate away. I still haven't talked to her since she joined the team. But then, it hasn't been awkward between us either. It's not like we dated for long, plus we were both young then. She was one of my first girlfriends. But equally, I will need to address it. Remy catches my eye and smiles softly at me. I return the smile. Scarlett notices and her face pinches.

"What's the job? The only thing Stirling has told me is that it's going to be the biggest pay day I've ever had, and that it will be dangerous," Remy says, breaking the tension.

Morrigan leans forward, her long straight hair pulled into a messy pile, a pencil shoved in to keep the bun in place. "My guess is they wouldn't have asked me unless it involved the Borderlands." Morrigan's deep tones drift from the back of the room.

"Delightful, Stirling, you failed to mention that little nugget of information," Jacob says, glaring at her. He unzips his race jacket and slides it over his chair.

"Yes, it's a job inside the Border," Scarlett says. Stirling hands her the stick and Scarlett points it at the map.

"The Queen wants her piece of map back. Her plan is to restore the maps and our city. No more Old and New Imperium. Just Imperium."

Remy leans back in her chair, and she runs a hand through her spiky white hair and whistles. "We're stealing from the Border Lord himself and the Old Palace? That's one helluva security job."

Her eyes flick to mine, surprise widening them. She knows who I am, of course. We dated when we were teens. She knows everything, and thankfully, she's wise enough to realise the predicament I'm in. Of course, Remy was long gone from my life when father became the Border Lord. But unlike everyone else, she knows me from before, which means she knows who he is to me, too. I pray she keeps her mouth shut. I give her a stern stare, the message clear. *Keep your mouth shut.* She raises an eyebrow at me and gives me an almost imperceptible nod, and my shoulders sag in response.

"We are. Our focus will be the main palace, not the smaller residential palace, as we have intel from the Queen that implies the map is stored in a vaulted room on the top floor," Scarlett says.

"No wonder you needed us," Jacob says. "Has anyone ever driven through the Border?"

No one answers.

"Not that I'm aware of," Morrigan says, examining the Collection tattoos on her arms. "I believe I'm the only one with experience inside the Border?"

"Not quite," I say, my voice quiet.

Everyone turns to me. A nervous little titter of a laugh spills out. "I used to live there. I was there when..."

There's a collective gasp drawn, but no one asks me for more detail. Thankfully, Remy reads the situation and comes to my rescue, changing the subject.

"Right," Remy starts and slots her arms behind her head. "What *is* the payoff?"

There's the Remy I remember. She's as lean and wispy as she was when we were teens. I try to crawl my memories from our time together. It was a few months at most. We were never well matched. Both of us are too ambitious, too desperate to get out of our area and find bigger things, live bigger lives. She left first, that's why she wasn't there when The Tearing happened.

"The Queen will offer us a royal favour," Scarlett says.

Morrigan sits straighter, tilts her head, and stops examining her tattoos to focus on Scarlett.

"If we pull this off, we could ask for anything. The Queen will bestow insane amounts of coin on us. We'll be set for life. All of us."

"Yes," Morrigan drawls. "And if we fail, the Border Lord will slit our throats and shower in our blood."

I shiver at the thought. I know father has done some bad things in order to keep order inside the Borderlands, but I don't understand why everyone has such a negative opinion of him. He's not that bad. When no one else came to help us, he saved thousands of magicians. He should be lauded, not made into a pariah.

"We won't fail," Scarlett says, and the ice in her tone sets my teeth on edge. "Remy, you're going to be in charge of getting us into the Palace. Morrigan might be able to help with that. She's got Palace magic."

The pair of them nod.

"Jacob. Your job is to research transport options out of the Borderlands. Quinn, you mentioned being able to help with routes in? The problem we have is that this is a covert op. The Queen can't be seen sanctioning a mission against the Border Lord without inciting civil war. Therefore, we're on our own. No Border passes, no paperwork."

Jacob whistles.

I take the stick and aim it at the map. "We can't go in along any of the trade routes or defended guard gate houses. Of which there are many."

A grumble ripples through the room.

"That doesn't leave a lot of options. We could travel south and across the sea? Come at the Border from the other side? I have a ton of ship contacts," Stirling offers.

"No," Morrigan snaps. "I don't know the other side of the Border as well as this side." Scarlett glances at Stirling. I follow a silent exchange between them, shared expressions and gazes only twins understand.

"How about you, Quinn?" Morrigan says.

I shake my head. "I think it would put us at a tactical disadvantage."

"Fine, no boats," Stirling raises her hands and drops them in her lap.

"I think we're going to need to go in on foot. Through

one of the less well guarded areas. We'll need fast escape routes, though." Jacob nods at me.

"Could you talk me through whatever transport lines still work in there and some routes in and out?" Jacob asks.

"Absolutely. There's not much in there that works, but I can have a think and perhaps we can come up with some solutions together."

Scarlett takes the stick. "Stirling, that leaves you with resources. We're going to need supplies, food, sleeping equipment, medical packs."

"I have the medical packs. I can bring those from the stores," I say, pointing at the racking pushed against the warehouse walls.

"Excellent, one less job for me," Stirling says.

"That still doesn't give us a route in," Morrigan says.

"Or any information about the Old Palace security?" Remy adds.

"Well, the Queen gave us some old schematics for the palace security, which is better than nothing," Scarlett says and nods to Stirling, who shuffles the papers and slides a schematics map to Remy.

"And I might be able to help," I say.

Scarlett catches my eye, her brow raised.

"Well, one of my family members works for the Border Lord, remember?"

Scarlett nods. "Do it. Make contact and see what you can find out."

For the next two hours, we debate routes into the Border back and forth. Every time we thought we'd come up with a solution, someone would poo poo it. Either Morrigan had intel we didn't or I knew father had put security traps in or it didn't work logistically.

"Fuck," I say louder than I'd intended.

"What?" Remy says and rubs her face, exhaustion setting in.

"We don't go through the Border, we go under it. There's another route in that I'm ninety-nine percent sure will get us in undetected, but you're not going to like it."

"Go on..." Scarlett says.

I take the pointer stick from her, our fingers brushing as it rolls into my palm. I aim the stick at the Never Woods and the mansion that guards the entrance.

"No fucking way," Scarlett says. "Are you trying to get us all killed? That mansion was lethal back in the day."

"Yes, but the mansion is dying now. And as for the woods, well, you're a trained High-Assassin so you've led me to believe..." I'm goading her, but she needs to accept this because, truly, I don't see what other choice we have. Every other entrance is guarded, and all the other routes aren't viable.

"That's a dangerous move," Morrigan says, cutting the silence. "It's a militia-owned mansion, and from what I can remember, it's power was rooted in time magic. It could really screw us."

"Do you see another option?" I ask.

She shakes her head. Me either.

Jacob has been quiet for a while, taking in all the options. But he sits up now. "Militia?"

"As in, not the Border Lord's men. These are the worst of the worst. Those left with nothing after The Tearing. People who care not whether you live or die or become animal fodder. If you stand in their way, they'll gut you. If you have something they want, they'll gut you. And they have nothing to lose, which means they'll fight dirty. If we are going through the Never Woods, and given there are no other options, then we'll need to be prepared. We'll all need to fight." I glance at Scarlett, my stomach clenching and knotting. I can hold my own, but I'm not a fighter at heart. Even though it was my suggestion, the thought of going through the Never Woods terrifies me.

"Hold on, there are groups of people against the Border Lord inside the Borderlands?" Scarlett says.

I nod.

"Then why can't we team up with them?"

"Scar," Stirling says, a warning in her tone.

"You're going after the Border Lord?" Remy asks, and her eyes skirt to mine.

I glare at her. My stomach clenches. *Keep quiet.* I'm screaming the words silently at her, praying she can understand.

Scarlett shrugs. "If he falls on my blade while we're in the Old Palace, I won't cry about it."

My pulse quickens. This is it. This is the moment I find out what she's planning. "Is killing the Border Lord part of our plan, then?" I say, picking at a nick in the fabric of my crop top where Scarlett held the blade. I daren't glance up in case my expression gives me away. Remy's eyes bore into me. It twists my guts into knots. What if she says something? What if she tells everyone?

"Damn right. That piece of shit deserves to pay for what he did," Scarlett says.

"What did he do?" I ask, my voice barely above a whisper.

"He took everyth—"

"Scarlett," Stirling barks. "Enough. Yes, killing the Border Lord would be deeply gratifying, but that is not the mission and not what we are focusing on."

Scarlett spins her blade on the tip of her finger and nods at her sister. But the way her eyes narrow at the knife, I don't believe for a second that she'll drop it. I glance at the hilt, realising it's the same one she stole from me that first night I met her. The one my father gave me. If she knew it was his...

What if she does?

No, I decide.

She can't. Because if she knew who the Border Lord was, if she knew he was my father, I'd be dead already.

CHAPTER 17

QUINN

Scarlett sits up and slams her blade into the table. "Then let the training begin. We knew we'd have to train. The Never Woods, the militia, all they do is increase the importance of everyone being able to fight competently. Right, everyone up. We'll do a couple of hours now, and then you can all go for the night."

I get up, my brain still swirling with thoughts of Remy. I grip her arm.

"Promise you'll stay quiet?" I breathe.

Remy raises an eyebrow at me, her lips pursed. "It's a disaster waiting to happen."

I dig my nails into her arm, pull her closer and hiss, "Promise me."

"Fine," she shucks me off. "I promise. But if they find out and they ask me, I'm not taking the fall for you."

She stalks off to find a place on the mats. And I'm left wondering what happens when Scarlett discovers who I am? I didn't use to care. Let her find out because all we wanted was to kill each other.

But now... Now things are changing. I don't want the games to end. I don't want... whatever we have—

"Quinn, move your arse," Scarlett says, using the blade to spank my cheek.

I scuttle to the middle of the warehouse where Stirling is laying mats out that she must have sourced from somewhere.

Scarlett pairs everyone up. Remy and Jacob, as they are almost as tall as each other. Though part of me wonders if she's paired Remy with a buff guy in the hope she gets her arse handed to her. Scarlett doesn't have to say she's jealous, I can tell from the stiffness in her jaw every time she sends a glance Remy's way. If she feels like that, maybe she'll forgive me for not telling her who I am.

Scarlett puts Stirling and Morrigan together, a terrible idea if you ask me. And by the vicious glare Morrigan gives Scarlett, I'm actually worried for her safety, given Morrigan's power.

But that leaves me partnered with Scarlett.

The chance to throw her around would usually appeal, but my mind is filled with thoughts of what if, and what happens when?

Scarlett takes a deep breath and her voice booms around the warehouse. The tone changes. More serious, deeper, stricter, commanding.

I like it. I want to do exactly what she says, *whatever* she says. She enjoys being in front and teaching. I can tell because of the way a tiny crinkle appears in the corner of her eyes. It's only ever there when she's content. It's rare Scarlett gives away anything facially. She's usually stoic, part of her original Assassin training, no doubt. But I've spent enough time with her now to notice the differences, and this, she loves. I decide, for whatever reason, to try a little harder for her.

"First, we learn defence. The chances are the militia will attack when we're least expecting it. We need to be prepared to defend ourselves," Scarlett says, projecting and gesturing with big movements.

Everyone nods, and Scarlett continues.

"Number one. Do not defend with the squishy soft parts of your body. You defend with hard bones and absolutely no areas where you have arteries. For example," she points to the outside of her forearm, "you use the outer edge as it's all bone. If you expose your wrist to an attacker, and they have a knife, they could cut your wrist and you'll bleed out."

I move from foot to foot, the realisation of how serious the game I'm playing is dawning on me. This is life or death: mine, father's, the militia's, the teams. Scarlett demonstrates a variety of blocks, low ones to block kicks, high ones overhead to block arms dropping axes and weapons on us.

"Now, I want you to practice these blocks in turn. If you're defending, finish your blocks with an attack. Whether that's a punch or kick, whatever you can get out. Run each block ten times a piece. And then swap attacker and defender. I want the attackers to go for it. Really attack with all your body weight. Do not hold back. The militia won't. I expect you all to be bruised by the end of this session," she pauses, examining each of us. "Well? what are you all waiting for? GO."

The room erupts. Scarlett rounds on me, her eyes glinting, her smile a thin snarl. "You ready for this, baby?"

"No."

"Good."

She launches herself at me without telling me which attack she was going to do. And by all rights, I should have been pissed at her. I could have been hurt. But I guess the militia won't tell us how they'll attack, so why should Scarlett? Not if I stand any chance of being able to defend myself.

Scarlett's arm swings at my head. I don't have time to think; I react. Bam. Forearm out. Block. And before I realise what I'm doing, I've launched a punch straight at her solar plexus.

It doesn't make contact. Scarlett cups her hand around my fist, catching it as it was going to make contact.

She steps aside, an eyebrow raised, a lopsided smile. "Not bad."

"I didn't mean to. I just reacted. This is weird... usually we..."

"We're trying to actually punch each other?"

"Yeah," I say laughing.

"Really try to punch me. That was a good swing you got. But let's go again. I promise you can't hurt me."

"Is that a challenge?"

She licks her lips. "I'll sweeten the deal. You land a punch on me, and I'll let you do whatever you want to me."

I raise an eyebrow. "Whatever I want? Oh, now that's a deal I can take."

"You and your deals."

I launch myself at her. Legs, fists, body. I give her everything. Scarlett blocks, ducks and then comes for me. This time she reaches for my collar to scruff me and put me on my arse. But this is one I recognise.

Malachi used to do this to me as a kid. I land my hand over the top of her arm, yank her forward and off balance, and then throw a kick to her ribs. But Scarlett saw it coming. She disentangles and slaps my leg away. While I can defend myself in a scrap, I'm not trained, not like her. I lose balance and take us both down.

Scarlett lands on top of me, her arms pinning me to the floor, her chest pressed against mine.

She's right above me, her breath flowing over my lips. It's sweet and deep. The press and weight of her body on top of mine makes my cunt heat. I'd much rather strip her clothes off and roll around the mats than fight her.

"You seem to enjoy being on top of me, don't you?" I say, a cheeky grin peeling across my lips.

Scarlett closes her mouth, her gaze exploring my face. This is how I get her.

"You're right where you should be," she says, grinning, and slides her knee between my thighs and against my crotch. I let out a moan.

I lean in; she leans down. I want the kiss, but I want to win more.

As her eyes close, I clench my fist and slam it into her ribs. The blow knocks her off balance, and I draw my knee up and use all my weight to flip her onto her back. I close my legs around hers, like I did with Malachi. I pin her arms to the ground, making sure she can't move.

Her cheeks are bright red. Fury tremors through her expression.

"Two nil to me, baby."

She wriggles out and rolls me off her. She clears her throat and addresses the team, the rage dissipating. "This is another great lesson. You want to stay on your feet. This isn't a judo ring. We're not here to wrestle, and you don't want to wrestle the militia. You get on the ground and shit is going to get far more dangerous. We'll deal with those techniques next time. Continue."

Scarlett rounds on me, her eyes darkening. I tiptoe my fingers up her waist, between her cleavage and onto her chin, which I pull down.

"Anything... I... want..." I place a soft kiss on her lips. "Someone once told me all the best deals are sealed with a kiss."

She huffs out a laugh. "Someone wise and beautiful and—"

"—And egotistical and irritating and—"

"—And enough of that. Let's say we raise the stakes? Double or quits. If I can land a punch, I get to do whatever I want to you?"

"I'll take it under consideration."

She laughs. "Are you ready?"

"No."

"Good."

She flings forward, a jab, jab, hook. I block, block, block and attack. Turns out, while I might not be quick, I'm really, really fucking strong. And by the end of training, both Scarlett and I are blowing hard. She makes the group run through another set of attacks and another set of defences, And by the time we get to the end of the session, everyone is red faced and glistening. Sweat runs down my neck and temples, I have big splodgy wet patches on my clothes, and every single muscle is screaming.

Scarlett folds her arms, taking me in, her eyes running me top to bottom. "If I were a betting woman, I'd say you had some kind of training. Especially given some fights we've had on jobs."

I laugh. "No, but I did have a physically bigger, younger

brother, who pretended his sister was a brother. But no, no formal training."

"Then I'm impressed." She turns to the room. "Let's leave it there for tonight. Tomorrow, I want you here in the afternoon once you've worked on your own mission research. Once you've cracked the basics of self-defence, we'll run weapons training. If any of you have sense, you'll go down to the open baths in the centre of town and jump in the ice bath and then get in the hot pools. It will help your muscles because I can assure you by the end of this week you're all going to be in agony."

"Phsst," Jacob says. "I have to stay fit for racing. I'll be fine."

"Is that a bet you'd like to make, Mr. Jones?" Scarlett says, pouting at him and folding her arms.

Jacob opens his mouth but shuts it again. "I'm a betting man. What's the stakes?"

"If you're not in agony by the weekend, I'll cook dinner on the last night before we leave for the mission."

"And if I am in agony?"

"Then you cook."

Jacob rubs his chin but then nods. "You're on."

Scarlett's face darkens at the same time as smiling, and it's mildly terrifying.

"Oh, Jacob, you're completely and utterly, royally fucked now, sunshine," Remy says, laughing as she picks up her jumper and heads out for the night. "I'll see you all tomorrow."

Jacob follows her out, and then Stirling says, "Are you coming?"

"Coming where?" I say, confused.

"The bathhouse? Trust me, you'll need it before

tomorrow unless you want to feel like a carriage ran you over."

"I... umm."

"Much to my chagrin, I'm going," Morrigan says and picks up a pile of books and deposits them into her bag.

I glance at Scarlett, who nods agreement.

"Fine. Let me lock up."

Twenty minutes later, as my muscles are seizing, we arrive at the bathhouse. It's an old relic left behind by histories lost to our memory now. They're open to the public, but it's dead tonight. There's only one other person in the far corner. That, at least, is a saving grace.

"The changing area is over there," Stirling says, pointing to an open stone corridor.

"Where are you changing?" I ask.

"I'm stripping and diving right in. The quicker I get in, the less I'll hurt tomorrow."

And just like that, she whips off her top and trousers and jumps into the cold pool feet first in only a sports bra and knickers. When she bursts to the surface, she squeals.

"FUCCCK, it's freezing." Her teeth chatter, but she doesn't get out.

Scarlett is looking at her watch. "Forty seconds to go."

"Fuck you and your fucking watch, Scarlett."

Morrigan cackles.

"You won't be fucking laughing when it's your turn," Stirling spits. Which only makes Morrigan laugh harder. Perhaps there is still a chance for them both.

Stirling turns a delightful shade of red as she grips the sides of the drop pool. It's only big enough for one of us to get in at a time.

"Ten. Nine..." Scarlett counts down, and the more

numbers she says, the more ferociously Stirling glares at her. I swear she's going to knock her sister out. But as the timer hits one, she scrambles out of the pool, cussing, and jumps into the hot tub. The relief instantly relaxes her expression.

"Morrigan, you're next," Scarlett says.

Morrigan strips. She's curvy like me, but when she drops her clothes, the woman on the other side of the bath-house stops what she's doing and stares, her mouth parting.

I can see why. It's not the perfect hourglass Morrigan has, though that is a sight to behold. It's not even her waist-length jet black hair. It's the fact that 75% of her skin is covered in Collection tattoos. She has to be the most powerful magician I've ever met. I thought only royals had the ability to wield that much magic. Even though I knew Morrigan was powerful, even I can't stop my mouth from dropping either. Both of her legs are sleeved in tattoos. Her back too. Only her chest and abdomen are clear. It's an incredible achievement for someone only in her early thir-ties. I can't even fathom the power she will hold when she's a few decades older.

She takes a few deep breaths, Stirling catcalling from the hot tub. Morrigan gives her the birdie and says, "Shut your trap, Grey."

Then she jumps in. She bursts through the water screaming obscenities and I can't help but laugh at her. Only this time, it's a nervous laughter. Scarlett is smirking as she tracks the time on her watch.

"Three. Two. One... and time."

"Fucking Stirling. This is your fault," Morrigan snaps, glaring at her.

"You'll thank me when you're not dying of lactic burn in

the morning," she says and gestures for her to get in the hot tub.

She does, and although it's clear she warms up immediately, she's still scowling at Stirling. Is this how it's going to be the entire mission?

Scarlett, still smirking, turns to me. "Your turn."

I press my lips together, knowing this will be the coldest sixty seconds of my life.

"Don't worry, you only have to do it three times tonight," Scarlett says, practically hyperventilating. Tears of laughter leak out and run down her cheeks.

"You're an epic arsehole. I'll be timing for you after. Extra ten seconds, I think."

Which only makes Scarlett laugh harder. She stops, though, the moment I strip to my underwear. She tries to keep her eyes on mine. Though the minute I reach the edge of the plunge pool, they rake down me. This, at least, makes me smile. I like knowing I have an effect on her.

That I can stop her in her arrogant tracks.

She's not invincible.

I steady myself, take a deep breath and then leap into the pool feet first. When I break through the surface, a scream rips from my lips. It is ferociously cold. My entire body burns. My extremities are immediately numb. The cold steals my breath and I have to concentrate to avoid panicking. It takes about forty of the seconds for me to calm down, and then this strange sense of tranquility envelops over me. The cold loses its sharpness, and I settle into an almost delirious elation. Then, the timer is up, and Scarlett offers me a hand to pull me out.

I take it and as soon as the air hits my skin, I'm freezing all over again. Stirling and Morrigan clap me from the hot tub. I snatch the watch out of Scarlett's hand and say, "Your turn, motherfucker."

Scarlett laughs and strips while I climb into the hot tub with the other girls. And it is no word of a lie when I say it is the most blissful and glorious few seconds of joy I've ever experienced while my body adjusts.

"Ready with the timer?" Scarlett says.

I suck in a small gasp as I glance down Scarlett's body. I don't think I've ever actually seen her so undressed. Whenever we've fucked, it's hurried, frantic, a mess of limbs and fighting.

The tight lines of muscle, the abs carving up her stomach. Everything is toned, her thighs meaty and muscular despite being long. She doesn't really have a waist, she's straight up and down. She wears men's pants and a sports bra, and her nipples are hard beneath the fabric. It takes all my strength to tear my eyes away and hit reset on the watch.

"Ready," I say, unable to look up again.

"Go," Scarlett says, and then splashes into the pool.

"My Gods, you two are sickeningly into each other. Anyone would mistake you for being head over heels in love," Stirling says.

"Leave them alone," Morrigan growls. "Love is always beautiful."

"Love?" I say, confused, and glance at the pool, wondering why Scarlett hasn't come up for air.

"Excuse me. I'm going to go home. I'm tired and need to rest up before meeting Remy tomorrow." Morrigan gets out of the pool and leaves.

"She won't surface. Hardcore show off," Stirling says.

"She stays under the whole time?"

"Disgusting display of willpower, isn't it?"

I glance at the clock. Fifteen seconds down. I can't even imagine how cold it is with her head submerged too.

"You love her, don't you?" Stirling says.

"What? No. I..."

Stirling smiles. "I thought so."

My mind flits to the racetrack. Stirling's words, *you'll regret*.

"You don't hate me, then?" I ask, my voice quiet.

"Why would you think that?" she says, frowning.

"I..."

"Of course I don't. I want Scarlett to be happy. You seem to make her happy. I think you bring out the best in her. You soften those hard edges."

She grips my shoulder as Scarlett breaks the surface bang on sixty seconds.

"Show off," I spit, but I can't stop thinking about what Stirling said. Of course, I don't love Scarlett. That's ridiculous.

I don't.

Do I?

This is business. It's all a game. A ploy to stop her hurting my father. A way to get my journal back.

Scarlett wades into the water, her face relaxing as much as each of ours did as we slid into the warmth.

"I'm off," Stirling says. "Catch you soon."

When she's gone, I glance at the corner of the bathhouse. The other woman has left too. Scarlett and I are alone. In nothing but our underwear in a hot tub with a clear sky and stars twinkling.

"You did well this afternoon," she says.

"Thanks," I say, running my hands across the surface of the water. My skin already smells of chemicals.

Scarlett catches my hand and pulls me through the water until I'm right in front of her. My heart thuds against my ribs. I want to reach out, run my fingers over her wet skin. Follow the rivulets of water beading and falling down her neck, her chest, her breasts. But this feels different. I don't know how to sleep with her like this. I've only ever fucked her angry. My mouth dries.

Scarlett folds my fingers into a fist. Kisses the knuckles.

"One thing. When you punch, make sure your fist is like this." She turns my hand until my knuckles are straight, thumb at the side tucked underneath.

"Not like this." She tilts my fist a little up.

"You have a habit of angling the punch up a little. But if you really hit hard like this, the pressure goes all the way down your wrist, through your arm bones. If you land a blow hard enough, you could break your own bone."

She draws her fingers down my wet skin, pointing at the bones and tilting my hand. Everywhere she touches me, it leaves a wake of tingles. For the first time, I notice that her hands and knuckles are scarred. I trace the lines of the old wounds, wondering how she got each one of them. Some are fresher than others, but most are faded, echoes of jobs and missions.

"How old were you when you started training?" I ask.

She sighs and leans back against the edge of the tub. "I don't remember ever not training. I think even as a toddler I had instructors."

"You didn't have a choice?"

"It wasn't that. I showed an aptitude for it, I guess, so my parents encouraged it. And I willingly complied. Who doesn't enjoy being the best at their skill of choice?"

I nod, knowing exactly what she means. I displayed a

talent for herbs and alchemy from a very young age. "Sometimes I wonder if we're all just self-fulfilling prophecies. Rather than giving us a chance to explore other options, we're all herded into whatever field we show the most promise in, and that's it."

"What field of magic would you go into if you weren't a medic?"

"Honestly? I'm not sure. I love poisons, but I don't think I have the physique to be an Assassin."

Scarlett's expression turns serious. "What you lack in cardio speed you more than make up for in strength. There are ways to compensate."

I smile. That's sweet. Sometimes I look at Scarlett and I wonder who she really is. What's beneath the hard shell exterior?

"I also don't know if I'd have the kill switch gene in me. It's one thing supplying poisons to people because I'm not doing the kill. But it's different when you have to look the person in the eye as you take their life."

"Well, you seem to want to kill me often enough."

I chuckle. "Touché."

She smiles then leans her head against the poolside and kicks back, floating. "It's quite something, the first time. I think the guild trained the feeling out of me. The first kill was hard. But there's no room for emotion in the field. You feel, you die. Over time, they drill it out of you."

"I wonder if you'd find it easy to kill me now."

She drops her legs and sloshes her way towards me. She picks me up by the thighs, and I lock my legs around her waist.

"Oh, I could kill you." She leans into my neck and bites the flesh, eliciting a moan from me.

"Liar," I say.

"Narcissist."

I laugh. She runs a finger along the bottom of my sports bra, the pads gently pressing into my skin. She pauses when I continue talking.

"The other part of me thinks I would have taught. I love academia, and I'd be happy lecturing in the guild training new recruits. But then I'd have to work for someone. I'm too independent for that. Perhaps my self-fulfilling prophecy was right after all. What about you?"

Scarlett looks up at the stars. The sky is inky black now, the crisp night air an exquisite shock against the warmth of the tub. I shiver, so she holds me tighter. Tangled together, we submerge our shoulders into the water. Staring at the sky reminds me of father, the observatories in the old palaces. We used to spend time there at night. The skies were usually clouded, of course, after The Tearing the Borderlands were usually freezing or full of storms. But on the odd night when the skies cleared, father and I would go to the observatory and try to spot constellations.

"There's only one place I'd go if I weren't an Assassin..."

She doesn't finish the thought. At first, I'm annoyed. I'm sharing. Why isn't she? But then I realise I already know the answer. "The track?"

She looks down at me. "I'd race all day, every day."

"Maybe you can. Maybe you should."

She shrugs at me. "Perhaps. But I wonder if I raced full-time whether that would steal the joy from it. Right now, I love it because it's a treat, a reward, but if I had to turn it into a job, I'm not sure."

We're silent for a while. And my mind wanders to my father. I need to understand why she hates him. Why is she determined to kill him? But I'm frightened if I ask it will change everything. I like these moments. The spaces in between when I catch glimpses of the real Scarlett, not the one she presents to the world.

"I need to ask you something," I say, a quiver beneath my words.

"Okay," she says, drawing out the syllables. She sits me down on the ridge beneath the water and gives me some space.

"Before we go on this mission. I have to ask. Is it really about the map? Or is it about m—" I clear my throat, covering up what I was going to say. "I mean. Is it about killing the Border Lord?"

Scarlett stiffens. She edges closer. "Does it matter?"

"It does to me." The backs of my eyes sting, and I'm not sure if I can keep the tears down. I love my father. I cannot let her do this.

"It's about both," she sighs.

"Why do you hate him? Every time his name is brought up, I can see it. It changes your face. There's a darkness or a shadow or something, but it passes through you and your whole demeanour changes."

She doesn't look at me. "I'm not supposed to…" Her eyes scan mine, searching. Though what she's hunting for, I don't know. "I'm trusting you, okay?"

I nod, solemn.

"There was a mission years ago. A job for him that was surrounded by secrecy. A solo commission. He'd sought me out personally because I'd finished top at the academy."

"Okay," I say, scrunching up my face. I didn't know father had ever commissioned an Assassin. I mean, his soldiers have killed defending the trade routes, but commissioning an Assassin is different.

"I can't tell you the details, obviously."

I chew my lip because the devil is always in the detail, and I want the specifics of exactly what my father asked her to do.

"Anyway, when it came down to it, I couldn't go through with the job. Not properly. One wrong decision and it changed the course of my life and Stirling's. I'm pretty sure that he is the one who set up my parents as a punishment for failing his mission. He's the reason my parents are dead. The reason I lost my legacy."

I suck in a sharp breath. It cuts its way down my throat and burns its way around my body. No. It can't be true. He'd never be that cruel.

"Are you sure it was him?"

"In my gut and with my whole soul."

I shake my head. I don't want it to be true. And if that's really what happened, I need the truth. Something awful quivers in my gut, my ribs tighten as my mind races through all the things my father has done, wondering whether it's possible. Whether I'd misunderstood him all this time.

Scarlett lifts my chin. Her expression strained, a small furrow between her brows. She wipes a tear away from my cheeks with her thumb.

"Never thought I'd see you cry for me, Quinn."

"How do you know it's not for the Border Lord?" Because it is. In part. Maybe it's for her too. Maybe it's for me. The loss. The betrayal. Recognising my father might not be who I thought.

She scoffs. "Please. We both know they're for me."

She leans down, closer and closer, tilting her head. She's going to kiss me. I'm sure of it. All my oxygen leaves. I can't breathe. I want it and I don't. This is dangerous ground. I'm supposed to be here to stop her, not to kiss her.

But what if what she's saying is true?

That my father really set her parents up.

Her lips brush against mine. "I believe you won a bet..." she says.

CHAPTER 18

SCARLETT

"Anything I want?" Quinn purrs.

"For you, Quinn Adams... I'd do anything." I lean down and caress her collar bone with my lips, her skin warm against the biting chill of night air. Water flows over my body, drenching my braid.

"Take off your clothes, Scarlett," Quinn says, and it's the most commanding thing I've ever heard her say. I baulk, realising I've never relinquished control, never let myself be vulnerable.

This is a first for me.

For us.

The air around us feels different, as if tonight, instead of fighting and fury, we're united, we're one, moving the stars and galaxies. Aligning the universe to where it always should have been.

"Now take mine off," she says, never looking away. Her eyes locked on mine as I dutifully do as she says, slipping her sports bra and knickers off. The intensity bridged between us is infinite, as if we are the only ones left in the world, as if she is my everything and I am hers.

My heart pounds against my ribs, but not because I'm angry, not because I hate her. But because I don't.

Because I want this in a way I've never wanted it before. I want her in a way I've never wanted her before.

It consumes me. Fills my body and sets me alight. The need, the yearning, it burns in every cell. I lunge forward, but she holds her hand out, stopping me.

It's torture. The restraint tears at my muscles, and she knows it. She is beautiful naked, the soft flesh of her belly, her rounded breasts and pert brown nipples. I would spend the rest of my life making her come, and it wouldn't be enough. I don't think I could ever get enough of her.

She shifts her bum to the edge, her legs clamped together, graceful, ladylike. I can't see her core, and I need to. I need all of her.

"Touch yourself," she says.

I open my mouth to protest, desperate to taste her, to have her. But she waggles a finger at me. "A deal is a deal."

So I slip my hand beneath the water and part my legs. I touch the swollen nub of my clit, but I keep my eyes on her, watch as her lips part, a breath escaping. My nipples bob in and out of the water, the cold air hardening them to points. I bite my lip, rub my clit faster, allow myself the softest of moans.

She goes rigid, her jaw flexes. It's hurting her to hold back as much as it's hurting me. I step closer, lay my other hand on her thigh. I can't touch her where I want, but I can drive her wild.

I moan louder. I'm getting close.

"Stop," she commands.

I do. Fire burns through my eyes. Fuck, I was close.

She points to the side of the pool. "Lean over the edge."

I glide through the water and lay my stomach on the cold poolside.

"Now spread your legs."

I suck in a breath, open my legs, baring myself to her. She takes my thighs in her hands and then she slides her tongue over my wet cunt. I let out a guttural moan as she flicks her tongue against my clit, over and over. She slides her mouth over my flesh. The more I soak her mouth, the harder she grips my legs and the faster she laps at my core.

"Quinn..." I pant, breathless.

I can't hold on anymore. Her mouth is like lightning and ecstasy, the rhythmic beat of her lips and tongue, over and over, harder and faster until I break apart in her mouth and I'm crying out her name.

I pant against the stone pool, tingles coursing through my body. And then I spin round, turning on her. But she's already sat on the edge of the pool, her eyes dark and devious.

"Come here," she says and draws me closer with her finger.

I do as she asks.

"Kiss me."

I rise out of the water, slide my lips over hers until I can taste myself and my wetness on her tongue. I bite her bottom lip, suck it as I pull away. She moans against me, then pushes me off.

She stares at me, and slowly, she opens her legs, millimetre by millimetre, as if this, like everything else we do, is a game.

You win, Quinn. I'm yours.

When her legs are spread apart and I can see her wet

pussy bared in front of me, it takes every ounce of strength to stay put.

"And now?" I say. "Now, what would you have me do?"

She tuts and pouts her lips. "Eat, Scarlett. Now it's time to eat."

I grin, because I've never been so fucking hungry in all my life.

CHAPTER 19

SCARLETT

The days blur. An exhausting haze of training, the bathhouse, eating—food, not Quinn, sadly— going through the house and packing the last few boxes, and researching. With a week to go, Stirling has already sourced all the supplies we need for the hike across the city. Food, sleeping and kit bags, medical supplies from Quinn and weapons. Remy has located Old Palace schematics that are newer than the ones the Queen gave us and located a tunnel we can use to enter below the palace. Quinn thinks we should be undetected, and Morrigan also gave the thumbs up. Which means we have an entry point for the mission. Stirling and I don't, however, have a house to go to once the mission is complete. The unease creeping into my gut is growing into an ugly noose. I'm sure we can sofa surf for a few days when we're back, but after that, we're going to need to sort a new place to live.

Between some Border Walker Stirling knows and Morrigan's knowledge of the palace, Remy is busy deciding the best route to break in and get out, as well as how to combat the security runes both on the inside and the outside of the palace.

Jacob, however, is having less luck. Given he spends most of his time racing, he doesn't have any contacts inside the Border, so getting accurate information is trickier for him.

This evening I find him with an array of spanners and bolts surrounding him, his hands surrounded by pearlescent flames deep in my bike's engine.

"Should I be worried?" I say as his head pops up.

"Upgrades, you're welcome."

"Thanks? Do I owe you beer for this, or should I purchase an upgrade on leathers and a helmet?"

"Maybe both. I had to think. I've not found much on transport. Had to put my hands to use, fixing something to give me the headspace for ideas." He grins, and I help him tidy away his tools.

"Quinn has talked me through most of the basics. Carriages are few, most broke during The Tearing, and bikes are few and far between, too. She said it was like an EMP went off and fucked all the electrics. Which is not proving helpful to me."

"But there's hope?" I ask as I put the last tool away and we make our way inside. Morrigan sits in the corner of our planning table, her nose buried in a book with a pile next to her, and Remy is levitating moving cog parts made of copper thread in front of her. Stirling and Quinn are already on the training mats.

"There's always hope. I'm thinking I'll try to salvage a carriage while you're actually inside the building. I'm not wild about splitting the team up, though."

"Hmm, me neither. But at this point, I'm not sure we have a choice."

He takes his tool box and dumps it with his belongings and joins the rest of the group in the middle of the warehouse.

"Tonight, ladies and gentleman, we're moving onto weapons training," I say and shift on the spot. This was the session I've been dreading. It's one thing practicing with arms and limbs, of which most of theirs are now a delightful mottled mosaic of purple and green bruises. But when you add weapons in, I'm expecting chaos.

"We're going to start with close combat this evening. I'm going to pair you up differently. Morrigan, you're with Quinn. Sister, you're with me. And Jacob, you're with Remy. I'm doing this because your attacker may not be the same size and weight as you, and you need to defend yourselves against whoever we're attacked by."

"Yeah, most of the militia are male, or they were when I still lived in the Borderlands," Quinn says.

"Close combat, small blades." I roll out my blade case along the table and gesture for everyone to pick up a blade of their choice.

Once everyone has a blade, I turn to the group. "This is where we put all the blocks we've been practicing into play. These blades are real. They're sharp, and you will fuck yourself up if you don't block effectively." I draw my blade across the pad of my finger and let my blood spill onto the mats.

Quinn is skittish. Her feet dancing. She needs to get a grip because Morrigan won't hold back. I wonder briefly if I made the right choice switching the pairings, but I know without a doubt that we could get attacked by anyone in the field. Of any size. The team needs to be prepared.

"Block with your bones, not your blood. And to up the ante, the first one to draw blood gets to skip the plunge pools tonight."

"And the loser?" Jacob asks.

"Hundred burpees."

A low whistle rips around the room. No one wants the burpees. Literally no one. But they truly are one of the greatest body exercises. And if this lot isn't fit enough by the time we head into the Border, then it will be all our asses on the line.

Quinn's eyes widen and then narrow, a dark smile spreading across her lips. I can smell the fight in her. There is nothing sexier than an angry Quinn, all pent up and ready to murder.

My body reacts to her. It yearns for her, urges me forward. But I refuse. We haven't slept together since the first night at the plunge pools. Something shifted between us that night and now we're... I don't know. Different. Before, it was just lust and hate. But the more I get to know her, the more I doubt all my game plans. I don't want to ruin her anymore. If I ruin her, I ruin my heart.

"One attacker, one defender, now is the time to put all your skills and drills into practice. Ready? Go," I bark, and the room ignites into a rush of blade swings, jabs, and grunts as bodies slam into each other. The clatter of metal knives dropping to the floor echoes around the warehouse. Good. That means they're successfully disarming each other.

Stirling hops from foot to foot, grinning at me. "Ready, sister?" she grins.

"Always."

She lunges, but she's slow. Or at least slower than me. I spin out of the way and kick her legs out from beneath her.

And then I look at her crumpled body on the floor and laugh.

"When will you learn?"

She grunts some inaudible profanity at me and scrambles up. A hot flare burning in her expression. This is the best way to beat Stirling. Piss her off enough, she makes mistakes.

She lunges again, blade out.

"Sloppy," I tut as I lean out the way and bat her arm out of reach.

She snarls, baring her teeth, and it makes me laugh. "You know you won't win."

"You know *you're* not going to win," she flicks her gaze to Quinn.

Her words catch me off guard. Quinn is sweating profusely, her jaw locked in concentration. What happens when this is over? What happens if everything returns to the way it was? I don't want that anymore. I want to ho—

I'm on my back, a knife at my throat. Stirling's victorious smirk leering down at me.

"Found your weakness," she says, glancing at Quinn.

"Ahh, but dearest Stirling... I found yours first." And with that, I nudge the blade. She hadn't noticed I'd slipped it against her side and into her ribs, just enough to draw blood.

Her eyes widen. Then she sags onto my chest and mumbles, "Wanker," into my chest.

"You never could stop yourself gloating." I roar with laughter and roll her off me. "That's no plunge pool for me tonight, and," I raise my voice, "hundred burpees go to Stirling."

Everyone stops to see Stirling clutching her ribs. But Morrigan is so deep in sparring Quinn she doesn't hear me.

Quinn turns to face me. And then the world slows. Morrigan's face drops and scrunches. She realises what's about to happen, but too late for her to stop herself.

I'm up, running, reaching for Quinn. But I'm slow. Too fucking slow, and the blade plunges into Quinn's shoulder.

Her face pales, a strangled cry escapes her mouth, and then the entire room is silent. An eerie blanket wrapping around us as the realisation of what's happened sinks in.

Quinn's eyes roll, her knees go, and then she's in my arms and I'm running her to the medical room.

There are shouts and noise behind us, but I don't care. I need to get the blade out of her shoulder and make sure she's not nicked anything vital.

I lay her on her front, slice through her training shirt and sports bra, letting it fall to the sides in one smooth motion.

"STIRLING," I bellow, but she's already behind me, holding one of the medical packs. I'm not medically trained, but the guild taught us enough to treat traumas in the field. We were always being injured, my body is littered with the scars to prove it. While I can't operate or do half the shit Quinn can, I can assess whether the blade has nicked anything vital and if not, get it out and stitch it.

"Iodine, needle, thread and pressure wound kits," I say, but Stirling is already ahead of me.

Morrigan appears, her face ashen. "Scarlett, I'm sorry, I didn't mean—"

"It's fine. I know. Let this be a lesson for all of us to never, ever take our eyes off the blade."

Quinn rouses. Tears stream down her cheeks.

"Stay still, Quinn."

"Quinn, I'm so sorry," Morrigan says, kneeling beside her.

"You get to hold her hand when I pull the blade. That can be your punishment."

Quinn manages a staccato laugh, but it's only half-hearted and edged with the hesitation only nerves can bring.

"Is it going to hurt?" she says.

"Yes," Stirling and I say simultaneously.

"I can help ease the pain if you'll let me. I'm not a fully qualified medic, I can't get rid of it all, but it might ease it a bit," Morrigan says.

Quinn nods. Morrigan stands, holds her hands over Quinn's shoulder and bends and contorts her fingers until a pearlescent light coats her shoulder and the tension leaves her muscles.

I lean over Quinn's body, examining the placement of the blade and the depth it's penetrated, the position.

"It's not fatal. In fact, it's not even that deep. A couple of inches. You'll be sore. But I suspect you have a potion in that shop of yours that will help speed up the recovery."

She groans into the bed.

I find Remy and Jacob hovering, and Stirling's ribs dropping her own set of blood on the floor where I nicked her.

"Oh, for Gods sake. Morrigan, go patch Stirling. Everyone else, out." There's a scuffle, but a few seconds later, the door clicks shut and we're alone.

"You need to grip the bed. I know Morrigan has helped, but this is still going to hurt like nothing else. But I need to get it out. Okay?"

She squeezes her eyes shut and nods into the bed.

"Ready?"

"No."

I laugh. "Good. Three... Two..."

I yank the blade out and apply the pressure dressing.

She screams. It's a piercing shriek that makes my bones shiver.

"What the fuck happened to one?"

"Never, ever go on one. If you're pulling a blade out of someone, they're expecting the pain. If they know you're going on the one count, they'll tighten their muscles and that can do more damage."

"I knew that," she growls. "I'm the fucking medic."

"Not right now, you're not."

"It burns like a son of a whore."

I bite my lip. "This is unlikely to be the worst injury you suffer. Not once we're in the Borderlands."

"Aren't I the medic? Shouldn't I be the one stitching me up?"

"Are you also a contortionist? Because if you're not, good luck bending to reach this. Now lay still. I need to straddle you."

That shuts her up. And then, she giggles. It builds and builds until she's shivering. It's shock, of course, settling into her system after a stab wound. Before the shock shuts her body down, I need to get her stitched. I pull the needle and supplies closer and carefully hoist myself onto the bed. I slide my thighs over her arse. Her cheeks are firm between my thighs, and it is more than a little distracting. Warmth floods my groin, my knickers immediately wet. I push thoughts of pulling her trousers down and slipping my fingers between her flesh away.

I lift the pressure dressing off and lean forward. My hands find her skin. She gasps, shocked at my touch.

"I'm going to need you to tilt up, if you can."

As she tilts, there's a flash of brown plump skin and the briefest hint of dark nipple, and I swear to Gods, my mouth dries. My body taut with the urge to flip her over. To run my hands over her skin. To tug her nipples until she cries my name.

This is a dangerous position to be in. She keeps her arm up. I swear she does it on purpose. I have a delicious view of one breast, and it makes focusing intensely difficult.

I force my gaze onto the wound. "I'm going to lift the bandage off. The bleeding has stemmed enough I can start stitching. This is going to sting. But you can take meds after."

"I suppose this is what I can expect when this is all over?" she says.

I frown as I puncture her skin over and over. "What do you mean?"

She's stopped shivering finally.

"A knife to the spine when I'm least expecting it. You won't let the client thing go, and I won't jeopardise my business. So I guess that's it, isn't it? I'll need to watch my back for the rest of my life."

I purse my lips. Because yes, two weeks ago, that's exactly what I'd have said she needed to do. But now? Now I know her, now I'm not really sure what I want. I stitch the skin together, knitting it into a neat line. When I'm done, I tie off the thread and place a bandage over the wound. Then I help her upright, until we're facing each other.

"One, I think you'll find I've already stabbed you once before." I finger the faint line a centimetre below the stitches. This scar was from when I pinned her to a wall with a blade so I could finish an assassination without her interfering or making me puke or blind. "And two, I'd never be so petty as to stab you in the back. If I was going to assassinate you, I'd do it to your face."

There's a moment where the space between us stills. There's no one but us. The noise of the warehouse dulls, vanishes. Until all I can hear is her heart beat. All I can feel is her blood on my hands, the sweat between our skin. Her mouth parts, her breath heavy.

Fuck. What if the blade had been lower? What if it had caught her lung, her heart? What if it hadn't been a shallow wound?

What if I'd lost her?

Her tongue skitters over her lips. "How many times have we hurt each other? Stabbed, punched, poisoned?"

I shut my eyes, anything to stop the yearning. "Too many to count, almost as many orgasms as we've given each other. I guess it's our foreplay."

She smiles and leans into my neck. "I always did like foreplay."

In this moment, right here, this is when I realise how much I want her. How much I need to taste her skin, feel the caress as she wraps her arms around me, have her by my side as I fight, when I sleep, when I race. I want to fight for her, with her, win her over and over.

I want all of that, not just today, not just tomorrow, but even after this is all over.

I pull away and help her into a gown to keep her warm.

"But you won't kill me, will you?" she asks.

"No. I stopped wanting to kill you a long time ago. Doesn't mean you don't drive me to fucking madness, though."

She laughs, runs her fingers along my jawline, her thumb over my mouth, and pulls me close. But before she kisses me, she stops. Her shoulders sag like they're weighed down with secrets and unsaid words.

"There's something I need to t—"

The door opens. Stirling coughs.

"We need to go. We've got a house viewing tonight,"

she says and then has the audacity to actually look apologetic for interrupting yet again.

I give Quinn a last glance. "See you tomorrow." And I walk out, shoulder barging into Stirling as I exit the medical room. I don't stop and march right out the warehouse.

"You are a cock blocker of the highest fucking order," I growl at her as she catches up to me outside.

"Yes, well, this time we do have a house appointment. But why is it I cock block, again? Right, because of what you told me you wanted to do and how much I want you to be happy. I don't want you to dive in with her unless you're really ready."

"Keep your fucking voice down. I changed my mind. I won't kill her."

Stirling shakes her head at me. "Oh great, well, you still have a giant fucking problem. When this all ends and the mission is over, what are you going to do? We're going to go back to our lives. And if we're not successful, what then? You're going to have to choose the girl or the business. Because you can't have both."

"Then I guess we have to make sure we're successful, don't we?"

CHAPTER 20

QUINN

We leave for the Borderlands tomorrow. Just like that, three weeks of training and preparation evaporated. Which means, BBQ night. Of course, Scarlett made sure that Jacob was not only in agony by the end of the first week of training, but in agony after every single session. Meaning, he's cooking. He learnt the hard way; you don't bet a Grey twin. Not if you want to keep your dignity.

My shoulder, thanks to a potent and vile tasting elixir I brewed, is all but healed. There's a scab on my skin where the knife entered, but I made sure to rub herbs on the wound and drink the elixir daily. By the time we leave tomorrow, even the scab should be gone.

So tonight, we're back in the park. Jacob is cooking on a rented BBQ under the stone arbour. Remy hands me a beer. "Cheers," she says.

I clink my bottle against hers. "Cheers."

We're silent for a while, sitting and staring out at the surrounding park. I know what's coming. It's hung between us this entire time, a weighted secret, thick and dirty. We still haven't talked, not properly. Sure, we've spoken at length about the plans, about runes and routes in, about supplies and security traps, but we haven't spoken about us.

"Given we might die tomorrow... how you are, really? How have you been since...?" I say.

Remy snorts. "I'm alright, you know how it goes. Escaped the flats, found my way to the rich part of town, realised it wasn't all it was cracked up to be, still found myself on the wrong side of the law. But I'm here, I'm surviving."

"I'd say you were thriving. Where did you learn about runic systems?"

"I apprenticed to one of Roman's rivals. Wasn't the smartest move to be honest, but I learned a lot and tried pretty hard to stay politically neutral. But enough about me. How about you? Are you... happy?" Remy's eyes flit to Scarlett, who's standing by Jacob and the BBQ.

I sigh. "It's complicated."

"It's always complicated," Remy says and nudges me.

"Oh, come on, we were young. It was brief and decidedly uncomplicated, we would never have worked."

"No. We wouldn't. Even so, it seems... tense between you."

I turn to her and lay my head on her shoulder. "That's what I like. She's nothing like anyone I've ever dated before."

"You are dating, then?"

"Gods, I have no idea."

"You need to tell her. Given her penchant for kil—"

I sit up, glaring at her. "Quiet." I glance at the BBQ but Scarlett has moved further away, talking to Stirling outside the stone arbour.

Remy continues, "I'm just saying. I've left it, stayed quiet this whole time, but what the hell are you doing? What do you think is going to happen when you reach the palace and," she drops her voice, "she's about to knife the Border Lord and you're defending your fa—"

"Don't say it out loud."

Remy shakes her head. "I know we haven't stayed in touch much over the years, but I still care about you, Quinn. I want to see you happy with her, but if you don't tell Scarlett, then this won't end well."

"Tell me what?" Scarlett says.

My blood runs cold. Where the fuck did she come from? I glare at Remy, who purses her lips at me. Then she gets up and leaves. The message obvious. Tell her. Tell her who you are.

Scarlett holds out a hand and pulls me up.

"Tell me what?" Scarlett says again, her brows drawing together.

I want to tell her. I do. But as I open my mouth, all the words lodge in my throat, and nothing comes out. Did she hear? Does she already know?

"Quinn? Tell me what?"

I lower my head, but Scarlett's fingers find my chin and pull it up, her thumb brushing my lip.

"That I don't want this to end." It's the truth. Not the truth I should have admitted, but it is a truth nonetheless.

"And what... is this?" she says.

I look up, my stomach swirling and knotting. "I... I don't know. But I... I don't want it to stop. I don't want us to go back to the way we were... do you?"

She closes her eyes, takes a deep breath, and when she opens them again, they're focused.

"No, I don't. And I didn't think I'd ever say that. But it does create complications."

Before I can respond, Stirling barrels into us, knocking us apart. She flings her arms around both our shoulders. "Whaheyyyy, alright love birds."

Scarlett pinches Stirling's arm fabric and flings her hand off like a filthy rag.

"Starting the mission with a hangover is a bad idea, don't you think?" Scarlett says.

Stirling shrugs. "That's why we've got Quinn. She can potion the hangover out of me. Hey, babe?" She winks at me and my lips twitch, trying to suppress a laugh.

Morrigan appears. "Not sobered up yet, then?" She tuts and sashays away.

Stirling's face falls. "Why do I gotta love that one? She's never going to love me back. So I'm drinking." She raises a bottle and glugs the rest of it.

"If you spent more time making it up to her, things might progress," Scarlett says.

"I am not taking romantic advice from you. You are… you… ugh." She heads towards the barbecue, stumbling over thin air and alcohol as she walks.

"I hope you have a hangover cure," Scarlett says.

"I'll figure one out for her."

"About before, when this is over, we should talk about us."

"Okay," I say, and she heads off to speak to Jacob.

I sidle up to Morrigan, who's sat on the edge of the hill with a beer.

"Hey," I say, sitting down next to her.

"Hey, yourself." She's cut her hair, not much, but the

ends running down her back are pinned straight and as blunt as her fringe.

I glance at her roots. "Oh, you're not naturally dark?"

She smiles, raises her hands above her scalp, bends and contorts her fingers, and the black seeps into her roots.

"I take after my mother, curves and hair. Her skin is more olive than mine. I get my fair skin from father."

"Do you have siblings?"

"A sister. I haven't seen her in a while, though. We don't get on. In truth, she's an absolute bitch of the highest order. We've spent a lot of time apart for... reasons. You?"

"A little brother, we're close. I spent a long time looking after him. My mum, she's... she drinks."

Morrigan takes my hand and squeezes. "I'd tell you about my family, but you wouldn't believe it. They all have issues, though. Every family is the same, legacy or not."

I scan her face, Collection tattoos peeking out of the collar of her shirt, and that's when I figure it out. "You're a legacy, aren't you?"

She gives me a soft smile.

"I couldn't work out how you had collected so much power, but there's no other way. You have to be a legacy magician."

"Yes, of sorts. I don't like to talk about it though because I worked damn hard to get where I am. I'm the one that studied and grafted to earn the power. I don't want that work undermined by the fact I'm a legacy."

"I respect that," I say and clink our drinks.

"I'm not the only one you respect, am I?" She nods in Scarlett's direction. She's still standing with Jacob.

"She's more talented than she realises. I reckon the loss of her legacy really affected her confidence. One minute she's commanding and decisive, and the next, she can't see what's right in front of her."

"Don't undersell yourself. She knows exactly what's in front of her. She's afraid of how much she wants it, how much she wants you."

I don't want to think about Scarlett anymore. It's complicated. I notice Stirling slumped in a chair under the arbour. "I take it she's drunk because you rowed?"

Morrigan notices Stirling, huffs and lies down on the grass. "How can you love and hate someone all at the same time?"

I laugh. "Apparently, quite easily."

Scarlett's eyes find mine across the park. It makes my heart pump. She makes my heart pump.

I squeeze Morrigan's shoulder. "We're all a little fucked up. Maybe it's time to forgive her."

Scarlett gestures for me to walk with her.

"Excuse me, I'm being summoned."

She waves me off and I get up to meet Scarlett on the other side of the arbour.

"Will you walk with me?" she asks. The late afternoon air is chilly already. A breeze whips around us the minute we leave the sanctuary of the arbour. She's carrying a rucksack, but she slings an arm around my shoulder, anyway.

"Always cold, despite that fiery heart of yours," she says.

"And you're always warm, despite that cold killer heart of yours."

She laughs. "You're lucky I don't pull a knife on you now."

"Foreplay in the park?" I grin up at her.

We make our way down the hill and take a path through the woods. The sun is setting and the last rays of light stream through the canopy of trees, spraying the forest floor with speckled beams of light. The trees rustle and sing a nighttime lullaby as if calling the evening closer. I shiver against Scarlett's side, so she pulls me closer. How different we are to a month ago.

We walk in silence for a time. Scarlett's fingers brush against my arm. This is silly. I know what I want. I reach up and loop my fingers through hers.

Words build in my chest. I need to say the things worrying me. The things we need to sort before we go into the Border. Perhaps if I explain to her that the Border Lord is my father, that will be enough to change her mind. Besides the fact it's dangerous in there, and if we're not a united front, we're all going to be in danger. We continue to stroll quietly through the woods, happy in each other's company until we reach a clearing and I can't hold back the words anymore.

I pull us to a stop and face her.

"What if he didn't do it?" I say.

Scarlett sighs. "Why do you care about the Border Lord?"

"I don't. It's... What if he didn't?"

Scarlett takes my hand and rubs her thumb in circles around my palm. "The thing is, even if he didn't. What he has done. What he asked me to do... it's... it's unforgivable. No matter whether he dies because he took my parents or for his other crimes, he's not a good man."

My eyes sting. She doesn't understand what she's saying. She doesn't know him, not like I do. Aren't we all faulty in some way?

"None of us are innocent. Not you or me. We've both killed people. This isn't a game anymore. We could go in there and die."

She frowns, the furrows making her ice-blue eyes bright. "Life is a game, Quinn. We're here until we're not. We're winning until we lose. Doesn't everything feel sweeter when you've fought for it?"

She's right, but this feels like much more. We're tied in knots, and I don't know how to get us out.

"I need you to promise you won't kill him."

She steps away from me. "Why? What aren't you telling me?"

I rub my forehead, my mouth drying. This, right here, is when I should tell her, but I know even as the thought trickles through my head that I won't. That if I do, I'll lose her. Instead, I tell a lie wrapped in truth.

"Because I can't bear the thought of you dying. He's dangerous, the Borderlands are dangerous, and I want us both to come out alive. If for no other reason than I can kill you myself and destroy your business."

This makes her roar. "Liar."

"Narcissist." I'm smiling, but inside I'm breaking.

"Don't ask me to promise that. The one thing I never want to do is break a promise I've made to you."

I lean my forehead against her chest, wrap my arms around her waist and pull her in tight, wishing that I could pull her so close our atoms merge, close enough that the space, the lies and the secrets disappear and there is only us left. There, safe in her arms, thoughts of my father surface. Memories I'd suppressed. I don't want to believe her. But the closer we get to this mission, the more memories surface, and, like a parasite, I'm doubting myself.

Doubting him.

Thing is, after The Tearing, you had to live under the Border Lord's rule. Father took charge, he saved lives, provided clarity and leadership when there was none. He made everyone feel safe and like there was hope again.

It's easy to a cling to a leader when they gift you hope. Maybe he took things too far. I was young; I didn't see the change in him. That line between corruption and justice, leader and dictator.

"I brought you something..." she says, pulling me back to reality.

"You did?" I ask, disentangling myself.

"Let's make a deal..."

"Isn't that usually my thing?" I say.

"What can I say? Your games rubbed off on me." She kneels by the bag, pulling the strings.

"Alright, you piqued my interest. What are the stakes?"

"Our hearts?"

"Those are some high stakes."

"Well, someone once told me every deal has stakes."

"Did they now?" I'm grinning down at her, trying to sneak a look inside the bag, but she scrunches the fabric so I can't see. I sigh. "Fine, what do you desire...?"

"I don't think it's polite for me to confess what I desire." Her expression softens. She stands, sliding the item behind her back. She trails a finger up my neck, slides her hand around my head, and pulls me close. My heart slams against my chest, a rhythmic siren calling one name only.

"I believe all the best deals are sealed with a kiss."

I gasp. "One kiss? From your sworn enemy?"

She smiles. "Just one."

"A fair price."

So I lean in and stretch up on tiptoes, and then she leans in to meet me. Her fingers tangle in my hair. Her lips move over mine, soft at first, then harder. She sucks and tugs on my lower lip. My nipples graze against my top as they stiffen. Her hand drops to my bra, her fingers playing with my steely nubs. I drag my kiss down her neck, along her collarbone.

"A worthy kiss, indeed," she says, finally pulling away. "I believe this belongs to you."

She pulls the object out. Its dark leather cover, worn and degraded with love.

"My journal." And this time when I gasp, it's not fake. "You're giving it back?"

"I'm not the same person I was when I took it... I didn't feel right keeping it anymore."

I leap into her arms. She stumbles, but catches me, and when I kiss her, it's with everything I have. My lips glide over hers hard, then soft. My tongue pushing into her mouth, tasting the sweet smoke of her. Her arms slide around my arse, gripping me tight. She walks me until my back hits a tree. The journal thuds to the floor, but I don't care, it won't break.

Right now, I want her.

All of her.

Tonight.

And every night for as long as I breathe.

She strips my top, and her mouth finds my breasts, my stomach. She unbuckles my trousers and slides her fingers into my knickers to find my clit.

But even as she pushes a finger, two, inside me, over and over, until I'm breathless and moaning into her neck.

Even as I soak her hand and dig my nails into her shoulder, my world dissolving into electric tingles, my core breaking apart for her.

There's something deep inside my soul. Something dark and insidious. Something full of doubt and fear that when she finds out who I really am, all of this will be over.

CHAPTER 21

SCARLETT

It's ball-breakingly early when we meet the team at the edge of the city. I can't bring myself to actually check my watch, but the morning birds haven't started singing, and I know it wasn't even five when Stirling crawled into my room and poked me awake, grunting about a hangover.

I mixed up a set of herbs Quinn gave me and force fed Stirling, who perked up immediately. I guess The Poisoner is a dab hand with potions after all.

Jacob arrives first, a giant rucksack on his back. Remy next, a slimmer pack on hers, with a wire water tube running from the pack clipped up to the strap.

We're all dressed in a combination of black combat trousers, sweat-proof tops and hiking boots. Finally, Morrigan and Quinn arrive. Quinn has pinned her hair up into a quiff. The sides look freshly shaved, her neck exposed. I want to run my lips down her skin, along her collarbone, listen to her moan.

"Scarlett?" Stirling says, snapping me out of my thoughts.

"What?"

"Stop gawking, and pull the map," Stirling says, wrenching me around and pulling the map out of my rucksack pouch. "Let's run the plan one more time, Scarlett?"

"Okay, Stirling is scout with the map. We're going in through the derelict mansion in the south quarter of the city and then through the Never Woods. We get in and out of the woods today. We do not camp there. The pace today will be hard and fast. Understood?"

Everyone murmurs agreement.

"We'll enter the city here," I point to the southern end of the Border map. "From there, it's a two-day walk across the city and we expect to camp in this area." I slide to another section.

"Quinn and Morrigan agree the best approach to the actual palace is through the escape tunnels. Quinn says they're unguarded, though she suspects there will be runic security. That's where you come in, Remy."

Remy nods.

"It's here we split. Stirling and Jacob, you'll head off to find bikes or carriages. And you'll have how long to get them up and running?"

"Three hours, tops," Jacob says.

"Excellent. Then we enter the palace through the basement. Quinn, you take it from here."

She squeezes into the middle of the group. "We're going to use the wall cavities. There's one section between floors where we'll have to pass an open corridor. That's the riskiest part in terms of exposure. We'll make our way through to the east wing of the palace and then head to the observatory. That's when Remy and Morrigan will take over to locate the hidden room. From there, you two will need to override the security systems to reveal the room and get us in. We take the map and get out via the nearest exit. We'll likely trip security taking the map, meaning a dog fight out of the palace gardens. This will be the most dangerous part. And we're regrouping where?" Quinn glances at Jacob.

"We'll meet you at the end of the west gardens. Hopefully, we'll have bikes ready and we can follow the tracks out of the city and through the Border."

"Great, everyone ready?" Scarlett says.

There's a mumbled nod of agreement.

"Alright, let's head out. We're taking the sub to the city limits and then we're on foot," Jacob says.

Half an hour later, we're climbing off the subway and heading down a deserted track. The air is crisp and sharp, the dawn warmth not quite ready to tickle the horizon. It's coming. But we need to be inside the mansion tunnels before the light rises or we'll be too easily caught.

Stirling sets a relentless pace marching down the track at speed. Twenty minutes of keeping up with her and there's a line of sweat running down my spine. Quinn has a sheen over her forehead, and even Remy and Jacob are pink on the cheeks.

Stirling stops, waves her hands at us. We scoot into the trees and hustle up next to her.

"That's the mansion," she says, pointing about half a click across the field. There's a decrepit building that looks more like a demolition hazard than a previous mansion.

"We're going in there?" I whisper.

"You bet," Remy says, crawling forward to the threshold of the trees.

"Can you reach security this far out?" Quinn asks.

"No, but I can assess whether there's any outer perimeter we need to watch for," Remy says.

She adjusts herself till she's kneeling and takes her backpack off. I hold it for her, and she inches towards the edge. She takes a deep breath, runs her hand through her white spiked hair, and settles herself. She holds her hands out, palms flat towards the direction of the derelict mansion.

"If you want to see what I see, touch my arms," she says.

The rest of us glance at each other and then scramble to get to Remy first. Stirling, Morrigan and I touch one arm, and Quinn and Jacob lay their fingers on her other one.

Remy's hands shudder, moving faster and faster until the vibrations are so rapid there's a hazy halo all the way around her palms, and then my vision blurs.

When it clears, the view is like nothing I've ever seen.

"Cool, huh?" Remy whispers.

"Beyond," Quinn says.

I hear her words, but I can no longer see her. My chest tightens. I gnaw on the inside of my cheek. It's fine, we're all fine, miles away from anything.

I turn back to the mansion, and the copper mesh of cogs decorated with runes surrounding it. It's vast, stretching the entire way around the mansion grounds, and at least fifty feet in the air. Then, much closer to us, there's another mesh fence made of the same rune covered cogs. Each of them connected to the other, a network of spinning russet moving in a hypnotic pattern.

"I knew it," Remy says. "If we'd gone ahead, we'd have tripped the mansion's outer security system."

"How do you disarm it?" Morrigan says, the excitement for new knowledge, a new skill she can collect, evident.

"Like this."

I can't see her hands, but I can sense the movement beneath my fingers. The cogs in the closest security fence move, twisting this way and that. Sometimes halting. Occasionally, one turns blue or deepens from copper to fiery red.

"Shit," Remy says. Her arms shake under the pressure of magic threading through her veins. Warmth from the muscle strain crests through her top.

She backs up the series of rune movements she just made and the cogs drop from red to a burnished brass.

"Little fuckers had a secondary runic subsystem buried in the interlocking threads."

She shunts her body forward. A cog vibrates in the centre of the fence and then poof, the whole mesh of cogs and runes dissolves, evaporating into the rapidly vanishing night.

My vision returns to normal. The forest, the team and all our kit reappears.

"Nice one, Remy," I say and give her a tap on the back.

"I've never seen that done before," Quinn says.

We pick up our packs as the stars wink out and a flourish of molten orange and yellow stripe the horizon.

"Okay, let's go. We need to get into the house before the sun rises, and we still have the mansion's local security to get through," Remy says.

"Follow me," Stirling says and once again sets a gruelling pace.

We keep to the fence lines, and even though it takes a little longer, we go around the outside of the field rather than crossing it directly. Though there isn't meant to be any security here, we can't take any chances.

The closer we get to the mansion, the more my senses tingle. The wind is too still, too quiet. Bird song vanishes, noise mutes like the air in high winter after a snowfall. It sets my teeth on edge. When we're close enough to the mansion, Remy can access the security. She signals for us to drop and wait. She steps toward the mansion and repeats a similar series of movements as she did in the forest. This time, none of us touch her but watch instead. Her eyes lighten, the pupils turning grey and then morphing into black as her magic flares to life and pearlescent light as white as her hair circles her fingers.

There's a shift in the air, a loosening almost, and then she returns to us.

"Idiots," Remy said. "Whoever set the security here is an amateur. They thought making the outer fence tighter would prevent anyone from getting in, but the building was practically an open door. We're good to go."

The six of us get up.

I take the mansion in properly for the first time. It's old, so old the stone doesn't look real. Decayed enough that it's no longer brown, but not quite grey either. The exterior doesn't seem to be solidly anything, rough in some places, smooth in others. Like the house is showing us whatever it thinks we want to see. There are half a dozen turrets dotted around the roof, this house taller than normal. Most are only one or two stories high, this one is four at least.

In the middle of the front facing wall, near the highest floor, is a circular hole. As if some carving or sculpture or maybe a clock lived there.

We don't need to go up that high though, the tunnels that run under the Border and through to the Never Woods are in the basement.

The windows nestled in the brick are cracked and broken. Air should rush through, as there was a biting chill this morning, but there's no sound, no movement save for a cluster of blackbirds sitting on the broken roof, half of the tiles caved in like a beaten face.

I shudder.

The birds don't sing.

They just watch us.

Beady, judging.

The skin on the back of my neck hackles, ridges of goosebumps rising. I hate it when things are too easy. Nothing is ever easy. Not if it's worth it, not if the prize is big enough.

I scan the area. Push my hearing, try to sense movement, anything unusual, bodies moving in the wind, feet crunching soil and gravel. There's nothing. No movement. No motion. We're clear.

I nod my approval, even though every ounce of training I've ever had is screaming at me that something is wrong, that I shouldn't trust the ease by which we're progressing.

"Wait..." I put my hand out, and everyone halts. "Keep your wits about you, okay? This place gives me the creeps."

We approach the door as the sun peeks over the horizon, yellow rapidly filling the sky and the warmth of morning settling on our faces.

Stirling steps out and pushes the door an inch. No creak. No, nothing, just the same muted air.

I edge closer to Quinn, instinct driving me to protect her.

"What was this place?" Jacob asks.

"Castle Clock House," Morrigan says. "I can feel the tick, tick, tick of the mansion's magic. But it seems... off somehow. The beat of the magic isn't rhythmic, it's skipping a beat."

"Is it safe for us to go in there?" Remy says.

"I don't see another way through to the Border, do you?" I say.

"Not without being seen. Not without alerting the Border Lord. Not without the Queen's sanction, and definitely not in the time scale we have," Quinn answers.

"Then we don't have a choice," Remy nods.

She shoves the door wide open and we creep in. Unlike castles and mansions still living and full of magic, this one doesn't welcome us in the same way. Instead of intense pressure as we enter, it greets us with a silken touch, a featherlight caress that throbs against my skin. And then in a blink, it evaporates.

Jacob is the last one in and closes the door, plunging us into darkness. Morrigan opens her palm and a fist-sized flame fires to life. But no sooner is it roaring in her hand than she throws it up and away. It's sucked into a lone lightbulb hanging from the hallway ceiling.

Spiders crawl under my skin. Everywhere I look are clocks. Tall ones, broken ones. Small wrist watches litter the floor in fractured pieces. Ornate antique ones stacked on rickety shelves. Smashed cogs, screws and tools smother the floor and furniture.

The walls beat. They warp and swell. Beat. Beat. Pause. Like the castle has arrhythmia.

"We need to move. Let's get into the tunnels as quick as we can."

I slide my hand into Quinn's. It makes me relax knowing she's close, that I can protect her if something happens.

Stirling leads us deeper into the house. Room after room, derelict, decaying, paper peeling off the walls, clocks smashed, abandoned. The unnerving click and tick on the edge of our hearing.

There and not there.

We reach the heart of the house, and Stirling pulls open a wooden door with a staircase that leads into darkness.

"Morrigan, light?" Stirling says.

She throws hovering flames down to the basement. Stirling moves to enter. But I pull her back.

"No. Me first." I'm the most trained, I can react the fastest. I draw a blade from my hip and push in front of her. She nods and slides in behind me, taking her blade out too.

I step down, down, down.

Until the flames searing light against the fathomless blackness makes my eyes ache. The tunnel swallows everything: light, sound, thoughts, sanity.

The tunnel floor is dank. Shallow puddles of darkened water splash my boots. The walls are slick and wetter than expected. Mould is so thick in here, I can taste it clawing at my throat. When the first breeze whips in from the Never Wood, it brings the tang of iron, of blood. My muscles tighten, my body listening, straining for clues and warning sounds. But there's nothing except the growing stench of coagulating blood.

We reach the end of the tunnel. Slow and steady, I push the door, and I know instantly something is wrong. The air when we entered the house was warm, the morning sun blooming and pouring heat over New Imperium. But as the entrance eases open, it's a frigid chill that whips in. And while the light is the same dim orange, it's not morning. I step out and glance at my watch.

"Fuck," I growl as the rest of the team pours out of the tunnels.

"The castle fucked with us in there. It's already 5pm."

"5pm?" Stirling shouts.

"Keep your fucking voice down, Stir. We don't want to alert anyone."

Morrigan steps close. "I think it was the castle's residual magic. It felt off when we went in. I didn't feel any animosity from the house. I don't think it meant to harm us. It's just sick."

"It's put us a day behind," I say.

"It's worse than that," Jacob says, staring at the map in Stirling's hand.

"He's right, we're not going to get through the forest tonight," Stirling answers.

"Fuck." Jacob wipes his mouth. "Now what?"

"We'll have to camp in the woods," I say.

"They're full of militia, though," Quinn says, her voice quiet. Everyone turns to her.

"We don't have much choice. If we walk through the night, we'll be exhausted tomorrow." I kick the ground with the toe of my boot, a flare of heat bubbling in my gut.

"I can set up a security field around our camp, and maybe Morrigan can juice me up so it holds for the night," Remy says.

"Great idea," Jacob says. "And we could rotate sentry duty, keeping an eye out for militia."

"Fine. We move out now and walk for as long as possible. We'll camp and sleep for six hours, and then we'll get up early and make it as far through the city as we can."

"Agreed. We can camp early tomorrow and recover in a safer area," Stirling adds.

"Into the woods we go then," Quinn says and pulls up her snoody.

CHAPTER 22

QUINN

The clock house gave me the creeps. I spent the entire time wanting to cling to Scarlett, praying we get out alive.

We trudge through the woods as fast as we can, which still feels glacial to me. Now we're deep in the Never Woods, the unease that started in the house has hung a noose around my neck.

I can't breathe.

I want us to walk through the night and get out of here. Even my father doesn't fuck with the militia. They're a law unto themselves and the kind of magicians who would gut their own mothers if it meant a bag of coin. Most of them were scorned by my father. It was his own fault the militia formed, to be honest. If he were a more merciful man, perhaps it wouldn't have happened.

But most of the people in the militia either betrayed my father or he didn't deem them worthy enough to join his soldiers. Eking out your existence, living off scraps and begging. Understandably, those banished didn't like it much, and so the uprising began. It took two years of savage fighting and countless lives lost before they settled into an uneasy truce. The militia lived in the Never Woods and the Border Lord's men stayed around the Old Palaces, manning the trade routes.

My mind wanders to Scarlett, the fury that burns in her veins for my father. I know she thinks he's done wrong, and I understand why she thinks that. But sometimes people in power do bad things for the greater good, and I really do believe he was doing it for the good of the magicians abandoned inside the Border.

She has to be mistaken.

Movement through the woods is slow. Slower than I'm comfortable with. The rain pours, soaking my clothes and chilling my body until I'm certain I'll never stop shivering.

Jacob brings up the rear, walking backwards, mostly scanning the trees, watching for movement. Remy and Morrigan are in front of him. Then me. Stirling and Scarlett leading the front. We don't make it more than fifteen minutes before the group grinds to a sudden stop.

Scarlett signals for us to move off the path and into the forest line. The canopy above us gives us a small respite from the constant drip of rain. It patters now, the plush leaves taking the brunt of rainfall.

She points to her eyes, then points both hands in opposite directions. Then she lays her palm out flat and indicates for us to get down. Scarlett and Stirling scoot into the forest and to the other side of the path. My skin itches and crawls like we're being watched. But I scan every direction and there's no one there. I'm being paranoid.

Scarlett catches my eye. "Be safe," she mouths, and then the pair of them creep up the path and disappear from view. The longer we lie here, the more the damp earth seeps into my trousers. It crawls into my bones like the dull, insistent throb of a toothache.

Scarlett and Stirling reappear, a grim expression on their faces as they kneel next to us.

"There's people up ahead," Scarlett whispers.

"Militia?"

Stirling shrugs. "Doesn't matter. They're dead. Very. Very. Dead."

"So the militia are near?" Remy whispers.

"Given the bodies are only holding a small amount of heat, I'd say they've been dead a good few hours already. The militia may not be in the immediate vicinity, but I doubt they're far away," Scarlett says.

"We need to keep going. See how much further we can get before we're forced to camp," Stirling says.

We continue walking for what seems like an eon. My feet and knees throb with the hours of movement. My eyes are sore because I've been awake for too long, and my lower back and shoulders are blazing from the weight of carrying the bag. But despite that, despite the fact my muscles are on fire, the damp earth is still leaching into my skin and sucking at my marrow. When I think I can't take another step, Stirling veers off the path and into the trees. The shrubs and bushes bite at my trousers, thorns stabbing and poking through the fabric. And then, as soon as we stepped off the path, we move into a small clearing.

"Nice one, Stir," Remy says as she drops her bag in the middle of the clearing and gets to work. "Everyone in the middle while I work. Morrigan, you're with me."

Morrigan steps up and slips her hand into Remy's. Stirling's eyes slide to their clasped hands. Scarlett gives her a curt shake of the head.

"Have you collected illusion magic?" Remy asks.

"Of course," Morrigan replies. Her husky tone drifts through the woods and, as if they sense the vibrations of her voice, the forest leaves rustle in response.

"I can lock into the field you create and then turn it into a reflection. It should render us invisible," Morrigan says.

"Excellent. Let's do it," Remy says.

Morrigan's eyes darken and then flame blue like fire and snow and oceans. Strands of her hair flicker and hover, pointed with static. Remy's eyes shiver into grey. Her hands, one holding Morrigan and one out front, vibrate so fast they blur.

It takes seconds, but I know the minute the shield is up, the severe chill eating away any shred of warmth I had vanishes as the dome closes in around us. The noise of the forest calms until it's a quieted muffle somewhere in the distance.

When Morrigan and Remy are done, they turn to us.

Jacob is at the edge of the barrier, his hand reaching out. "This is eerie as fuck."

Morrigan grips his shoulder. "Don't break the boundary. You break it and we're sitting ducks. While we're inside, we can't be seen or heard by anything on the outside. But you break that dome and we're screwed."

Jacob inches back. "Noted."

Morrigan sets about making a fire, flames falling from her palms. Once it's on, I boil water. I scavenge the area and find some mint leaves to crush up and sprinkle in, making a brew. I hand cups out while Jacob takes over the fire and starts cooking dinner. When I give Scarlett her mug, her fingers press against mine.

"You sure this won't kill me?" she says, a smirk on her lips.

"I figure if I have my journal back, I can make you a tea."

She smiles and takes a sip of the tea. "Not bad for a medic."

I roll my eyes at her and take the final mug for myself. The liquid slips down, warming my insides and making me yearn for home. It's not my tea, but my mother's. She used to make Malachi and I this sweetened mint tea in the early days after The Tearing. Before father had control of the Border, there was no order, no one farming or growing anything. Once those rations were used, everyone here starved. On those long wintry nights when father fought to gain control, mother would make us mint tea and sweeten it with flowers. Father would drink it too, when he crawled in, in the morning, broken and bruised from a night of slaughtering men, and mother and I would tend his wounds.

After we've eaten, we pull out our sleeping bags. I grab my journal. I sent Malachi a note last night as soon as I got in and he's finally replied, relieved I'm okay. But he doesn't say much else, and to be honest, given how tired I am, I'm relieved because I don't have the energy to reply. I slide it into my pack.

Jacob and Morrigan take the first sentry duty shift, Stirling and Remy are second, and Scarlett and I last. We can't risk all of us sleeping at once. We take two-hour shifts. The floor is hard, and no matter how many rocks and twigs I brush aside, I'm still deeply uncomfortable. But I'm also so exhausted it takes me all of about three seconds to fall fast asleep.

It feels like I've been asleep for as many seconds when Stirling nudges me awake.

"You're up, kid," she says and winks at me.

I groan and haul my frozen carcass out of the sleeping

bag. Stirling doesn't bother to unroll hers again. She slides into mine and falls instantly asleep. I glance up at Scarlett.

"We should walk the perimeter," she says. "It will keep us warm."

"Okay," I say, my breath coming out in rolling white puffs.

We walk in the same giant looping circle for half an hour. But it doesn't matter how fast we walk, my lips turn blue and my teeth chitter chatter where I can't seem to warm up.

"Can you get that under control?" she says.

"Ah-ah-ah-parently not," I stammer out.

She scruffs me and pulls me into her arms. "It's almost as if you enjoy being in the arms of your enemy."

I snuffle out a laugh and lean into her chest. How she's warm enough for her body heat to wash over me through clothes, I don't know. But it's not long before the chattering stops and the tension in my body eases.

"You're not my enemy anymore," I say.

Because she's not. It doesn't feel like it. Not anymore. I know she holds a grudge over what I did to her business. But I'm sure there's a way to work it out when we're back.

"Perhaps once the Border Lord is dead, the world is healed, and my parents avenged, then maybe we can be something else."

I have to physically stop myself from tensing up. How could I forget what she wants? The closer I get to Scarlett, the harder it is to remember why I'm here. That the only thing she really wants to do is kill my father. And that's the one thing I can't let her do.

I let go and pull away, but she tightens her grip on me, her arms suddenly iron vices. I open my mouth to speak, but she shakes her head. Her eyes skirting the dome.

She releases me and places a finger on her lips. Her whole demeanour changes. She pulls not one, but two blades out and runs to the other side of the dome and drops into a crouch.

I swallow and pull my snoody up to cover my face. If there are militia nearby, one of them could recognise me, and that's the last thing I need.

I drop to a crouch, too. Though why, I don't know. This dome is supposed to be invisible. But it seems like the right thing to do.

Scarlett twists to face me and points to the rest of the team sleeping.

"Wake them," she mouths. "Keep them quiet."

I nod and, keeping low, make my way over to the team, sliding my hand over their mouths and gently rousing them.

Using hand signals and gestures, the team is up and packed in less than two minutes. But when I'm done and everyone is awake, my blood turns to ice.

Scarlett has vanished and so has the dome.

CHAPTER 23

SCARLETT

"Wake them," I mouth. "Keep them quiet."

They're here.

I know it. I can't see the militia, but I can sense them. The Assassin master used to call it our knowing. It's how he could tell the High Assassins from the mediocre. He said I was born with a knowing that was unparalleled. Too bad they stripped me of my Collection tattoos. Sure, I have my residual talent left, but it's nothing like it was.

My arms tingle. A crawling sensation that's creeping over my skin like silk and thorns. I know they're watching. I just need to find them.

I'm at the edge of the dome with a decision to make. Step out, risk being attacked. Stay inside and leave us sitting ducks.

I pull Chance out, rub her ridged edges, the gilded words.

"Don't fail me." I flick her up. She slams down and I drop her onto the back of my palm.

Yes.

She confirms what I already know: I can't stay put. It's the bigger risk. I need to break the dome and go on the offensive. If the militia are here, they've figured out we are here too. The only tactical move I have is to get out and get ahead of them. I crawl out of camp and sit just far enough out of the way I can reach the team, but I'm hidden from the militia, tucked under a shrub, camouflaged by leaves and forest detritus.

This is the dangerous part, using the team as bait. But it's the best tactical move, draw the militia in and slaughter them all. Quinn is the first to realise I'm gone. Her face splits. Terror widens her eyes.

I'd never leave you, Quinn. Have faith in me.

Quinn starts, but only makes it a few paces before Stirling grabs her arm, fury drawing lines in her face.

"I need a piss," Quinn snaps, shucking Stirling off.

Stirling raises her arms. "Fine, but don't go looking for Scarlett. She knows what she's doing."

They're being too loud. Far louder than they should be given the circumstances. Which means Stirling must have caught on to what I'm doing. She knows they're the bait. So why be quiet?

Stirling grabs Quinn's hand and pushes it onto the hilt of Quinn's blade. Quinn nods, and then says far too loud, "Won't be long."

She parts from the group, and my breathing shallows. Adrenaline shoots through my system, making my muscles tighten. I know she can look after herself, but I'm not rational when it comes to Quinn. I want to leave, to run to her side and slay anyone that comes near. But if I do that, we lose our tactical advantage. I have to believe that she will handle herself. Hell, she's put me down enough times.

I hesitate.

But Stirling turns out to the woods, staring off into the distance. Looking for me, I suspect. She flicks her head in Quinn's direction, draws a knife and stashes it up her sleeve. Morrigan comes into view now, rubs her hands and stretches her fingers. Remy and Jacob draw their own weapons. They turn their backs on each other, each one facing a different direction, forming an inverted circle.

Makes sense. There's more of them. They protect the kit; I protect the girl.

I skirt around the edge of our camp, careful not to snap any twigs, to keep my feet light and my wits sharp. I stay low to stop my figure from breaking up the shrubs on the forest floor.

When I reach Quinn, she really is peeing.

Gods, woman.

She's crouched down, her knickers round her ankles, a stream of water flooding the forest floor. I look away, trying to give her privacy, seeing as she doesn't know I'm here. The stream of water stops, there's a rustling and then...

Quinn gasps.

My body tenses. My vision tunnels and focuses. She's standing. A man holding a blade to her throat.

I lift my chin and flex my fingers around my Katana. A familiar calmness weaves through my mind, fire and flames stitching into my muscles.

The knife at Quinn's neck is at least five inches long, sharp too. I can see that from here. Quinn's jaw is hard, her eyes burn the same fury stitched into mine. She's not afraid. She wants blood.

"Move," he barks.

My chest shudders under the pressure of suppressing my breathing and the adrenaline coursing through me.

He moves her towards the group. Two more figures appear from behind trees and surround the group. There's a clink and grind of metal, leaving a sheaf, and then six more bodies join the militia. We're outnumbered.

But I take a minute to assess. Although clothed, all of them are edges and points, clothes hanging off boney shoulders and hips. Their cheeks are hollow, eyes filled with haunted shadows.

They're not dangerous because of their numbers, they're dangerous because they're desperate.

That makes them unpredictable.

The man holding Quinn is directly in front of me now. The fool didn't bother checking his surroundings.

There might be more of them, but they're not strategic. We can win this. The man holding Quinn hasn't noticed me.

"The rucksacks," he growls. "Give them over like a good little girl, and you don't have to die."

"Go fuck yourself," Stirling says.

The man holding Quinn sniffs out a laugh. "Ballsy little cunt, aren't you? You really willing to risk this little bitch's life for a poxy rucksack?"

He pulls the blade tighter up Quinn's throat, and she inhales sharply. My teeth grit. This is it.

I inch my way out.

Directly behind him.

Silent, swift.

He dies now.

I hold my sword to his neck vertebrae. "You touch her again, motherfucker, you die."

He stiffens and the rest of his group twitch. All of them noticing me for the first time.

"Pat, mate..." one of them says. "Easy lad."

Pat spits on the ground, and his hand jerks, nicking Quinn's neck.

Oh, that was silly.

I slam the palm of my hand on the hilt of the sword. It slices through skin and cartilage right to *Pat*, here's, spinal cord.

He goes rigid, standing bolt upright. You'd compliment the posture if it weren't for the fact he was a dead man standing.

I rip out the sword and a fountain of claret sprays my face, my nose filling with the sweet tang of iron. Gods, I've missed killing.

I smile, look up at the rest of the militia, my eyes darkening as Pat falls and thuds to the forest floor.

Quinn swipes her fingers over her neck, smearing the blood.

"Cunt," she screams and kicks his body, spitting on the carcass.

I crick my neck, left, right. Roll out my shoulders.

The remaining militia freeze. Their leader lying motionless on the floor, no one sure of the next move.

But I am. It's playtime.

"Stay down, Quinn," I say.

"Fuck that," she snarls, and something inside of her snaps. She draws out a blade, kicks him hard in the face, and then sinks the blade into his chest. She yanks it out, screaming obscenities.

Over and over she plunges the blade hilt deep into his chest.

They say that love happens slowly.

That falling is really the slow knitting and meshing of souls and lives. Of heart beats finding a rhythm to share for eternity.

But in this moment, right here, as Quinn reaches for her raw power, her inner rage. As she shows me exactly who she is, the darkness in her soul, I know I'd lay down and die for her.

I'd cut open my chest and deliver my dripping heart in open hands.

My soul yearns to feel her rage, to let her take me and make me bleed for her. I need to taste her fury, to drink it, devour it.

Falling in love doesn't happen slowly, it happens in moments of clarity and revelation. In fleeting sparks of action and displays of our true selves.

It happened right there.

At the same moment, the forest erupted in an explosion of metal clashing on metal. A crescendo of violence tearing through the night.

The team leaps out, swords swiping and jabbing. Bolts of pearlescent magic slamming into bodies and trunks, splinters of bark filling the air.

Jacob lunges for one of the militia, Remy at his back veering the other way. Jacob delivers a vicious sword through the man's neck. There's no time for me to stand and admire the team. Three men charge at Quinn.

I drop, swiping a leg out, knocking one instantly to the floor. I whip out a second blade, plunge it into his chest as I raise my longer blade to block a blow driving down on me.

The clang and ricocheting tings of blades a melody of death sung for the forest. Iron fills the air, bitter, sweet and delicious.

My favorite.

The smell of victory.

The smell of grit and power.

The smell of games won and lost.

I glance up. I've been separated from Quinn. Shit.

She throws her arms out. Blocks a brutal lashing. Her legs are trembling, the rage from the attack subsiding, leaving her exhausted. She won't be able to keep him off for long. Fights like these aren't about strength, but stamina. How long can you push through the baking heat in your muscles, the charring exhaustion that rips through arms and thighs?

The man now attacking Quinn feints left and drops a savage punch to her gut. I'm up, my legs powering me across the shrubs. I jump, kick, and land a savage metal-toed boot to the temple. He drops to the floor unconscious, but not before the arm he's swinging slices through my bicep.

I hiss. Blades always hurt, but this is nothing compared to some of my wounds. I reach down and help Quinn up. She's coughing and red-cheeked, but she's okay.

She bats me off and pants, "Help the others."

The mossy forest floor is splattered in red. Morrigan has a man levitated in front of her, his face swollen and purple. Pearlescent ropes hang him by the throat. His veins bulge and darken, his eyes bloat, and then, nothing. He hangs limp.

Satisfied, Morrigan drops him to the floor, joining his comrades in death.

The six of us stand in silence, save for the heavy breathing. Each of us smeared in moss and dirt, blood and sweat.

"We good?" I say, eyeing each one of them.

"I'm good, minor cuts, but I'll live." Jacob nods and wipes his face. "How the fuck do you move that fast?"

"I guess I was born this good," I grin. It's total bullshit, of course. I mean, yes, I've always had a natural affinity for Assassin skills. But equally, I still have some residual Assassin magic, much to the guild's irritation. They can remove the Collection tattoos, but they can never truly sever the connection. Not once a house has chosen you. Not once it's accepted you. Unless you piss the house off, that is. But that's a whole other barrel of problems.

"Remy, you okay?"

She nods and stretches her arm out. "Twinged something in my back, few bruises, but I'm okay."

"I'm fine," Morrigan adds.

And Stirling gives me a thumbs up. We gather our kit, Quinn patches up Remy's cuts and then the slash on my bicep while Jacob, Morrigan and Stirling haul the bodies into a pile. Morrigan draws flames up from the earth and sets light to them. Remy creates a boundary around the bodies so the flames won't spread to the trees, and we leave them burning.

When the team is ready, only Quinn remains standing by the fire. I take her hand, and she jumps.

"You okay?" I say.

"Yes, sorry. It's..." Her eyes fall to the face of the man closest to us.

"I... I knew him."

I frown. "Pardon?"

"That man there." She points at his face as it's swallowed by orange flickers. "He was... well, he worked with my family a long time ago. I knew him, not very well. But I didn't expect he would turn and become militia. It's unexpected, is all."

We move through the forest in silence. Everyone lost in their own thoughts. The reality of the mission we've taken on sinking in. Dawn drifts in the air, the faintest hint of warmth chomping at the icy night. The canopy above us mottles, beams of soft light drifting through, shining on undergrowth and shrubs. Illuminating the mess we've made of our clothes and faces.

After two hours, as we reach the edge of the Never Woods and the trees grow sparser, the gaps longer between the leafy arms of giants, morning light hits our faces as Jacob speaks.

"Can we clean up?"

Everyone mumbles agreement.

"There's a lake off the main road about five hundred meters from the entrance to the forest. I saw it when I was appraising the exit routes. If it's still there, and not toxic, then we should be able to use the water with no problems," Stirling says.

"I can check the water toxicity," Morrigan says. "I studied in a botany mansion for a while. With a bit of luck, I should be able to parse out most toxins."

We move in a slow grinding thud, thud, thud. The silence is still thick between us. When we break through the forest and onto tarmac, the team visibly sags. As if the density of the forest was suffocating, as if smoke and death clung to the leaves and shrubs. And now that we're out, we can finally breathe.

"I've never killed anyone," Remy suddenly says as we cross the road and head down an empty street. "I've robbed mansions, stolen magic, drained dying castles. But I've never actually..."

"It gets easier," I say, and rub her shoulder. "It was them or you. Were you willing to die for them?"

"Never." Her eyes are fierce. "If I die for a cause, it will be a noble one. One of my choosing."

I squeeze her shoulder again. I feel that drive deep in my soul, the grinding yearn to live a noble life, fight for a worthy death. I realise how far we've come. The fact the first time I met Remy, I genuinely considered slicing her throat in her sleep. I don't wear jealousy well. Never have.

"The raw horror of this morning will fade. Whether you let what you did define you is up to you."

She gives me a weak smile, and we continue in silence. As we near the lake's shore, the bulbous grey clouds open, and rain splatters the surface, dappling it with pretty round rings. Somewhere in the distance, lightning flashes and the sky roars an angry song.

Morrigan's hands hover over the water. She bends and contorts her fingers into strange shapes, pearlescent ribbons lancing the surface and powering through the lake.

A few moments later, she smiles. "Bath time, ladies."

"And gentleman," Jacob protests.

Remy, Morrigan and Jacob strip fast, throwing their clothes in a giant pile and running into the water. Their gasps and shrieks rip through the morning air.

Quinn undresses more slowly, her hands and legs shaking as she attempts to peel off her blood spattered clothes. When I can't stand the sight of her pitiful body trembling any longer, I tut, and make my way across the mud.

I hold out my hand. She hesitates, but accepts, her fingers curling around my palm. The soft pressure as she uses me as a counterbalance. I hold her steady as she pulls off a boot, but then she fumbles with the buckle of her belt, her fingers too unsteady to detach it.

"Stop. Just stop. Let me help."

"I'm exhausted, and it's freezing."

"I know, it's okay," I say and help her out of her trousers.

When she's in her underwear, she mumbles, "Thanks." And then heads to the shore and tiptoes in.

Stirling's at my shoulder. There's a heaviness in the way she breathes. Gods, I know what's coming. I step forward. I'll get in the water fully clothed before I have this conversation.

"Don't. Even. Think. About. It. Sister. You've given up the game, then?" Stirling says, as her nails dig into my shoulder and drag me back. Her voice is low although the others are too far out to hear anyway. They've drifted further into the lake and are throwing a soap bar between them.

"Yes, no more games."

"So you've told her how you feel?"

I toe the ground. "Not exactly."

Stirling sighs.

"What do you want me to say? I don't have all the answers."

"Well, you better find some, because what happens when our titles are reinstated and you're drawn back into the guild? How will you run your business and hers without some kind of territory war?"

I open my mouth to answer. But I don't have any. So I shut it again. I don't want to hear this; I don't want to hear any of it.

"Leave it, Stirling. We don't even know if we will make it out of here alive. Let's concentrate on the fucking task at hand, shall we?" I glare at her and rip off my top, boots, and trousers and jog into the freezing water.

"Mother of fuck," I hiss as I drop my waist and shoulders into the frigid water. "It's so cold I'm pretty sure my pussy just shrivelled itself into celibacy."

Remy erupts, laughing so hard she kicks her head back. Jacob, too, as he wipes a tear from his eye. I glare at them. It's not even slightly funny.

"Payback for the plunge pool," Jacob wheezes.

Morrigan, bless her sweet soul, is the only one decent enough to throw me the soap.

Quinn, still quiet, still lost in what happened, I suspect, trudges back out of the water. She doesn't meet my gaze, and I lean toward her, wanting to go to her, to wrap my arms around her hurt soul and pull her in. Tell her it's going to be okay. That we're going to get through this. It breaks me seeing her look like this. Seeing her shrink into herself.

A few weeks ago, I'd have loved it. Knowing something I —or anyone—had done had pushed her into a pit. I'd have lauded it over her, one nil to me. I knead my temples. I don't know how to do this version of us.

It—us—we were always meant to be a game. Meant to fuck each other as much as we *fucked* each other over. When the hell did we get to caring how the other felt?

I wash the rest of the blood off my hands and sink my face into the icy water. When I surface, I realise I'm the last one left. So I get out and dress as fast as I can.

We wander through the city, hour after hour of deserted streets, broken buildings and desolation. Miles upon miles of abandoned city.

"What happened here?" I don't realise I've said the words out loud until Quinn responds.

"The Tearing was bad. As the ground and buildings shook, there were physical places ripped instantly in half. The places worst affected, we left. Too many ghosts, death in every corner."

Street after street is derelict. Buildings crumbled into piles of ash and dirt. Others remain partially standing or with holes and gouges in the sides. Streets littered with the aftermath of years of decay. Broken bricks, metal, abandoned toys half rotten in the road. We pass another street and a dolly lays death-still on the path, neglected, like the arm hanging off it.

I shudder. It's a war zone, only no war ever happened. For a split second, I understand what the Border Lord did, why he was pushed to take such drastic measures.

"How many died?" I ask.

Quinn's voice is barely above a whisper. "Thousands. Ten. Twenty? The shaking lasted for three days. The weather never quite returned to normal. We have vicious storms here, snow that falls eight feet high. Sun that burns the tarmac and scorches skin until it blisters."

"I'm sorry," I say. And for the first time, I really mean it. "The Border Lord... I don't condone everything he's done. But I understand why."

Quinn nods, her face solemn. "He was trying to keep his people alive."

Hours pass. We walk through miles of abandoned streets. The rain continues to pour, thunder booms, echoing around the empty streets, and lightning tears the sky apart. Quinn explains that the majority of the city is empty save for a few industrial buildings they continued to use to help manufacture what they needed to live. Most of those left living here moved into the centre of the city, claiming homes that were vacated during The Tearing.

Stirling pulls us to a stop late in the afternoon.

"We should make camp. Tonight is the last night before we attempt the palace. We should eat and try to sleep as much as we can. Tomorrow will be a long day."

She studies the map for a while longer and then folds it away and heads off. A few minutes later, we pull into another deserted street. I've seen so many I can't tell the difference anymore. They all look identical.

She peers into the window of what looks like it used to be a cottage and smears dirt off the glass.

"It's empty," Quinn says. "They all are."

"Just being safe," Stirling answers, squinting through the dirt. She jimmies the door, and after a moment, it creaks and groans, but with a shove, opens. The door frame is matted with cobwebs. Stirling visibly shudders as she wipes the sticky white threads away and pushes the door open for the rest of us.

The house smells musty. Like ancient paper and earth. There's a rotten L-shaped sofa on one side of the room and a door to a kitchen on the right.

Stirling and Remy are marching in and out of each room checking for Gods knows what. The only thing we'll find in here are skeletons and shadows.

When they're satisfied, they reappear. "There's one bed in the back room and the sofa. Two can use the bed, two on the sofa, and the other two take sentry duty," Remy says.

Stirling has bags under her eyes. I hadn't realised how tired she'd gotten as scout. But now we've stopped, the toll is obvious.

"You and Stirling sleep first," I say. "Morrigan and Jacob, you're on the sofa. Quinn and I will swap out after a few hours."

Stirling doesn't even attempt to protest. She nods and vanishes into the back room, followed by Remy.

Quinn and I busy ourselves in the kitchen. Nothing works, but Morrigan creates a false gas hob, using the original oven and some elemental fire magic. Jacob cooks up some supplies of chicken broth and tea—he's taken on the mantle of keeping us fed. Most of his work won't happen until we leave him and enter the palace. I guess he wanted to be useful.

When it's time, I wake Stirling and Remy and show them the broth, which, thanks to Morrigan, is still warm for them. Despite the food, or maybe because of it, exhaustion has eaten into my bones. Quinn looks as wrecked as I feel, and the two of us make our way to the bedroom in the back. I close the door and stare at the bed.

It's a single.

CHAPTER 24

QUINN

Of course, there's only one bed.

Scarlett glances at me. Her shoulders sag, face wrinkled. She sighs as she drops her rucksack.

"You look exhausted. Take the bed."

She lays down, making her rucksack a pillow. I lay on the bed, my belly in knots, a coldness I can't shift seeping into every cell. I lean over the bed and glance down at Scarlett.

I trail my fingers over her shoulder, down her bandaged bicep. She startles.

"Would you... I... Will you hold me?"

Her features soften as she climbs onto the bed and tugs my back against her belly. I don't need to see her to know she's smiling. The heat of her breath trickles down my neck. I swear she lights up the world when she smiles, or maybe it's my world she's lighting up.

"What if I wanted to be the big spoon?" I say, my tone light.

She chuckles against my back. "As if I'd ever let you be the big spoon."

"Good thing I let you win then," I grin.

"If by *let*, you mean making me think I've won so you can steal my body heat while you sleep, then sure. Why not?"

I laugh. "What twisted thoughts you have."

"About as twisted as our relationship."

I hitch over to face her. Her eyes are the blue of glacier waters and shallow beaches made of crystal and sand. Usually they're cold. Distant even. But tonight they burn like white fire and stars.

My stomach folds in on itself. I want to tip my chin, press my lips to hers. But I also want to pull the blade from my belt and push it into her hard abs. This torture needs to end. The pain of knowing I'm keeping secrets from her. Secrets that are going to come out tomorrow. Secrets that will end everything we have. I should end it now.

"I hate you," I whisper.

She smiles. "No you don't."

"I do," I say. But it's weak. She knows I don't mean it as much as I do.

"I know you," she says.

"You don't know shit," I say, and move closer.

"We're trained... In the guild. To read body language. Subtle clues. The guild wanted us to predict our enemies' every move. We're taught to read bodies. Of course, they meant it for fighting. But I prefer using it in other ways."

Her arrogant eyes draw down my face, hover on my neck, and skim down the rest of my body.

"See, I know... right now, your nipples are hardening

beneath that lace bra you're wearing." She brushes her fingers across the fabric, and it's like lightning. I have to bite down a moan. I want her to shred my clothes and fuck me until I can't walk.

"And what of your nipples, Ms. Grey?" I reach out, slide my hand under her top and pinch her nipple. She sucks in a breath.

"What about the growing heat between your legs? Hmm?" I slip my knee between her thighs, lifting it until I meet her groin. She swallows hard, a long blink.

"I will play any game you bring me, Scarlett."

She leans down, presses her lips against mine. Her kiss is different, deeper. It tugs at my heart, my soul, like wildfire and roses.

"Yes," she says. "You will because you are my match. Because when I close my eyes it's you I see. When I fling my sword, it's you I want to protect. And when I breathe deep, it's you I want to inhale. It's always you, Quinn. It always was, and it always will be."

My chest dulls. Not because I don't want to hear this, but because I do. The backs of my eyes sting, and my throat closes. I have to tell her. I have to tell her now before it's too late.

Her lids flutter shut, her breathing slows.

"Scarlett, wait. I need to tell you something," I whisper.

"Anything," she breathes.

I close my eyes. I can't bear to watch her reaction when she realises I've lied, that I'm not who I said I was, that I've betrayed her, us, everything we've worked toward.

"The Border Lord... he's my father."

I wait. Wait for the knife slipping between my ribs, the rage ripping from her throat, but I'm met with silence.

I peel open an eyelid.

Scarlett's face is expressionless, still. Lost to sleep and dreams.

"Fuck," I breathe, and then sleep drags me under into a fitful world of fretting and wondering whether this game we play together was ever really worth it. Because right now, it feels like we're both about to lose.

CHAPTER 25

SCARLETT

By the time Stirling shakes us awake, Quinn's limbs are wrapped in mine. Our legs are tangled, and she's buried under my chin in the crook of my neck. The air is freezing, my fingers feel swollen from the cold, and I ache all over. But the gap between our bodies is hot. She rolls off me, yawning. I look at my sister who is grinning.

"Stirling."

"Good morning, Scarlett. Quinn," Stirling says and winks at the pair of us. "There's some porridge in the kitchen, thanks to Jacob and Morrigan."

After we eat, we gather our belongings and leave the abandoned cottage.

We take three hours, but eventually, we reach the palace perimeter.

"The tunnels to my, um, the palace—the queen's old palace—run the entire length of the grounds. Supposedly, they were political escape tunnels built into the palace, should the realms ever go to war."

Morrigan brightens. "That's right. They're there in case anyone attempts to assassinate the royals during political meetings or balls. The queen is a suspicious woman... so I hear."

I frown at Morrigan. "How do you know the queen?"

Her eyes widen, and she shrugs. "Just a bookworm." She points at a palace Collection tattoo peeking out from under the sleeve.

Of course.

The six of us crouch low on the edge of the grounds. The rain has, at last, taken a break. Though the clouds still smother the sky in a patchwork of muddied grey. Remy and Jacob hunt up and down the field searching for the tunnel entrance.

Quinn picks at some grass. She speaks, but her gaze doesn't leave the floor. "My relative said they hadn't ever been in them, and they can't remember the last time they were in use. We're probably looking for an entrance buried under a decade of plant growth."

"Got it," Jacob says, jogging back to us. "We need blades."

The rest of us draw out our knives and blades and head over to help hack up the plants. It takes twenty minutes before we've pulled enough green away to really see the entrance tunnel.

"This is where I leave you," Jacob says when we're done gardening.

"Wait, I brought gifts," Remy says and hands out little round flesh-coloured beads.

"What's this?" I ask.

"Goes in your ear," Remy says. "It will enable us to stay in contact with Jacob while he hunts for vehicles."

Stirling checks her watch. "We have a little over thirty-six hours to get the map and get back to the Queen's Peace Ball. Three hours max inside the palace, okay?"

We all place the beads inside our ears. It's an odd sensation, cold, slimy almost, and then it disappears into my ear canal and that whole side of my face grows warm.

"Everyone's up and working?" Remy says.

I jolt, the dissonance of having her voice inside my head and seeing her mouth move right in front of me.

"Yeah, it's a weird one," she laughs. "You'll get used to it. Made of medical magic, these, and a little dose of sound conducting waves from a music chalet. Anyway, I won't bore you with the details."

"Well, thank you, Remy. Jacob, Stirling, do you have everything you need?" I ask.

They nod. Stirling holds up the map she's been using. "Map, comms, and good old engineering magic." She elbows Jacob in the ribs.

He rubs his hands together, sparks flying out from his palms. "I haven't hot-wired in years. This should be fun."

"And Plan B if you can't find anything?" Scarlett asks.

"Use the tunnels to make our way to the Border and bargain our way through?" Stirling says.

"Sounds like a terrible idea," I say.

"Which is why I'll find us a car," Jacob winks.

"Between Jacob's skills as an engineer and mine as a Resourcer, how can we fail?"

"Rendezvous in three hours by the west end of the gardens. Good luck."

"Don't need it," Stirling winks at me, then yanks me in for a hug. "Love you like the plague."

"Idiot." I shuck her off. "Be safe."

With that, Jacob buckles his blade, picks up his ruck-sack, and together, he and Stirling move off.

"Okay, time to change into staff uniforms," I say and pull my uniform out of the bag. They're not quite the same as Border Lord uniforms, but between Quinn's knowledge of having lived here and her relative who still works for him, she thinks they're a close match. I guess we will see.

When we're all dressed and our bags repacked, Remy says, "My turn."

She stands square on to the tunnel entrance. She kneels, places her hands on the floor and takes a deep breath. Her hands vibrate and sink into the earth until there's barely a knuckle left. The earth rumbles under my feet. Her eyes fill with grey. Silver white threads pierce the earth matting and meshing over the tunnel entrance. Sweat runs down Remy's temple. I dig Chance out of my pocket, rubbing the gilded words for luck.

The metal rods sealing the tunnel vibrate faster, dirt and dust fall from the tunnel roof and splatter on the sodden floor.

Time evaporates. It's taking too long. It won't work. We're going to end up getting caught.

I grit my teeth, grinding them into each other, my stomach hardening. But as I taste bile, the metal rods blocking the tunnel entrance evaporate, and the entrance is clear for us to enter.

"Well, that was a fucking challenge and a half," Remy says, wiping lines of sweat from her face. "I wish I could stay and study the security systems. They're so old and intricate, I was worried I wouldn't be able to hack them."

"Thank gods we picked a genius for a team mate then," Quinn says, slapping Remy on the back.

And so we enter the tunnels, plunging ourselves into the gloom, and the mission begins.

CHAPTER 26

QUINN

The tunnel under the old palace grounds is nightmare dark. I take the lead, then Remy, then Morrigan and Scarlett following up the rear. The closer we get to my father's territory, the louder my heart beats. This was a stupid idea. I'm never going to get through the palace undetected. And what happens when one of my father's staff realises who I am?

It takes half an hour to cross the grounds and reach the palace cellar. I shuffle as close to the cellar door as possible and nudge it open inch by inch.

I place my hand on the door, praying the palace remembers me. It should. I spent enough time here during those early years after The Tearing. I know it's been a while since I visited, but I'm hoping its memory is long. The door is heavy, but it opens without resistance. I audibly sigh, relief washing through me as the familiar pressure of magic slides over my skin, testing, assessing and finally greeting me with the sweet scents of cinnamon and mint, woody smoke, leather-bound books and metal. This palace's power is more eclectic than the one in New Imperium. After The Tearing, its magic was... volatile shall we say. Two men had various limbs severed because they pissed off the palace. Entrance is not guaranteed. I stroke the wood, silently thanking the palace for welcoming me.

"The walls are hollow," I mouth and pull out the floor plan. Scarlett sketched on the route she thought we should follow back in the warehouse. I trace the route with my finger, trying to remember the route through the house. Once we're inside the walls, there won't be room to pull maps out and check. I'll be guiding us from memory.

"Have you got it memorised?" Scarlett says.

I fold the map shut. "The riskiest part is the stairs. There are no stairs inside the walls, so we have to exit the walls, go up the staff staircase and then back into the walls to the other side of the palace."

"I remember the palace floor plan, and I'll be right behind you in case you forget," Morrigan says.

I move to the back of the cellar and feel along the walls until I find the ridge under the wallpaper.

"There you are." I push on the ridge and then push both hands along the edge. The wall clicks open and swings wide.

But the walls are narrow, and we have to enter single file. When Scarlett pulls the wall door shut, it seals us in a darkness so acute it takes my breath away. The rising bubble of panic fissures under my skin.

Morrigan reaches out and finds my fingers and squeezes them. "Hold on, I'll help." An ember encased in a bubble flies up above me. It showers the narrow space in a warm light. I almost wish she hadn't done it. At least in the dark, I couldn't see the spiders crawling along the wood beams.

I take a deep breath and start walking. Foot after foot, we inch our way through the palace. No one speaking, all of us trying to keep our breathing slow, calm, and quiet. All of us lost in concentration as we make our way deeper and deeper into the palace.

We turn left and right so many times that keeping track of the turns and which room we're in is excruciatingly difficult. I have to stop and close my eyes multiple times to make sure I haven't led us astray, there's no way to pull the map out in here, it's too tight. Instead, I pull on all my childhood memories, the play time running about, and the hours I spent studying the floor plans before we left.

It takes an hour, but we reach the staff quarters and the staircase that should be located outside the wall. Scarlett leans against the wall and strains, listening for anything, pushing her Assassin trained senses to hear further, to feel deeper.

She nods, and I push and click on the wall door. It springs open, and the palace appears.

Home.

I want to run, find mother and Malachi and grasp them tight. I want to find my room, pull Scarlett inside and strip her. But more than any of that, I want to find father and tell him what Scarlett has planned.

But I can't do any of those things.

I step out, making sure my snoody mask is pulled high, and I head straight to the staircase. It's enclosed inside a turret wall, so thankfully, we're only exposed for a short while.

Remy shuts the wall and follows me. We head up the turret, moving as fast as we can while remaining quiet.

We reach the second floor and it's empty, save one member of staff.

"Shit," I mumble. I keep my head low, trying not to make eye contact. The last thing we need when we're this close to the map is for a member of father's staff to recognise me.

We walk past the staff member, all of us feigning the arrogance and confidence of a magician who fought their way through The Tearing and survived.

The closer the staff member gets, the more blood roars in my ears, my heart hammering against my ribs. I glance up.

Fuck.

Her eyes land right on mine. I know her. It's Marissa. She's been a member of father's team from the start, works as a farm hand. She knows me too. Though whether she'll recognise me when I'm dressed in father's staff uniform, I don't know. I pull my gaze away from hers; I don't need to give her any more time staring at me than necessary.

I risk a quick look back. The woman stops, a flicker of recognition runs through her expression. I keep walking, holding my breath, praying to the High Magician that she doesn't put it together before we're out of sight. She turns away, shaking her head, and I increase my pace, walking as fast as I can without arousing suspicion.

As I round the corner, my shoulders sag. One more corner and I'm punching the wall hard and fast, ripping the wall open and dragging everyone inside. I lean on my knees, not caring if I get covered in cobwebs.

Scarlett grips my shoulder. "We good?"

"We're good. I just need a second because I knew her. I wasn't sure if she recognised me."

"What exactly is it your relative did for the Border Lord again?" Scarlett asks, her eyes narrowing at me.

Shit.

CHAPTER 27

QUINN

Once we're through the next section of wall, we step out into the east wing, the most isolated. There's nothing here save the observatory at the top of the building. I check my watch. We've used over an hour of time making our way through the palace. Every footstep feels like a ticking clock, a countdown to an inevitable end.

We reach the observatory and walk in. The room is as it always was. Star maps sprawled across the walls in navy blue and gold lines. Above us, the ceiling is made of glass, the sky stormy and grey. Always grey here, never high summer or spring, just the constant grind of in-between.

Remy paces around the room, her eyes narrow, glaring at the walls at the floor.

"It should be here, right?" Scarlett says.

"There's a hidden room, yes, but I'm not sure where."

Remy slams to a halt. "Everyone stop," she says and runs a hand through her spiked hair.

"What's wrong?" I say.

"It was too easy. We walked right in here. The Border Lord wouldn't let his map be so poorly hidden."

Her eyes darken, her hands move fast, twitching and bending knuckles and fingers as she pulls on invisible building threads. She buckles to her knees, sparks of electricity crawling across her skin.

"Er... Rem...?" I say, stepping forward.

"Don't touch her, let her finish," Morrigan says, grabbing my wrist and pulling me back.

Remy groans, an aching sound ripping from her throat. Her forehead furrowed with cavernous lines.

"We have to help her," I growl.

"Hold on," Morrigan says.

As I break out of Morrigan's grip ready to yank Remy back, she snaps out of it, panting, sweat running down her temples, her eyes bloodshot, a drop of blood running from her nose.

"Shit," she says.

"What happened?" Morrigan asks, clasping Remy's face.

"I was right. This isn't the room we need. Whoever created this observatory was intensely devious. They've melded another room into the fabric of the building, like a displacement. It mimics the look and feel of a hidden room."

"But?" Scarlett says, giving Remy a hand up.

"It's not actually here. It's an observatory with some clever illusion magic."

"So we have absolutely no idea where the map is?" Scarlett says. "FUCK." She kicks her rucksack, and it skitters across the tiled floor.

I stare out the single observatory window, the other

palace in my line of sight. A replica palace, one for each of the princesses. A memory surfaces. Father taking me to the observatory in the other palace. Trying to star gaze on the odd night when storm clouds didn't rule the skies.

"Do you know why I love the stars?" he said.

"Because they're beautiful?"

He laughed. "No, kid. Because they all look the same. If you're untrained, you'll see what you want to see, find patterns, illusions. But unless you understand what you're looking for, you can't use them as a map."

"Does it matter? Can't you just appreciate them?" I asked, staring into the telescope again.

"Perhaps. But part of being a leader is showing your people what they want. It gives them hope."

I push the telescope away. "But isn't that a lie? You're not really giving them hope."

"Aren't I? Hope isn't something you can hold, Quinn. It's intangible. It's what hope can make you do that's important."

"So it's an illusion?"

"Perhaps." He squeezed my shoulder.

"But aren't you failing your people if all you give them is an illusion?"

He presses his lips together, his eyes downcast. "Not if the illusion is enough. Not if giving them hope makes them fight on, fight harder."

The memory fades, the observatory window coming back into focus.

"It's not here," I say.

"I thought we'd established that," Remy says, her jaw flexing.

"No. I mean, I know where it is. There's another observatory like this one in the other palace. And that one the

Border Lord uses as his personal residence. This is the working palace. He'd keep the map close to him."

"How do you know so much? I thought it was your relative who works here?" Scarlett says, a note of hesitation in her voice.

"I... it..."

"Does it matter? We've got less than two hours to get out of this palace and into the other one. Let alone still finding a way into a hidden room," Remy snaps.

But I'm out of suggestions. While I know where the map is, I don't have a clue how to get us there from here.

"What about the sky bridges? Weren't there bridges connecting the palaces?" Scarlett says.

I shake my head. "Collapsed during The Tearing."

"And the garden is teeming with staff, so we can't walk out the front door," Remy adds.

"I know a way," Morrigan says. "When I li—studied here, I... that is so—"

"Spit it out Morrigan, we haven't got time," Scarlett says.

"Sorry, basically someone created short cuts to each palace. There were lectures in both. And we were lazy and didn't always want to walk between the two. One of the fabric weavers teamed up with an engineer, and they created these portals by bending the fabric of space, weaving it with a form of engineered subatomic cellular travel. A sprinkle of magic and poof. It's kind of ingenious, really. When you look at the dynamics of the t—"

"Morrigan, darling, I have exactly no idea what you said. But what would be delightful is if you could tell us where they are?" Remy says, kneading her temples.

"Right, yes. There's one at the end of the corridor."

"Well, let's go!" I say. "Lead the way."

Scarlett enters the corridor first, blades tight in her hands. She makes sure it's all clear, and then we follow her out.

"Remy, you have to be the one to open it. It's locked with a runic system. It's not hard, you should be able to see it once you touch the door. You'll need to align the lock this end with the lock that end. Once you do, you can open the door. Otherwise, you'll open it into whatever room is behind the door."

Even as we're walking down, Remy's eyes are deepening to grey, her hands glowing silvery-white. They vibrate fast, her fingers moving too quick to discern the movements. We reach the door and she has her palms out. Sweat runs down her forehead and cheeks.

"Bingo, motherfucker." Her eyes flash back to brown, and she grins, places her hand on the door and opens it.

"Ladies," she beams and holds her arm out for us to enter.

We run down this corridor and straight to the observatory door. I glance out the window, looking at the palace we were in seconds ago, wishing I'd known about these doors when I lived here.

Finally, we reach the observatory door. "Remy?"

A sheet of slate drops over her eyes, the familiar pearlescent whip of magic vibrating at her hands. She snaps out of it almost immediately and turns to Scarlett, her face the same ashen colour her eyes are when she uses magic.

"We have a problem."

"Another one?" Scarlett says, her fist balling.

"I can open the room, but it's going to trip the security."

"For fuck's sake," Scarlett growls. "There's definitely no way to get in without it tripping it? No fancy hack?"

"Not unless you're the Border Lord himself or a relative."

My blood freezes. My back rigid.

"Wh—what do you mean, a relative?" I ask.

Scarlett cocks her head at me, her face a picture of lines and furrowed thoughts. I can feel my grasp on my secret slipping. Tiny fragments tearing off and drifting away and into Scarlett's orbit. She's piecing the scraps and shreds of information together. I know it. I can feel her tumbling away from me. All this time, our universes were pulled together, our galaxies crashing into each other, fighting, exploding. And now they're drifting apart, the strands connecting us ripping under the taught tension.

"There's a failsafe. I can't prevent it from tripping security... unless we have a blood key. And that means the Border Lord himself, or a close relative."

"He has a son," Scarlett says.

"No," I bark, too harsh, too fast. Scarlett's eyes land on me. They're hot, and more of the puzzle pieces are slotting into place.

I can't let her go after my brother. But what alternative do I have? Tell her, tell the team, risk them all hating me for the rest of time, but get us into the room, retrieve the map and get the hell out of here.

Or don't. Trip the security, risk my father coming and finding us and them still finding out. Either way, this is the end of the road.

If father arrives, Scarlett will try to kill him.

Thoughts swirl. I'm paralyzed by the indecision of it all when Scarlett pushes her finger to her ear and says, "Jacob. Do you read?"

Her voice echoes in my ear a millisecond after I hear her in the room.

"Roger that, Scarlett. It's Jacob here. We're having a few technical difficulties on the vehicles."

"Technical difficulties? You want to explain exactly what the hell that means?"

"Scar. Chill." This is Stirling's voice. "We've got the situation handled, but you're going to have to meet us at a different location. Ask Morrigan if she knows where the disused rail track is. There's one near the back of the second palace."

Scarlett glances at Morrigan, who nods. If she doesn't know where it is, I do. But explaining that will be tricky.

"Second palace? For once, a bit of good news," Scarlett says.

"What do you mean?" Jacob asks.

"We're in the old palace now," Scarlett says.

"What, why?" Stirling says.

"Long story. We'll meet you there." With that, Jacob and Stirling's voices vanish from my head.

"How long do you need to get the vehicles running?" Remy asks, interrupting.

There's a loud thudding in the distance, a sharp, screeching grind, like metal clawing over metal.

"Half hour. Maybe forty minutes," Jacob says, huffing and puffing.

"You have fifteen," Scarlett says. "I'm done with this bullshit. Let's get the map and get out of here."

She removes her finger from her ear. "Get it done, Remy. Trip the security."

Remy nods, her eyes darkening before her hands even go up. "Morrigan, lend me your power."

Morrigan steps up and slips her hand into Remy's, and the two of them go still. Their hands vibrate, power pulsing between them.

The walls shudder, the floor beneath my feet ripples and shivers until it's not wooden any more, but marble and white. The walls meld and shift, the navy giving way to creamy marble striated with strings of black. Even the air changes, warming and tingling with cinnamon and herbs.

Then, in the middle of the room, the map appears.

Scarlett sucks in a breath. "I fucking knew it," she says, marching toward the box.

My eyes widen as I take in the sight because inside, there isn't one piece of map, but two.

No. No, no, no.

If both pieces of the map are here. Then...

"He set you up," I breathe. I glance at Scarlett. "The Border Lord really did set you up."

The realisation hits me so hard my knees buckle. If father set her up, what else did he do? What don't I know? I can't breathe. My chest clamps down, my breathing is rapid.

"Woah," Scarlett says, pulling me up. "What's going on in there?" She brushes my hair away from my face.

"Guys, we don't have time to play happy fucking families. I tripped security. We need to secure the map and get the fuck out," Remy says.

Morrigan grabs a hammer out of Scarlett's bag and slams it into the glass box.

"Fuck. Fuck. Fuck," Remy cries, her eyes still dark. "It's the same fucking system. Failsafe. We need the Border Lord's blood to open it."

"Or a relative?" I say, my voice quiet.

Scarlett's hands pull away, pieces slotting together, her eyes growing distant as the puzzle gets clearer.

"We're fucked," Remy says, punching the glass. "Security is on the way. Now what the hell are we going to do?"

A line of sweat runs down the back of my neck. We're not fucked because I can open the fucking box, but if I do, it all breaks. I'll destroy everything.

Open it.

Don't

Open it.

Don't.

But what other choice do I have?

In the distance, the first thud of soldier's boots slams against the corridor floor. Everyone's eyes glance down the corridor.

"Draw weapons," Scarlett says.

I lock eyes with Scarlett, try to burn her expression into my mind. It's the last time she'll ever look at me with respect, with lust, with love.

I walk over to her, put my hand around her neck, and pull her lips to mine.

"I'm sorry," I say.

And kiss her.

I kiss her like she's oxygen.

I kiss her like she's the sun and the moon, and the missing piece of my soul. Because she is, I see that now.

And now it's too late.

When I pull away, I take my blade out of my waistband and draw it over my palm. Scarlett's eyebrows draw together, a fleeting moment of confusion before realisation dawns on her.

"No," she whispers, her face crumpling.

My heart thuds in my ears, a rushing static of blood pounding in my head. I place my hand on the glass. It hums beneath me, the blood dissolving into the glass, and then the box clicks open and I pull the map pieces out.

Scarlett's eyes are wide as she stares at me. Remy and Morrigan wear similar expressions.

"You..." Morrigan breathes. "You're related?"

"She is," a booming voice appears behind me. Loud, commanding, deep.

And then father steps into the room.

Blades are drawn, and Morrigan raises her hands, her fists coated in fire. Scarlett holds two katanas, one in each hand. She glances rapidly from me to father.

Soldiers stream into the room surrounding us. Father steps forward, his colossal figure towering above me. It's been so long, I'd forgotten how big of a man he is. His dark curls and shaved undercut. I look more like him now than ever. And everyone in the room can see it.

He looks down at me and smiles.

"Hello, daughter."

CHAPTER 28

SCARLETT

Loving women with fury in their hearts has taught me that there are three types of anger. The first is at an injustice, a heavy rage that fuels rebellions and movements. The second is a protective anger. This one is dangerous. It's white hot and makes a woman fearless and capable of indescribable feats.

And then there's the last type of anger. A rage so deep, so furious, that it can crack a soul in half and smother its innards in scars. An anger fuelled by betrayal, by heartbreak.

That is the volcanic poison filling my body right now.

"Daughter? You're his fucking daughter?" I scream. "And you didn't think you should mention that?"

Quinn opens and closes her mouth, no words escaping.

I can't see. The only thing I can hear is the rushing slam of blood in my ears. My ribs rise and fall in haggard breaths.

"You?" the Border Lord says, pointing at me. "I recognise you."

The Border Lord. Her father...

Oh. Fuck.

In one instant, the furnace throbbing inside my body evaporates. Instead, I'm left ice cold. My mouth dries. My chest hollows.

Everything slots into place.

The Border Lord. The commission. His commission. The job that got my parents killed. I can't breathe. Static fills my vision, my limbs numbing. Because there's more. Much more that I haven't told Quinn. But she's betrayed me. Lied. Then again, so have I, and I didn't even realise.

"This whole time?" I breathe. My jaw is hard. I want to break something, smash the room until it's dust and ash.

I don't know whether I want to cry or scream or laugh. All three. I'm furious with her. I should kill her for lying, for breaking my trust. And yet, I've done exactly the same to her.

This isn't a game anymore. Not when everyone loses.

Quinn frowns, glancing from her father to me, realisation slowly dawning on her. "What was the mission you did for my father, Scarlett..." she asks, turning to me.

"Yes, Scarlett. What was it?" the Border Lord says, sneering.

Quinn's shaking her head, her knuckles white over her blade. Maybe I deserve to die. She glances between me and her father.

"If you tell her," I spit, "both of us will lose her." My body is tense, my muscles straining, as more soldiers flood the room, magic and weapons held high. I want to pounce, to let the ice in my veins ignite and kill them.

Kill them all.

"The only one with anything to fear here is you," the Border Lord says.

I shake my head. He doesn't get it. Doesn't understand. He's going to undo everything. I'll tell her because she deserves the truth. Because I'd give her anything, even if it meant losing her.

"Quinn, I'm so sorry," I say, the words faltering in my throat.

Remy and Morrigan are sizing up the soldiers, scanning the bodies, counting. We're outnumbered three to one. I assessed the second the room filled. It's going to be ugly.

"What did you do?" she says, her voice breathy.

"I..." I can't. I don't want to tell her. Her expression, the way she looks at me with such purity creates a war inside me. How could she have kept this from me? Why? And then I realise, to protect him, the same way she always protected her brother. No matter how hurt I am, she won't forgive me. Not for this.

"Your father commissioned me to take a life. A boy who was selling secrets."

She brings a hand up to her mouth, her eyes filling with tears. She knows before I say it. But I can't stop the words, not now that I've started. The truth spills from me.

"I came through the Border and took the commission. But when I found the commission, he was a child. No more than sixteen. I didn't want to go through with it... Instead I..."

Quinn drops to her knees. "You stopped him from speaking."

I nod.

"I cut his vocal chords. Left him close to help and prayed to the High Magician he lived. He was a kid. How could I kill him? It wasn't until I returned to the palace and told him what I'd done that I realised who the boy was. That the Border Lord had sent me to slaughter..."

"Malachi," Quinn says through her fingers.

I nod. "Quinn, I'm sor—" She holds her finger up to silence me.

"Don't you fucking speak to me," she roars. The light that always burns in her evergreen irises vanishes. And with it, any feeling she had for me. Instead, it's replaced with a fire so violent I edge back.

She stares at me, a knife dangling from her fist.

"You," she snarls.

Behind her, the Border Lord sneers. The soldiers edge closer, closer. I can smell the fight in the air, the grinding slice of swords drawing out of scabbards. My skin prickles with knowing. Someone is going to die today.

"You're the reason my brother can't talk. The reason he nearly died."

"I had no idea who you or the boy were. But I swear to you I tried to save him."

"Lies. You left him for dead. I was the one who found him."

"I did everything I could. If I didn't stop the boy from talking, then the Border Lord—your father—would come after me for not silencing him and then send someone else to finish the job. I had to make Malachi silent enough to save both of us."

Quinn pulls up. Her face torn, a raggedy mix of emotions flickering through her expression. The fury I came to respect and love filling me not with desire, but fear. This is where I lose her. Where our game ends and everything we've built comes crashing down.

We both lose. A betrayal for a betrayal. It's almost laughable.

She steps up to me, holding a blade under my chin. She reaches into my waistband and pulls out the blade I stole from her all those years ago. The blade I'd kept for this moment, for an execution, for retribution.

For him. I flick my eyes to the Border Lord, and his expression narrows. His lip curls, displaying yellowed teeth.

Quinn runs her fingers over the sharp edge, pushing at the ruby in the hilt. The same ruby he wears in a ring on his little finger.

The blade shudders in her hand. Its surface is shinier than I've ever seen it.

"That's why you took it, isn't it? At Roman's party. It's why you stole his blade from me, because you knew it was his?"

I nod. "I wasn't a hundred percent sure. But I recognised the ruby. I didn't understand how you possessed it. So I took it."

"All these years," she says, the fight going out of her voice.

I grip her wrist. "If you're going to kill me, do it. This means you win, Quinn."

I release her arm and she pulls back the blade, ready to strike.

"Know that I'm sorry and if I'd ever thought for a second... I wish I could change it... There was no other way..."

I should tell her the truth. Tell her what really happened. But she wouldn't believe me, anyway. Not now. Not telling her in the heat of the moment. Instead, I steel myself. If this is what it takes, then I'll die for her.

She tilts her head at me, her expression widening. Then she turns, blade still aimed at my heart, and faces her father.

"Would you?" she says to her father. "Would you take it all back if you could?"

"Take what back?" he asks, the gravel in his voice rumbling through my chest.

"If you could go back, would you decide against commissioning Scarlett? Would you find another way to stop the Queen from finding out your plan?"

He laughs, loud. It billows around the domed room, echoing, cold, and callous.

"Of course I would, Quinny."

Quinn's fingers tighten around the blade. She brings it to my chest, almost piercing the flesh. The heat of warm skin threatening to spill heating my torso.

"What... what would you do differently, father?" she asks, her voice quiet.

To my left, Remy is sliding another knife down her sleeve and into her palm. Morrigan squints at the roof. They're planning something. I plead silently with them to wait. Wait and see how this plays out.

Even though I'm livid with her for lying, right now, I have to believe in her. Believe that she knows me well enough, that I meant to save her brother as best I could, and this was the only way I knew how. I know she can't forgive me, hell I don't even know if I can forgive her, but maybe we can all walk away alive.

Her father falters, his eyes focused on Quinn. He huffs, as if the answer is obvious. "I'd kill him myself."

Quinn sucks in a breath.

"Don't be naïve, daughter. All we have, everything you're going to inherit, it's because we control the Border. You give the map back to the Queen and all of this goes away. Everything we worked for. Where the hell was the Queen when the world tore in two? She sent no one. Thousands died because of her selfishness and petty squabble with her sister. This is bigger than one life. It's bigger than you or me or Malachi."

"He's your son," Quinn screams. It's so loud and shrill I actually startle. Her hand shakes where she holds the blade to my breastbone.

I could snap it out of her hand. Could break her wrist and save myself. But what would that prove? What would it show?

No, despite everything, I still want her to see. Still want her to know that I never meant her or her brother harm. I'd give her my life if it meant her happiness.

"And he would have destroyed everything, Quinn. The Queen needs to pay for her weaknesses. She's not worthy of ruling a people. She left us to die. If it weren't for me, we'd all be dead. And my fucking son wasn't taking that away from me."

He's red faced. A vein wiggles down his forehead, pulsing. His eyes light with the same intensity as Quinn's do.

"Don't you get it, darling? That bitch of a queen took everything from us. My marriage is failing, my son is voiceless, you prefer her side of the Border to mine. So that what? You can dabble with some desperate throwback legacy trying to claw her status back?"

Quinn shakes her head. "It's not her that ruined everything you did. I'm just sorry I didn't see it before."

The blade releases. It flies towards the Border Lord. His eyes widen as the blade plunges into his arm. He winces and then throws his head back, laughing.

"You deign to try to kill your own father? Pathetic. I taught you better than that. You can't even throw a blade properly. SOLDIERS."

The soldiers move. Boots stamping on marble. I'm up,

swooping Quinn behind me, as the soldiers take offensive positions.

Morrigan strikes first, fire flaring and ballooning in balls towards the soldiers. The clash of metal on metal rings in my ears as the soldiers engage. I slice and cut, stab and puncture. Soldier after soldier. The whole time, father and daughter stand in the heart of the room, immobile. Glaring at each other while we fight around them.

Remy veers left, I stab right. Back to back, the three of us, a unit, a team punching, defending, striking.

Blood splatters the walls and floor, stains my clothes and seeps into the soles of my shoes. My muscles burn, but this kind of pain is good. It hurts, and I don't care. I want it to hurt like my heart. The acidic throb in my legs easing some of the ache in my chest.

Morrigan sets men alight, hangs them with pearlescent ropes and guts them without ever moving.

Finally, the last soldiers stare at the three of us: Remy, Morrigan and I, smeared in blood, teeth bared, gashes and slices in our arms and clothes.

The three of us pant like dogs. But I'm only just getting started. I want to cut mountains, destroy buildings, rip intestines from bellies, make the world pay for the bruise in my heart. The soldiers decide better than to attack us and flee, leaving only us, the Border Lord, and Quinn.

He sniffs, yanks the blade from his arm, and lets it clatter to the marble floor. He glances around the room, realising he's on his own.

And then, the strangest thing happens. A single bead of blood drips from his nose. He frowns, wipes it away and glares at his daughter. "You think this handful of girls is going to stop me? So they took down a couple of soldiers.

Who cares? I fought hundreds of men to get here. How the fuck do you plan to get out of the palace, Quinn?"

His face is pale, sweat lines his forehead. My blade lays abandoned at his foot.

"I'm not interested in stopping the soldiers," Quinn says. "Only you. I'm interested in making sure you never hurt Malachi again."

He laughs, but it comes out as a choked cough. Red-stained spittle flies out.

"Looks like you failed at that, too."

Except she didn't.

I glance down at the blade, the shine on the surface reflecting at me. It clicks. The blade has never been shiny.

Never.

I glance at Quinn. Her tear-stained cheeks. And I know what she did. I go to her. I slide my hand in hers. The poison takes hold of his insides, suffocates the air out.

"Quinny?" he says.

"I always thought you were doing this for the benefit of everyone, for the benefit of our people. But you weren't. This was always about you and what you wanted. And I see now. You're never going to stop. You nearly killed Malachi and for your own selfish gains. How can I let that go?"

The Border Lord drops onto all fours. He coughs up mucus and blood, spraying the floor with a halo of red.

He looks up at Quinn, his eyes dulling even as he reaches out to her. She steps back, letting his hand drop to the puddle of blood.

Their eyes hold each other. Quinn's nostrils flaring, her mouth twisted in disgust even as tears stream down her cheeks. I squeeze her hand and rub my thumb around her palm. Anything to make the pain go away. But I can't help because I'm half the reason she's hurting. She's the reason I'm hurting.

He slumps to the floor, sputtering, blood bubbling on his lips, and then he's still. A moan erupts from Quinn's lips as she kneels next to his head and leans over. She grabs his shoulders. Presses her face into his back and screams, pulling at his clothes. And then she picks up the blade and stabs, stabs, stabs.

All the while, she screams and screams and screams.

"Quinn..." I say, putting my arms around her. "Quinn, stop now."

I pull the blade from her hands, and she sags against me, sobbing until there's nothing left.

And then the room is as still and quiet as her father.

CHAPTER 29

QUINN

I flee the room, unable to bear the sight of them. I don't want Scarlett anywhere near me. Not after what she's done. I just want to see Malachi. I strip the snoody off, flinging it on the floor, and keep pounding down the corridor until I veer into the residential wing and find my mother carrying a tray of herbs and water.

I slide to a halt.

"Quinny," my mother beams, "we weren't expecting you." And then she takes in my clothes, my blood-stained outfit. Her face falls, and the tray of herbs wobbles in her hands.

"What... What happened?"

I will tell her. But not now. Not like this.

"It's complicated."

My eyes slide to the tray. It's packed. I recognise most of the herbs as things I've sent for Malachi to try.

"What's going on? Is Malachi okay?"

"Quinn," she exclaims, as if remembering. "Oh thank the gods, you're here."

My body chills, my chest and fingers tingling. She puts the tray down and pulls me into a hug. "He's not doing too well. Feverish and puking. But I'm hoping some of these herbs will bring him out of this sickness."

She pats my back, and with each tap I remember the knife plunging into father. The hollow thud as my fist slammed against his spine.

"I'll go make some tea. You sort Malachi out."

"I will, mama."

I should tell her about father. About the mess hidden in an invisible room. But he's safe in there for now. Concealed by his own tricks. I walk into the room. Malachi lays out on the bed, sweating and feverish. He sits up, coughs into his sleeve and tries to wave. But it's slow. Laboured.

I wasted all this time trying to steal bits of fucking maps and none of it matters. Not when he's been living here, under the rule of a father who wanted to slaughter him.

"I know about..." I touch my throat.

There's movement behind me. I smell her before I turn to see her. The scent of leather and hot skin, iron and power.

I expect Malachi to cower, to fear the woman who tried to end his life, but instead, his face lights up. He sits higher and waves at her.

"What... What are you doing? She... she maimed you." I turn to Scarlett. "GET. OUT."

Malachi frowns at me, reaches for my hand and pats it. Then gestures at Scarlett, waving in a circle. He coughs and wheezes a whispered, "Tell. Her."

Scarlett hangs her head, unable to meet my gaze.

"Tell me what?"

"Tell," Malachi says, a sharper wheeze this time.

"Okay, okay," Scarlett says, "stop trying to speak."

Stop trying to speak? What the fuck?

"When I accepted your father's commission, I didn't know it was your brother. I hadn't even met you then," she starts, and my fingers twitch, wanting to ball.

"Yes, you've made that clear. Get to the point, Scarlett, or get the fuck out."

Her jaw clenches. Malachi's hand slides over my fingers, as if trying to calm me.

"When I realised how young your brother was, I offered to bring him back with me across the Border. To keep him safe under the Queen's security as a refugee, if you like."

"What? Why didn't you go?" I say, turning to Malachi.

"He... he wanted to stay and fight. He thought that if he stayed, he could spy for the Queen. Become an informant of sorts. But he couldn't stay in the condition he was in. We both knew your father would find another way to kill him. Or get someone else to do the job."

I rub my brow. This can't be. I don't... And then a memory slides into focus. The Queen's meeting room, the thick journal she carried, was familiar. But I dismissed it. Everyone carries notebooks and journals. But it wasn't just familiar, was it? It was identical.

"You gave her a spelled journal," I say to Malachi. He nods and coughs, a bead of sweat rolling down his temple.

Malachi gestures for Scarlett to continue.

"It was his idea. For me to sever his vocal chords. Silence him without killing him. It was a risk, of course. We couldn't be sure it would be enough to satisfy your father. But he wanted to try, anyway. I did as he asked. Enabled him to become an informant..." She trails off. Oh, you sneaky bastard.

"You set this whole thing up, didn't you?" I say.

Malachi smiles, taps my hand and looks at his journal. I reach for it and hand him a pen. He coughs multiple times, so I set about mixing herbs, pouring liquid into vials. I can't look at Scarlett, though.

When Malachi is done, he holds up the journal.

She mentioned your name in so many letters, so many times. The information came in bits, but eventually I figured it was you. I knew Quinn had fallen for you, despite what she thought. And how could I not encourage that? My own sister had fallen for the woman who saved my life.

"She didn't save your life. She injured you," I spit. "Why would you let her do... do that to you? Why wouldn't you have told me? I would have helped you. We could have fought him together."

It's Scarlett that responds. "Because this was his way of fighting. Fighting for you both."

Malachi nods, agreeing with everything Scarlett's saying.

He mouths the words at me. "I chose this, Quinn. Scarlett reluctantly helped."

My head spins. I can't take any more of this.

"How long have you known?" I say to Scarlett.

She shakes her head. "I didn't. Not until your father walked into the room. That's when I put it together and realised who you were. Who Malachi was."

I let go of my brother's hand and march up to Scarlett.

"I hate you," I spit. "I always have."

There's a moment of hesitation. Scarlett never hesitates, but it draws in, wrinkling her eyes. And then she hardens.

"Was it ever real? Or was it all a fucking game to you?" she spits.

Her eyes are watery, the blue fierce. She shuts them and takes a deep breath.

Of course it was real. But I don't want to tell her that. I don't want her anywhere near me.

"Get. Out."

"Quinn, please..."

I shove her hard in the chest. "GO."

Scarlett's face breaks apart, and somewhere deep in my chest my heart shrivels, a spasming pain lancing through my ribs, making hot tears fall down my cheeks.

"Don't do this. Don't erase everything between us. I lo —" Scarlett says.

"Don't you dare say it. DON'T YOU FUCKING DARE." I'm screaming, the words raw and thorny in my throat.

She needs to leave.

I can't have her touch me or look at me. She's betrayed everything.

"This was never a game, Scarlett. This is my life. My family. How could you? You win. Okay? You fucking win. Just leave."

Malachi coughs, a hacking mucus. I turn my back on Scarlett, rushing to his side as he sprays blood across his duvet. He passes out in my arms. My chest clamps tight, a furious rush of panic filling me. There isn't time to deal with Scarlett. I have to fix Malachi.

I fuss with the herbs mother brought, assessing what's there. I have to create an antidote, a medicine, anything to take this fever down.

I take far too long to brew a tea, and by the time I'm tilting his head and pouring liquid down, his breathing has slowed.

"Come on, Malachi. Hold on."

I hold him, pouring medicine in, over and over. Holding, stroking the sweat away, applying cooling cloths to his brow.

Hours pass.

I don't know when Scarlett left, but when Malachi finally comes to, and the colour has returned to his cheeks, I glance up.

The doorway is empty, the palace silent.

And Scarlett is gone.

CHAPTER 30

SCARLETT

I stand and watch Quinn, my heart shattering. She never turns to look at me, never speaks, never acknowledges my presence. It's as though I've vanished out of existence.

Of all the things we've done to each other. All the times she's poisoned me, I've stabbed her, tied her up, the injuries and paralysis she's given me. This... this hurts more than all of them. I'd take a knife to the gut over this. How did we get to this place?

Her dark curls bounce around her head as she potters around her brother, crushing herbs and mixing ingredients. Her hands work in a rhythm of mixing, crushing, selecting. Years of experience and expertise enabling automatic movements. She mops his brows, tips potions down his throat, checks his pulse. Over and over. And never once does she turn around. I lose track of time, but eventually a hand finds my arm and pulls me away.

"Did you know?" I ask Remy.

She wrings her hands, her shoulders sagging. "She asked me not to tell you. I'm sorry."

I should rip a rib out and cut her throat with it. But I don't. I don't do anything. I follow Remy in silence, wondering how the hell everything went so wrong. We find Morrigan outside the observatory.

"I sealed each map piece in a separate bag and placed them in two different rucksacks. The Border Lord's soldiers have taken his body. I don't think there was a second in command. None of them know what to do."

"It's not our problem," I say.

"Everything okay?" Morrigan says.

"Not even close to okay. But I don't want to talk about it."

"Let's get out of here," Remy says.

Morrigan hands me a ring. The Border Lord's ring, gold signet with a ruby. I ball my fist around it.

"Thank you," I say to her. "I'd usually take his head and give it to the queen, but given our revelations this afternoon..."

"I figured as much," Morrigan says. "Is Quinn—"

"Staying put."

"I see."

We leave the palace via the rear exit and through the gardens in the open air. There are soldiers running scattered like ants in every direction. Somewhere in the distance a siren rings. But no one stops us, no one pays us any attention.

"Scarlett? Can you hear me?" Stirling says in my ear.

I press my finger to my ear to make her voice clearer. Remy and Morrigan follow suit as we make our way through the gardens.

"Loud and clear," I say.

"You need to get to the derelict station. Do you remember on the map there was a disused station to the right of the second palace?"

"I do," Morrigan says and heads off in another direction.

"Get to the station. You'll see us."

Morrigan is way ahead of us by the time Remy and I set off after her. If I strain, I can make out the overhead lines. The further I get away from the palace, the further I want to be. I need to get home and wash this place off my skin.

We enter the station. The station door hangs off the hinges, the roof is caved in, and as for the train tracks... Gods... broken sleepers and fissures crack the metal rails. There's a train parked on the rails, but it doesn't seem any more usable than the station. Half of the windows are smashed. There's silvery graffiti smeared down the outside of the carriage that looks like some kind of magic residue. The roof tiles are peeling off, and there's a hole in one of the carriage walls.

"What exactly are we doing here?" I say as Stirling pops her head out of the train.

"Funny story that," she grins. "On board chaps. Your carriage awaits..."

Remy and Morrigan glance at each other. "Is that a joke?" Remy says to me.

"I highly doubt it," I mumble.

The pair of them scramble up the half broken stairs and climb on board.

"Are you going to explain what the hell we're doing in this death trap?" I say, taking my sister's hand and climbing aboard.

"Wait, where's Quinn?" she says.

Remy and Morrigan wince at the sound of Quinn's name.

"She's... she's not coming. Let's just get home."

Jacob appears out of the engine cabin wearing a weird cap, a little lock of blonde poking out. I open my mouth to ask and decide better of it.

"Ready, ladies?" His eyes darken, his skin shimmers, and then his hands grip the train walls and the floor rumbles.

The train juts forward, and I shunt in my seat and almost slip off the edge. The carriage judders, shaking from side to side, but we stay put.

"I thought you could drive anything, Jacob?" I raise an eyebrow at him and grip hold of the seat.

"I'd like to see you magnetise a seven thousand ton train on rails that are barely functional and drive it out of here with no practice."

I shut my mouth.

The carriage continues to shudder and jostle until Jacob releases one hand and flips it over and twists two of his fingers. The carriage jerks forward in a violent motion, but it's released, and finally Jacob finds his rhythm. His shoulders relax, the tension in his fingers calms, and he moves into the main engine cabin. Freezing air whips in through the holes in the train walls.

Stirling joins me after a while and throws an arm over my shoulder and pulls me into the crook of her arm. I slide my head onto her shoulder and she rubs my arm.

"Remy told me everything. It's alright," she says and strokes my head. "It's going to be okay."

"She's his daughter," I sniffle out.

"I know."

"She killed him."

"I know. Hey, Scarlett...?"

"Yeah?"

"Stop talking."

"Okay." I slide down Stirling's chest and lay on her lap. She strokes my hair until the rocking of the train lulls me to sleep.

When we get home, the house is quiet, bare, and as hollow as my heart. We've spent days with a group of people and suddenly it's just the two of us. Remy, Morrigan and Jacob returned to their respective homes to rest, wash, and sleep off the mission.

I tiptoe around the rooms, wandering from the living room to the kitchen to the bedroom. Everything feeling wrong. Empty, save for the boxes piled high. The couple of days away stretched into an eon of time. I'd almost forgotten we have to find somewhere else to live. Stirling glances at me, the same worry lines etching wrinkles into the corners of her eyes as mine.

We should have sorted this before we left.

I traipse from room to room. Everything is too silent. No Quinn to irritate me.

Stirling appears at the living room doorway. The only thing left in here are the sofas and a bedraggled-looking plant.

"You can't give up on her."

I stop pacing the living room. "She lied to me. To all of us."

Stirling sits on the sofa, hitches her knees under her chin and rests her head on them.

"And if you'd been in her position? If you knew

someone was going after our parents...? Because when you think about it... everything we did w—"

"Yes, alright, I see your point. Either way, she won't forgive me for what I did to her brother."

"Sure she will."

I plonk down next to her. "And what makes you so certain?"

"Because her brother wouldn't be here if it weren't for you."

"She doesn't see it that way. She thinks I ruined his life." I pick at the threads of my sleeve.

Stirling shakes her head. "Scarlett, I adore you. But get a fucking grip. When have you ever quit? You don't lose. We —the Grey twins—do not lose. It's time to stop wallowing, suck your shit up, get in the shower and clean your frankly revoltingly smelly body, and win your girl back because I'm not a fan of this." She wafts a finger at me. "This Scarlett, she's tiresome."

I glare at her, but she wallops me in the arm. "What are you waiting for? Shower. Now. Heathen."

"Fine," I moan.

I spend so long in the shower that the water runs cold. I sit under the head, letting the water wash the dirt and grime and emotions off me. The whole time, it's Quinn in the fore of my mind. Images of her working on her brother, behaving like I don't exist, play and replay over and over.

I drag myself out of the shower and dress in my favourite suit, wearing the lacy bra I wore the night we spent in the Velvet Mansion. Images of her body melting under my hands flash through my mind. All of it aches.

I should have stayed. I should have made her listen to reason.

Three hours later, Stirling and I assemble outside the palace gates. Both pieces of map are tucked away safely, one in each jacket pocket. We enter the palace, white invite in hand. We're meeting the others tomorrow to give them their rewards. But Quinn should be with us. It seems like a lifetime ago we were handed the invites by that pompous butler, and yet, it was only a month ago.

The palace is decorated in sweeping ribbons, chandeliers sparkle like stars, and enclosed fire embers hover along the halls. Giant bouquets of flowers line the corridors and stand tall in the ballroom. Soft stringed music plays from a small stage on the right.

There are magicians dressed in fine robes, glittering ballgowns and fine suits.

I spot the Queen. She's at the back of the room wearing a red corset, her voluptuous bosoms billowing out the top. Her waist is tight, and the skirt fans out around her, a delicious slit up to her hip. She looks... familiar. Though I can't think why. She's the Queen, of course she's familiar. Everyone in New Imperium knows her face.

Stirling's eyes follow the Queen as she moves across the ballroom.

"Umm," Stirling says. "Did we know she was that hot?"

I laugh. "I'm not sure I noticed. But, she is smoking this evening. I'd maybe not try your luck, though. There are always the princesses you could date."

Stirling glares at me. "I mean, I am charming. But chance would be a fine thing. Even in my network, no one knows who they are. Anyway, go give the Queen the fucking map and get us our victory. I'm suddenly bored with this party."

"That's because there's no pussy for you to hunt."

"Just go find the fucking Queen."

She gives me the middle finger, and I laugh for the first time since leaving the Borderlands.

I reach the throne and kneel, bowing my head in deference.

"Approach," the Queen says.

"Your majesty," I say.

"Do you have it?"

"I believe you may prefer a more private location for our discussion."

A thin smile curls in the corner of her mouth. Perhaps Malachi told her about the maps?

"To the battle room then," she says. I gesture for Stirling to follow, and she meets us at the exit. We move down the same corridors we walked down four weeks ago, right into the centre of the palace.

My heart thuds in my chest as we pass down a corridor with long windows looking out onto the Sanatio's courtyard, the flowers lush and bulging. A hint of mint and lilac in the air. My chest squeezes. Would the Sanatio cure what I did to Malachi? We enter the battle room and the Queen takes a seat. She gestures to two chairs.

"You have the map?"

I reach into my jacket pocket and pull out a piece of map. "I do. But here's the interesting thing, your majesty. When we arrived at the old palace to retrieve the piece of map, we encountered something unexpected."

"Unexpected how?" she says and waves her butler to bring drinks. The butler dishes them out, and she raises her glass to us.

I lean back in my chair. "The map piece you hold, the

one you brought into the battle room when you commissioned us..."

She leans forward, her eyes darkening. She really knew. It was a test all along.

"It's a fake."

"Oh, and why do you think that?"

"Because we retrieved both pieces." I reach into my other pocket and take out the other half of the map.

She kicks back, laughing and clapping.

"Oh, bravo, bravo ladies. This truly is more than I could have hoped for. You've impressed me. Really, truly impressed me."

Her eyes glimmer as she looks at both pieces of the map. She examines the maps, searching for authenticity, I suspect.

Her head snaps up.

"You've done very well, indeed."

"Were you always aware?" I say.

She pauses, her face softening. "No. When the first map was stolen, I really thought the one I was left with was authentic. It's only when Malachi sent me a spell-worked journal that he told me to have the map authenticated. I resisted for a while, but eventually, that's how I discovered I was in possession of a fake. If I'd known... I assure you, I would never have ordered your parent's execution."

"It's why you invited us to the challenge?" Stirling says.

"I didn't think an apology would suffice. Not after all these years. Not after what I put you through. I don't expect your forgiveness, but I do hope I can make up for the damage I've done."

The Queen takes a sip of her champagne.

"He's dead," I say.

She sputters the gulp she just took. "I beg your pardon?"

"The Border Lord. Quinn, she... she was his daughter. We didn't know. But when she found out some truths about him, she took him out herself."

"High Magician," she says, gasping. She holds her hand to her chest, stands and paces around the room.

"Truly, this is most unexpected. I knew who Quinn was, of course. Malachi informed me. But I had no idea she would go so far when she learnt of his treachery. You have all excelled beyond my wildest dreams. With the Border Lord gone, we can heal the land and reunite the city. This is the start of a magnificent new era, ladies. I am incredibly proud of you."

Except, that's not at all how I feel. There's a cavernous hole inside me, gaping and vast. It's making my bones ache and my soul weary, and there's only one person who can fill it.

This is the moment I've waited for. I've spent half a decade hungering after the Queen's apology. Her recognition that she was wrong, that the Border Lord had set up my parents. And now I've got it, it feels empty.

The person I want to celebrate winning with isn't here. And I'm not sure there's anyway to get her back.

"Let us discuss your reward. Your royal favour. What shall it be? Reinstating titles? Money? Something else?"

My eyes widen. I know what I can do. How I can win her back. I realise winning is meaningless without her. Fuck the titles. Fuck the money. None of it matters unless she is with me. Because she is my win.

Stirling opens her mouth, and I place my hand on top of hers, silencing her. "I will make it up to you, I promise."

"Oh, fuck," she says under her breath.

"Your majesty, I'd planned to ask for the reinstatement of our titles and lands so that we could pay our team out of our inheritance. But I've realised that without Quinn here, none of it really matters. What matters is loyalty. Loyalty and love."

The Queen nods.

"I'd ask for a piece of Sanatio."

The Queen frowns. "You're sure."

"Scarlett..." Stirling says.

"I'll find a way to pay for their time, I swear it. I have to do this. We started with Quinn. We need to finish with her."

I return to the Queen. "I'm sure."

"But you're leaving yourself in debt with your team members."

"I am."

"So be it." She cocks her head at the butler and he vanishes from the room, presumably to collect a branch.

Stirling's leg is jigging next to me. I hold her thigh, pushing it into the ground to curb the movement.

"I like you, Ms. Grey. Your honesty, your display of loyalty, and your sense of moralistic virtue. I feel a deep sense of regret over my misguided actions. Here's my offer to you... Take your plant, but return to me, with your entire team, missing member intact, in forty-eight hours. I have a proposition for you."

She stands. The butler returns with a large clipping of the branch and hands it to me.

And with that, the Queen leaves and we're left wondering what the hell she wants with us.

CHAPTER 31

QUINN

When I told mother father was dead, she cried, but then those tears dried up quickly and she spent the last twenty-four hours walking around the palace in a daze, muttering to herself. They had a difficult relationship and I'm not sure she really knows how to feel. I don't think any of us do.

The soldiers keep vigil outside Malachi's room. For twelve hours, they waited for instruction, or for me to take my father's place. Neither of which is going to happen. I dismiss them. Tell them to leave and to stop manning the Border gates. The only instructions I'll ever give them.

The Queen will heal the land before long, anyway. They might as well go be with their families.

It takes over fourteen hours, but I get Malachi conscious again.

"We need to talk," he mouths when he's rested.

"Listen, before you say anything, I need to tell you

something. But you should rest first. It can all wait until you're better."

"No," he mouths. Then tilts his head. I recognise this expression. We slide into our old ways of communicating as if it hasn't been months apart.

"Father's dead?" he mouths and reaches for his journal.

"How... how do you know?" My stomach twists in knots, lumps cloy in my throat, choking the air from me.

He looks me up and down. My clothes are ripped, stained with dried blood. The lumps shrink. Right. It doesn't take a genius to infer.

I sag. "I'm sorry."

He opens his journal and writes.

Father wasn't a good man, Quinn. You loved him so much you couldn't see it. But even our mother understood. Gods, she had it hard enough with him.

> *That's not what I want to talk about.*

"What then?" I peer over his shoulder.

It's not her fault, he writes.

I stand straight. My shoulders are tight.

"You need to rest. Now isn't the time for this."

He raises an eyebrow at me. *Yes, it is.* He continues writing.

You shouldn't be mad at her.

"But I am, Malachi. She hurt you."

Yes, because I commanded it. She was doing what she thought was best. She didn't want to hurt me. And isn't that the point?

"I don't know. Is it? How am I supposed to forgive her?"

Do you forgive me?

"What do I need to forgive you for?"

For being an ignorant boy, thinking he can beat his father. For risking my life and placing it in Scarlett's hands, hoping she was skilled enough not to kill me.

"Of course I forgive you. There's nothing to forgive."

Then you don't need to forgive Scarlett, either. He took my hand in his, squeezed it, then continued writing. *I chose this. I need you to understand that. This isn't on her. It's on me. And right now, all I see is my sister's heart in pieces. You love her.*

"I do not."

That, at least, elicits a laugh from him, but it turns to coughing.

If I die, I want to know you'll forgive her, that you'll forgive yourself for whatever nonsense you've decided is your fault. That you'll let yourself be happy.

I take the pen from him. "Don't you dare talk like that. You won't die. This is... this is just some flu sickness. I will pull you out of it."

He takes the pen.

We're all going to die, Quinn. If I go, I'm going happy, knowing our father won't hurt anyone else. I'd be happier knowing my sister was happy, too.

"It's time to rest," I say.

He looks up at me, eyes round, expectant. Demanding.

"Fine. I'll consider it. Happy?"

He purses his lips and then lies down and sinks into sleep. That was twelve hours ago, and he's yet to wake. I sent a soldier to my shop for supplies. He hasn't returned, and every hour that passes feels like Malachi is slipping further away from me. I've been on the floor beside his bed since he fell unconscious, wishing the time would hurry and slow down all at the same time. I've checked all the medical texts in both palaces, and nothing is proving useful. My back and hips ache from the hard ground. My eyes burn from the lack of sleep. And I still haven't changed out of my blood-stained clothes.

Footsteps echo in from down the hall. But they aren't the booted clomps of soldiers or the shuffle, shuffle of my mother.

Feet appear at my eye line. I recognise the boots immediately and roll over so I don't face her. But inside, my heart is betraying me. A thousand beats forging a new rhythm. I want to get up, go to her. But I don't.

"Why are you here, Scarlett? I told you to leave," I mumble into the cushion I've been using as a pillow.

"I thought you'd like to know I collected our prize."

"Should I call you Lady Grey now, then?"

There's a pause. The silence is so thick and swollen, I actually wonder if she left the room. I sit up. She's in the doorway, arms behind her, looking more beautiful than I've ever seen her. She's braided her hair in a thick knot that hangs down her back, blue threads the colour of glaciers woven between the strands. The shirt she wears matches the threads, a stark contrast to her dark jacket and trousers. Her shirt is only done up to her middle, her breasts cupped in the most exquisite push-up bra.

I've never wanted to kill her and rip her clothes off more than I have right now. And that makes me laugh.

"What's so funny?" Scarlett asks. She reaches down, gives me her hand and pulls me standing.

"All those weeks we spent together. How far we've come, only to end up right back where we were."

"You want to kill me?" she says, her eyes dimming.

I tip her chin up. "If it helps, I want to fuck you just as much." I trail down her body. She brings a hand around to her front. She's holding a branch. The flowers are familiar, emblems for the High Magician monarchy. The minty-lilac blossom fills my nose.

I gasp. "How did you get that?"

She brings the branch up between us. "I won a challenge set by the Queen. The prize was a single royal favour. So I asked for a branch of Sanatio."

"But—"

"—and then I carried it here, to give it to you."

I step back, furious and desperate and devastated all at once. And then I'm rushing forward, hooking my hand around the back of her neck and pulling her down to my lips. Her hands curl around my waist, pulling me in tight. Our mouths and bodies swallowing each other whole. I breathe in Scarlett, the leather and metal and heat that follows her everywhere. I place one more soft kiss on her lips.

She hands me the branch and closes my fingers around it.

"Thank you," I say.

She shrugs. "I realised something..."

"You did?"

She nods. "I realised the only thing I ever wanted to win was you."

I grin. "Oh, you fucking charmer, not that different to Stirling after all."

She smiles, and it makes my stomach fold in on itself. My brother's demands clog my mind. As I stare at her, I realise I've forgiven her. I forgave her the moment she walked in. But nothing was ever easy between us. And I don't intend to make it easy now. Where's the fun in that? Where's the game? We've always played games.

"I need to help him," I say.

"I know. The Queen has asked that our team assemble at her palace tomorrow. Now there are no Border gates or guards. It won't take us long to get there..." She picks at her nail, not looking at me. "I guess I'll leave and see you there."

Her eyes flick to Malachi. "I hope it helps," she says and then vanishes from the door.

I stare at Malachi. His breathing has finally deepened to a steady rhythm. His words float through my mind. I place the Sanatio down and run out the door and down the hall. Fucking woman with her long legs. She's already halfway down the corridor.

I reach for her arm and grip it. "Wait."

She halts, her eyes dropping to my hand. "Stay," I say. It's not a question.

Hesitation flickers through her expression.

"I... I want you to stay. I need you to. Don't go. We need to talk. About business, about us... about everything."

"Okay." She squeezes my hand. "Go make him better. I'll wait. I have a feeling we'll make it all work... or kill each other trying."

I grin and huff a laugh out. "I missed you," I say.

I sense her smile before I look up at her. "I missed you too."

We walk back down the corridor to my brother's room, hand in hand. And as we do, I realise something, too.

I was wrong.

There are two things I love: playing games and Scarlett fucking Grey.

CHAPTER 32

QUINN

Malachi's fever is gone, his skin returned to its normal olive tone. When he woke, the fever had broken. While his voice wasn't fixed, he could make sounds, which was more than he's been able to do for years. I suspect with a few more teas mixed with the Sanatio, he'll be healed. But I've planted a clipping from the branch, in the hopes I can grow our own crop. Yes, it's not technically legal, but after what I did for the Queen, I think she'll turn a blind eye.

I shower, washing the stink and grime off me, cleaning the crusted blood and dirt from under my fingernails. The water washes through my hair, cleanses me of the last few days. I raze the hair from my calves and between my legs. When I'm preened and clean and smelling like a floral dream, I pull on some underwear and a silk robe.

I find Scarlett in my old bedroom. It has a four-poster bed with curtains that close the mattress off from view.

I lean against the door. "Comfortable?"

"I'd be more comfortable with your ass over here."

I smile, kick off the frame and shut the door behind me, turning the lock until it clicks. I walk across the room and drop my robe, leaving it where it falls.

"I guess we'll be kicked out of here soon. Once the Queen repairs the land and secures her palaces."

"Then I guess we better make the most of being here while we can," Scarlett says.

"Mmm. And how should we do that?"

"Well, first, I'm going to take these here hands." She waggles her fingers at me as I climb onto the bed. "And then I'm going to rip you out of those lace panties."

"Must you ruin a per—"

She grabs my arms and flings me onto my back. I giggle. "I do like it when you play rough."

Scarlett climbs on top of me, she draws my fists above my head and, with one hand, pins them in place.

"I won you," she says.

My pussy tightens at the command, the dominance, the ownership.

"Say it," she growls.

I shake my head, a grin forming on my lips.

"Say it, or I'll ruin these pretty little lace knickers."

I'm wet already, my core swelling at the thought of what she's going to do to me, how hard she might spank me. She pulls my knickers and releases them, letting the lace ping against my skin. I close my eyes, hissing at the sting and pleasure.

She slides her hands between my breasts, my nipples firming in response. She yanks the knickers so hard they split in half. I let out a moan of desire. She grins, the light glimmering in her eyes.

Her mouth roams my skin, her tongue sliding over my

chest. She bites my nipple through my lace bra. I gasp, the pain and pleasure mixing and flowing through me. She presses down with her teeth. Takes me to the edge.

"You won," I say, breathy tingles racing through my breast.

"Say it again," she growls against my nipple. The vibrations making the nub harder. I need her to take me, to run her hands and fingers over my skin and body like she owns me.

"You won me," I pant. "I'm yours. I was always yours, Scarlett."

She picks the middle of my lace bra and tears it in half with her hands. It falls away, my breasts freed. She runs her fingertips up my legs, slowly teasing. Sensations thrum in my veins, yearning for her.

With my hands released, I reach up and pull her to me, crushing our mouths together. My tongue slides across hers. She's sweet, like wine and honey. I kiss her hard, with the fury, and hurt, and fear I spent the last few days with.

I kiss her like I'll never kiss her again. Like it's the first time I've laid my mouth on hers.

She pulls back, slides her head close as if she's going to kiss me, and then doesn't kiss. She pauses, grinning at me.

It's a game.

I surrender, because while I'll never surrender outside, I will always surrender in the bedroom. I lay back, letting her take charge.

She places her lips on mine, slow and teasing, and sucks my lip. My body melts at her touch. I reach for her hand, push it down my hardened nipples, down my stomach and between my thighs.

She sucks a sharp breath through her nose. And then drives her fingers over my clit, again and again, the sensations building, my wetness growing. I curl my leg around her waist, making it easier for her to reach.

She pushes her fingers inside me, and I moan against her, my back arching as she pulses in and out. Everything builds until I've soaked her hand, and my nails dig into her shoulder.

I thread my fingers into her hair and push her mouth down my body.

"I need you," I moan.

She growls against my stomach, biting and nipping the flesh until I moan her name. Hearing it in my mouth lights fire in her eyes. She runs her tongue down my skin, and then as I pulse higher and higher, as she winds me tighter and closer to climax, she pulls her fingers out, leaving me empty.

Desperate.

She pulls me upright. I slide her jacket off, unbutton the rest of her shirt. I reach around and unclasp her bra and fling the pair away. I grin at her and then lie back, admiring the soft bulges of her breasts against the hard lines of her abs. The way the muscle cuts over her hips and disappears into her trousers.

I lock eyes with her and spread my legs, displaying my pussy. A deep guttural sound rips from her chest. She grips my thighs hard, and then she slides her mouth to meet my apex. I stop breathing.

The world melts away as she licks and kisses, sucks and moves her tongue between my flesh. I moan and my body arches. Her hands grip my arse tight as she pushes her mouth over me. I'm climbing higher, my pussy tightening under her control. And then she releases my ass and slides her fingers inside me, continuing to lap at my core.

I'm panting her name, moaning against her, rocking my

hips into her face until my world explodes and I come apart. Tingles ripple through my body, and I sag against her. She settles on the bed next to me and pulls me into her arms, kissing me, making me wet all over again.

I need to taste her, to feel her against my fingers. So I pull away, reach for her trousers and unbuckle them. She slips them and her underwear off.

When she's naked, I run my hands over her, letting my nails scrape against her skin. Goosebumps cover her body, her eyes roll back. I take a breast in my mouth, placing her nipple between my teeth until the coolness of my breath hardens it to a peak.

I can't take anymore. I push her down. It's my turn. She's laid bare in front of me, and I want her.

I want all of her.

I crawl up to her face, sinking my pussy onto her mouth. She moans into my heat as I soak her face. I arch back, sliding my fingers over her clit as she slides her tongue over mine. When I can't take any more, I release her and move down between her legs. I grip her knees and push them apart, sliding myself between.

I take her pussy in my mouth and suck at her core, tasting her sweet juices as she gets wetter. My tongue moves rhythmically, and as her nub hardens under my tongue, I slide one finger in, then two. I push until I find her spot, and then I caress and brush, throb in and out until she tightens against my fingers and builds against my mouth. Her panting making my cunt swell as she rides my hand, forcing my pace, forcing my movement. Still controlling me even as she cries my name and releases on my hand.

She collapses against me, satisfied.

I lean in, place a delicate kiss against her lips.

She smiles softly at me. "Okay, Quinn. You definitely won that one."

I laugh. "I love you more than games, more than winning."

She runs a finger against my cheek. "I loved you even when I hated you."

I lean against her chest, giggling. "Then I guess you win the 'who loves who the most' game."

She rolls her eyes, but she's grinning. "Shut up and spread your legs. I'm going to make you come all night long."

So I do.

And trust me, she does.

EPILOGUE

SCARLETT

We spent the night in each other's arms, fucking each other senseless until both of us felt uncomfortable walking and our mouths and jaws ached.

It wasn't until Malachi knocked on the door, finally well enough to be out of bed, that we showered and dressed. The Sanatio worked, or is working, I should say. While Malachi isn't completely vocal, he's well on his way. He's up and about, dismissing soldiers and disbanding everything his father built. Quinn's mother, though, is doing less well. She's taken to drinking and hasn't left her bed. Quinn, though, said this isn't unusual and that they'll make sure she gets the help she needs.

We left the palace, travelling in one of her father's carriages. She didn't speak much. Just stared out the window at the ruined city, her eyes hollow.

It will take her time. She hasn't grieved her father.

No one stopped us at the Border. The Queen has called for her guard to return to the palace while they prepare for "The Great Healing" as I hear the whispers say. But in all honesty, no one is sure what exactly is going to happen once the Queen repairs the map and heals the land.

Jacob let us use his spare bike garage for all our belongings. We were evicted as I was leaving for the Border, but Jacob and Remy helped Stirling put our belongings in his garage.

Neither of them impressed with what I'd done over the Sanatio Plant, risking their pay day.

We meet outside the palace. A guard shows us to the same meeting room this began in five weeks ago.

Queen Calandra welcomes us in. She's wearing a maroon pant suit the same ruby colour as the guard uniform.

"Your Majesty. Quinn and Stirling, you know. This is Remy, Jacob and—"

Calandra sucks in a breath. I stop talking, frowning as I observe Calandra's expression. She's fixated on Morrigan.

"What is...? I don't understand? Is this a joke?" Calandra says.

"Umm, no? This is—" I start, but she cuts me off.

"Morrigan. Yes, I'm well aware of who this is. What do you think you're doing?" Calandra barks at Morrigan.

Morrigan's cheeks heat. Stirling's eyes dart between the two, searching for an answer. I glance from Calandra to Morrigan, trying to work out what it is she sees.

The curves, the olive skin.

Oh. My. Gods.

"Hello, mother," Morrigan says.

My jaw hits the floor. Stirling sits down heavy in a chair, her hand wiping over her face.

"You're... you're a..." Stirling stutters and turns to Calandra, "she's a p..."

"Princess, yes. One of my two daughters. And apparently on your team."

"Don't make a big deal out of it. Let's get this over with," Morrigan says and waves her mother off.

"This is a very big deal," Stirling says, pointing at Morrigan.

Morrigan rolls her eyes. "We'll discuss this later."

There's a knock on the door.

"Enter," Calandra says, and a butler wheels in a trolley of food and six sealed envelopes. He distributes the plates of food, drinks and glasses. Piles of chicken and meats, salads and fruit.

"Morrigan, I will deal with you later. Everyone, please do sit, help yourselves to whatever you'd like and make yourselves comfortable. I wanted to thank you once again for going above and beyond with this mission."

She turns to Quinn. "I am truly sorry for your loss. I know that this is a difficult time for you, but I wanted you to know, New Imperium owes you a debt for your sacrifice."

Quinn, Remy, Jacob and Morrigan sit, though Stirling still hasn't moved. She's staring into the void from the armchair in the corner. I drag her up by the arm, pinching the skin underneath. She hisses at me, but it snatches her out of her daze. And she takes a seat beside me.

And then, under her breath, she growls, "She was a princess the whole time?"

"Hush," I breathe back.

Calandra takes a seat at the head of the table and opens her arms. "I've decided, by way of repaying the debt, to provide you all with an opportunity."

I glance at Stirling, and then narrow my eyes. "An opportunity?"

"What sort of opportunity?" Jacob pipes up, his creamy coloured hair slicked back today.

Calandra interlocks her fingers and takes a deep breath. "Work for me. As a team. Work for me on cases, discreet political business, missions if you like. And if you do, not only will I reinstate your titles, Lady Grey, but you may return to your land, holdings, and properties. Your parents' account will be unfrozen, and I'll ensure the banks give you access to what is rightfully yours and more."

She pours herself a glass of wine and holds it up. "I will even pay your team for their time for retrieving the map."

"But, why?" I ask.

She snorts, "I should think that's obvious. I will gain access to the most promising team of magicians I've ever had the pleasure of meeting."

I turn to the team. Could we work for her? Morrigan, Jacob and Remy are all nodding violently.

They're in.

But Calandra wrongfully ordered the execution of our parents. She's been the sum of everything I hated, everything I've spent half a decade trying to seek vengeance for. But now we're here... Now she accepts her mistake and that my parents are innocent. I'm unsure.

"I'd want my parents publicly pardoned. Their record absolved."

She raises her glass to me. "That would only be fair."

"You'd have to give up racing, Jacob. And Collecting, Morrigan. Do you really want to do that? And Remy, what about you? No more moonlighting."

She shrugs. "Life's an adventure. Just because we're a team for now, doesn't mean we have to give up everything.

Who knows, maybe Morrigan can Collect while we're working. Or Jacob can race on the side. But there's no higher honour than working for the Queen."

I turn to Stirling. Her jaw is flexing. She's scarcely moved her eyes from Morrigan. "Are you ready to move on?"

Stirling wipes her mouth. "This wasn't how it was meant to go."

"I know, Stir. But none of this went the way we thought."

Stirling tears herself away from Morrigan and stares out the window, watching the night clouds cross the moon. She's silent so long I fidget in my seat. Eventually, Stirling takes a breath and turns to me, grinning.

"Toss for it?"

My face pales, and I scoff a laugh out. "Of all the times, you choose now to place our fate in the hands of Chance?"

"Why not? Life's a game, is it not?"

I pull Chance out of my pocket, rub the surface, and give her a kiss. Silently praying that this time she plays fair. She warms under my fingers.

I flick Chance high in the air. My breath catches in my throat. I can scarcely breathe. What if it lands on no? What if it lands on...

It drops into my palm, and I flip it onto the back of my hand, covering the surface. I swallow hard and reveal our destiny.

My grin deepens. I show it to Stirling.

"The fates are with you, your majesty," I say.

"I think..." she says, "that if I'm not very much mistaken, the fates are with you, *Lady Grey*."

She stands and pulls down the screen behind her.

"Let us begin..."

As she explains the job, I slide my hand under the table and into Quinn's grip. My angry woman, now and forever.

And a smile creeps over my face.

I won.

Thank you so much for reading *A Game of Hearts and Heists*. If you'd like to read an extra steamy epilogue and find out how Scarlett and Quinn get engaged, you can do that by signing up here: rubyroe.co.uk/signup.

The story is not over! Discover what happens with Stirling and Morrigan in book 2: *A Game of Romance and Ruin*. Read on here: books2read.com/GRRR

Last, reviews are super important for authors, they help provide needed social proof that helps to sell more books. If you have a moment and you're able to leave a review on the store you bought the book from, I'd be really grateful.

THANK YOU

ACKNOWLEDGMENTS

My wife, I can't believe you read this one. And I really can't believe you loved it. Thank you for making me feel loved. I'd burn the world if it meant I could keep you forever.

Elli Z, I used to think people couldn't change. Then I met you and you changed me forever. There are no words to quantify the depths of my gratitude. I know you've heard me say this countless times, but truly. You are a master worker, a healer, a success creator. I have come so far since I met you. You make me believe I can move mountains.

Helen Scheuerer, my work wife. Who, without doubt, has had to deal with endless voice memos whining and cheering, crying, and delighting throughout this process. Thank you for being here throughout them all. Thank you for devouring the book and constantly reminding me I was doing the right thing. You're the work wife of dreams. Everyone else should be jealous that you're mine.

To my sister, Emma, for gifting me your talents and crafting me a stunning logo by hand and helping me brand Ruby. You're so talented, wasted working for our dad... you should come and work for me. ;p

To Katlyn Duncan for our morning sprints, for your consistency of just getting it done, that to my surprise, has now rubbed off on me! Thank you for your endless support, faith and always being there for even the silliest of questions. And, above all, thank you for being the queen of systems and helping me set up my own.

To Alessa Thorn, JJ Arias, Clare Sager, AK Mulford, and Crys Cain, thank you for your specific brand of "encouragement". The constant nudges that I was doing the right thing, that I should absolutely follow my heart. You guys made a difference. I pulled it over the line.

Meg and Katie, thank you for the daily encouragement, the caravan trips and being on the same journey of empowerment and self-improvement. You're powerhouses of positivity, and I'm grateful to have you both.

Becca, thank you for stepping in at the last moment and saving my bacon. You are incredible, talented, and a joy to work with. I'd actually be lost without you.

Last, but by no means least... To my friend. You know who you are. I foisted myself into your relator circle. Stop denying it. There aren't many people I let stand up to me. Consider yourself lucky. Now, stop dicking about. You're too talented for the world not to have your words. There's a little kid out there that needs traumatising before bed. Oh, and thank you for... Starbucks, cynicism, and sarcasm. My day would be a little less dark without you.

About the Author

Ruby Roe is the pen name of Sacha Black. Ruby is the author of lesbian fantasy romance. She loves a bit of magic with her smut, but she'll read anything as long as the characters get down and dirty. When Ruby isn't writing romance, she can usually be found beasting herself in the gym, snuggling with her two pussy... cats, or spanking all her money on her next travel adventure. She lives in England with her wife, son and two devious rag doll cats.

instagram.com/sachablackauthor

tiktok.com/@rubyroeauthor

Printed in Great Britain
by Amazon

46751016R00199